PRAI

"He has a gift for dialogue."—*New York Times*

"Really special."—*Denver Post*

"A crime fiction rara avis."—*Los Angeles Times*

"One of the best writers in the mystery field today."
—*Publishers Weekly* (starred)

"Ebullient and irresistible."—*Kirkus Reviews* (starred)

"Complex and genuinely suspenseful."—*Boston Globe*

"Credible and deeply touching. Russell has us in the palm of his hands."—*Chicago Tribune*

"He is enlightening as well as entertaining."
—*Tampa Bay Times*

"Enormously enjoyable."—*Ellery Queen Mystery Magazine*

"Russell is spectacular."—*San Diego Union-Tribune*

"This work by Russell has it all."—*Library Journal*

"Grade: A. Russell has written a story to satisfy even the most hardcore thrill junkie."—*Rocky Mountain News*

GIDEON'S RESCUE

BOOKS BY ALAN RUSSELL

Gideon and Sirius Novels
Burning Man
Guardians of the Night
Lost Dog
Gideon's Rescue

Hotel Detective Mysteries
The Hotel Detective
The Fat Innkeeper

Detective Cheever Novels
Multiple Wounds
The Homecoming

Stand-Alone Novels
Shame
Exposure
Political Suicide
St. Nick
A Cold War

Stuart Winter Mysteries
No Sign of Murder
The Forest Prime Evil

GIDEON'S RESCUE

ALAN RUSSELL

A GIDEON AND SIRIUS NOVEL

THREE TAILS PRESS
NEW YORK, NEW YORK

Cover design by Jason Blackburn

Three Tails Press, New York, New York

For author contact and press inquiries, please visit alanrussell.net.

I am lucky enough to have the greatest literary agent in the world, as well as the world's greatest editor. Thank you, Cynthia Manson and Caitlin Alexander, for everything you do.

HUNTING SEASON

Holly, Colorado
1,199 miles from Los Angeles
November 14

The Arctic air had brought bitter cold to the Colorado prairie. That was all right with Jim Grinnell. The birds would want to hunker down from the elements.

At a little before seven, dawn was beginning to show itself. Grinnell had set up his blind hours earlier in the darkness. One of the things he liked about duck hunting on the out-of-the-way eastern plains was that the area wasn't overrun with hunters, as it often was along the South Platte River. He liked the remoteness of the Holly State Wildlife Area. At the moment, he was the only hunter working this stretch of the Arkansas River.

Grinnell heard quacking and looked out from his blind. An approaching flock was circling his decoys. He tried to call the ducks down with a five-note call. Less was more, he was convinced, when it came to duck calls. He was trying to establish a dialogue with the ducks, and it worked. Grinnell and the ducks called back and forth until the birds were in range. Taking even breaths, Grinnell pumped his Remington Model 870 shotgun, drew a bead, and fired. One of the mallards, a drake, dropped from the sky.

"Yes!" he said, watching the bird hit the water.

This year Grinnell was birding without a dog. His old chocolate Lab, Brady, had finally died, and he hadn't yet replaced him. Part of that was laziness, but the bigger part was that he hadn't come to terms with old Brady's death. Over the years, he'd had better hunting dogs, but no better friend.

Even though he was wearing waders, Grinnell liked to avoid going into the water when he could. In Brady's absence he'd had to improvise, gathering in the downed birds with an old fishing pole equipped with treble hooks. So far this season, he had managed to snag every bird but one. The current had swept that duck away, but today the river was still; it was cold enough that the banks were icing up.

Grinnell stepped out from his blind, which was camouflaged to look like dead grass marsh. Nearby, he'd also set up what looked like weed cover. He was wearing camouflage himself, what the Brits liked to call a "ghillie suit." The bird wasn't far from the shore, probably no more than thirty feet off. He made sure the treble hooks were extended and in no danger of snagging on any of his body parts, then he swung his pole and released his line. It was a good cast. He began reeling in the line, changing its course a few times by redirecting the tip of the pole, until the large hooks snared the bird.

It was a big bird, at least three pounds. He took the mallard with him into the blind. Even though it was cold enough that he didn't have to worry about spoilage, Grinnell preferred to field dress his birds immediately after they'd been shot.

With practiced fingers, Grinnell reached to the middle of the duck's chest. He pulled the feathers apart, exposing the breast, and then cut open the skin. After placing the duck on the ground, he put one foot on its head and the other on the tail, and tugged upwards. The breast came up and out of the body, and with it both wings. Preserving the wings was necessary in the event a game warden came along. The wings allowed the warden to identify the species of duck that was taken. Of course, Grinnell seriously doubted any game warden would be coming along. They usually patrolled the more popular spots. Where he was hunting was considered the boonies; the Kansas state line was only five or six miles away.

Grinnell stored the breast in his ice chest. If a warden came along, that was fine by him. He had all his tags and licenses. And he wouldn't mind the company. Most hunters weren't solitary like Grinnell, but over the years he'd found solitude meant more ducks.

He rubbed his hands with some liquid soap, and then rinsed them with water from his bottle before pouring himself a cup of steaming coffee. It was his tradition to hold off drinking his coffee until after bagging his first bird.

The joe was piping hot, and he was forced to take it in little sips. That's when he heard the sounds.

"Oh my God," a woman moaned. "That's it. Don't stop. Yes, oh, yes."

Grinnell couldn't believe what he was hearing. It was twenty degrees outside and he was in the middle of nowhere. But damned if some woman wasn't crying out in the throes of passion.

He put down his coffee cup, unsure what to do. Where had the woman come from? And was she as close as she sounded, or were her acoustics being channeled from farther along the river?

"Ohhhhhh," she said. "Ohhhhhhh."

Grinnell decided he couldn't just stand there listening. It made him feel like a voyeur. The couple must not have noticed his blind, and he needed to remedy that. He opened the flaps and walked outside. His appearance put an abrupt end to the sounds. Grinnell expected to see a couple in flagrante delicto; an apology was already on his lips. But it was never offered. He stared at the rifle pointed at him.

Guns had always been a part of his life, but he'd never seen one from this angle, had never known how very ugly a rifle's bore was when pointed directly at you. That was the last thought Jim Grinnell ever had. An instant later, the view grew even uglier when the rifle was fired.

CHAPTER ONE

DOG FRIGHT

Four and a half months later

The two large dogs squared off. Teeth bared, spittle flying, they mirrored one another's movements. They were about the same size but distinct breeds. Their growls increased, and then they were wrestling on the ground, one on top and then the other.

A woman came running down the path, her eyes wide. She took a step forward to break up the dogs, then thought better of it. Peacemakers might be blessed, but that doesn't prevent them from getting bitten. The ferocious snarling made her keep her distance.

She challenged me with a look that said, *Why don't you do something?*

"It's all right," I told her. "They're playing."

She didn't quite roll her eyes, but it was apparent she didn't believe me. She hadn't seen the German shepherd initiate play with a little bow, or his preliminary tail wagging. The hound had happily accepted the invitation to play, and that had started the ruckus. The dogs had communicated with one another; each knew that no matter how loud their sound effects were or how realistic their pratfalls, it was all a game. The dogs were so good in their playacting that they should get a contract with the WWE. I probably should have told the woman that the shepherd was my partner, but I didn't want to step on his Hulk Hogan swagger.

Their grand finale looked choreographed; both dogs leapt, bumped chests, and then they hit the ground. They got up and shook themselves like dogs trying to dry themselves off. By mutual decree, they'd had enough.

"And that's a wrap," I said.

In Tinseltown you say things like that.

The two posers came running over to me, wagging their tails. Both were panting and in need of a drink. I waved to the woman and smiled. She didn't wave or smile back. And I imagine had she deigned to speak she would have said, "*We* are not amused."

I put a hand on Sirius's head and told him, "You could have been a contender." Then I accompanied Sirius and Angie to a nearby watering hole, where they slurped away.

This was my second visit to Angie's Rescues, a shelter that had been open for only ten days. The shelter had been Heather Moreland's dream. Heather had gone through hell and had sold her story for a lot of money, proceeds that had built Angie's Rescues.

Angie is Heather's rescue dog. Conversely, you could say Heather is Angie's rescue human. Angie is mostly bloodhound, a breed often described as a nose with a dog attached. She had sniffed out our presence the moment we parked, and had run from inside the shelter to play with her friend Sirius.

The dogs were finishing up their drinking when Heather appeared. "People were wondering if World War Three had broken out," she said.

Sirius and Angie ran up to Heather, and then the two of us shook hands. She was smiling and energized. Sometimes it's hard for people to come back from the kind of trauma she experienced, but she looked great.

"How are things?" I asked.

"Crazy," she said. "I never would have guessed how much work it takes to run an animal shelter, but every day I wake up with a smile on my face. This is what I was meant to do. I get goose bumps every time I see one of my animals leaving for their forever home."

I had heard that the day after Angie's Rescues opened, it was completely full with dogs and cats. It was a no-kill shelter, something the animals seemed to sense. Roughly half the animals taken in by Los Angeles County shelters don't make it out alive. In the city of Los Angeles the survival rate is better, but it's still nothing to brag about.

"How long have you and Sirius been together?" Heather asked.

"Like most of our state's citizenry," I said, "my partner came to California as an immigrant. That was five years ago."

My wife, Jen, had immediately babied the new arrival, and insisted that we change his name from the German *Serle* to Sirius. The big, bad wolf was putty in Jennifer's hands.

"And was it love at first sight?" asked Heather.

Sirius had loved at first sight, but it was my wife he'd fallen for. The two of us initially had a different kind of relationship. Work and training brought us closer and engendered trust. And then Jen died, and Sirius made sure I wasn't consumed in darkness; all that occurred before the two of us went through a crucible of fire to capture a serial killer. Five years of partnering had put us through a lot together. Each of us had saved the other's life.

"What's love got to do with it?" I said, quoting Tina Turner. "Sirius and I are cops. That means we're immune to puppy dog eyes."

"Science would dispute that," said Heather. "There have been several recent studies on oxytocin—the so-called love hormone—that show humans experience increased oxytocin levels whenever we gaze into the eyes of dogs. Canines also exhibit increased oxytocin levels."

"You need to be skeptical of all the junk science out there," I said. "Or at least that's what I heard at last week's Flat Earth Society meeting."

"Did you wear your tinfoil hat to the meeting?"

That got a laugh out of me and demonstrated just how much Heather had healed. She had gone from a somber, scared survivor to a happy and confident woman.

"Ready to work?" she asked.

"Lead the way," I said.

I had committed to volunteering at the shelter for four hours a week. Because of my work with Metropolitan K-9, Heather thought the best use of my time would be socializing with the dogs, taking them for walks, and working on basic obedience commands.

Angie's Rescues was a compound made up of several buildings. Cats and dogs were in detached buildings, with separate entrances for each. As we started up the dog path, we passed colorful cutouts of different dog breeds. There was also a familiar-looking object situated just off the walkway. At the grand opening party, I had presented Heather with a big box that contained a half-size bright-red fire hydrant.

"Your present has proved quite popular with our male dogs," Heather said.

Sirius must have been listening, because he decided it was a good spot for him to relieve himself.

"It was either the hydrant or a garden gnome," I said. "Personally, I'd prefer taking aim at the gnome, but I figured your clientele would want the gold standard."

"I'm afraid I will never look at those poor gnomes the same way again," she said.

There were benches along our walk; we passed under trees with greenery on each side. It felt more like a park setting than anything else. Before Angie's Rescues, I had never liked animal shelters, probably because they reminded me of prisons. Inmates describe their captivity as "killing time." It's an apt phrase—the passage of time is a slow killer. Whether it's in a shelter or a prison, those who wait behind bars are the forsaken.

When I was growing up, animal shelters were referred to as "the pound." A visit to the pound meant encountering cold cement, steel bars, urine and feces littering small pens, and the hovering angel of death. I always imagined that was why the dogs housed there barked incessantly—they were trying to scare away death.

Angie's Rescues had a very different feel from the pounds of old. Statues of St. Francis of Assisi stood at the entrances to the dog and cat buildings. Each featured a different St. Francis quote. I read the dog quote as we passed it: *All things of creation are children of the Father and thus brothers of man.*

If I ever return to the Catholic Church, I thought, it will probably be because of St. Francis of Assisi.

Throughout the shelter were painted murals (probably more for the workers and helpers than the animals), lots of planters and plants, fountains, and walkways that led into corrals. We began encountering dogs and their barking, but the noise didn't seem to travel far.

"As you can see," said Heather, "we've tried to offer dogs their own space by using planter dividers. We've also put in relatively high ceilings. Those, along with acoustic tiles, have cut down the noise."

I paused at an open space between the enclosures, took note of the sun and the sky, and said, "I'm used to seeing atriums in fancy hotels, not dog shelters."

"They bring in light and fresh air," she said.

As we walked, Heather greeted each dog we encountered. She knew the names of all her charges and offered me short histories on each.

"Hi, Pepe," she said, calling out to a Chihuahua mix.

To me, she said, "Pepe is a casualty of divorce. His parents moved to apartments that didn't allow animals."

We passed by Enrique, another Chihuahua. "Enrique was a stray found on the streets of East Los Angeles," Heather said. "Unfortunately, we have to limit the number of Chihuahuas and pit bulls in our shelter, simply because the supply far exceeds the demand."

The next cage brought us to a female shepherd mix, and Heather called, "Hello, Dolly."

Like the others, Dolly was a victim of human neglect. She'd been tied to a stop sign in North Hollywood and abandoned.

We paused in front of the next cage. The pit bull inside looked that much fiercer because of all the stitches and scarring, not to mention the cast on her back leg. "This is Emily," said Heather. "How are you, my sweet girl?"

The dog with the ferocious appearance began wagging her little stub of a tail. Because of her wounds and her cast, it took some effort to stand up, but Emily wasn't going to miss out on getting affection. Heather put her hands through the bars and started scratching a spot where there weren't any stitches.

"She looks like she's been through a war," I said.

"In a way, she has," said Heather. "We suspect Emily was a bait dog."

"What's that?"

"Emily was basically supplied as a sacrificial lamb to another fighting dog. She was a teaching tool for another dog to learn how to maul and kill. Even worse, Emily's muzzle was duct-taped closed when she was forced into the pit. She couldn't fight back even if she'd wanted to."

It was a story I found hard to hear; seeing Emily's condition made it even worse.

"Bastards," I muttered. It wasn't a harsh enough word to describe the criminals who fought dogs.

Because of Heather's own past, she probably sympathized with Emily's imprisonment and torture that much more. Both of them had proved to be survivors.

Even though she had suffered a mauling, Emily acted calm around Sirius and Angie. The dogs took turns sniffing each other through the barriers of the cage; there was a lot of tail wagging.

"Emily and three others dogs were tossed onto the side of the road in East Los Angeles and left for dead," said Heather. "The other three dogs with her had been shot. I guess the shooter thought Emily was already dead and didn't want to waste a bullet. When police responded to the dumped animals, though, they discovered Emily was still alive. Normally, a pit bull in her condition would automatically have been euthanized, but we were contacted and agreed to subsidize veterinary care. Because Emily was selected as a bait dog, not a fighter, my hope was that she would have a good temperament despite everything that happened to her. So far, that hope has been validated. She's shown no signs of aggression. I know someone is going to see past her scars and realize what a sweet dog she is."

I found myself scratching Emily. She looked like a patchwork dog; her flesh had been ripped open in dozens of spots.

There had been a time when I was a patchwork human. I still had a big scar on my face, courtesy of the fiery night during which Sirius and I had captured Ellis Haines, the serial murderer known as both the Santa Ana Strangler and the Weatherman. Haines had identical keloid scarring, although on the opposite side of his face from mine. I often catch people surreptitiously observing my scar, and there are times I can see reactions of uncertainty and fear. Of course, I'm probably oversensitive. To date, I haven't felt the need to do a John Merrick and yell out, "I am a human being!"

"You are a good girl," I said to Emily.

She responded with more tail wagging. Emily had ample reason to hate the human species. Instead, she had forgiven us. I doubted I could ever be as forgiving.

"Do you want to start by spending ten minutes with Emily?" asked Heather. "Because of her broken leg, I wouldn't walk her. I wouldn't even do much in the way of commands until she's healed up more, but we do want to give her as much socialization with different humans as possible. I can take Sirius and Angie and have them participate in temperament testing of other dogs."

I found myself nodding. Heather opened the cage and I stepped inside. "Careful scratching around her head," she said. "I think one of her wounds is still infected."

She pointed to the side of Emily's head. I could see where it looked raw and red.

"I'm surprised she's not wearing a cone."

"We took it off a short time ago because it seemed to be chafing her," said Heather, "but we'll be putting it on again later today."

I went inside the cage. When I worked Metropolitan K-9, we used to do squatting exercises so as to be able to get down to the level of our charges. I squatted down, which is supposedly

the natural resting position of humans. A lot of creaking and
cracking went into that natural position.

Emily sniffed around my face and gave me a little lick. Even
though she seemed glad for the company, she was alert, watching
all my movements. I spoke to her in a calm, subdued voice, and
between my measured speech and soft scratching and rubbing,
she decided it was all right to completely relax.

"What happened to you, Emily," I said, "was cruel and in-
humane. I'm glad you live in the moment. That's what I envy
about dogs. It gives you a freedom to go on with your life without dwelling on what occurred. But I promise you this. If I can
find the miserable excuse for a human being who did this to you,
I will make him pay."

My tone was meant to lull Emily; my words were meant just
for me. Emily was hearing "Brahms's Lullaby"; I was hearing a
vow. It was what we both needed to hear.

I spent time with a handful of other dogs. Each was given a ten-
minute walk, followed by training. All seemed happy just spending time with me. I tried to give each dog all of my attention, but
I found myself thinking about Emily.

Sirius helped me work with some of the dogs. When he
wasn't needed I had him practicing his exercises, including his
sits and waits. It was my responsibility as a handler to run Sirius
through his paces; we both benefitted from the exercise and the
time working together. Our ability to communicate and understand what the other wanted could save lives, including our own.

When I finished my shift, I was sweating. My partner and I
walked over to the office, where I jotted down a few notes in
each dog's file. Afterward, Sirius and I tracked down Heather.
We found her in a storage room, holding a clipboard and doing a

food inventory. Angie was sprawled out on the floor and Sirius went and joined her.

"How did it go?" Heather asked.

"Really well," I said. "You have a bunch of good dogs."

The proud mom smiled.

"Before I take off," I said, "I was hoping you had a minute to answer a few questions about Emily."

"I noticed you spent a long time in her cage."

I shrugged. "She had a lot to say."

Heather knew I wasn't being funny. Emily did have a lot to say even without words. "What is it you want to know?"

"I wondered if you could provide me the particulars of Emily's rescue. I'd like to know where she was found and if the police were involved. Dogfighting is illegal, and LAPD is part of the city's Animal Cruelty Task Force."

"I'm almost finished up here," said Heather. "After I'm done we can walk over to the office and make copies of Emily's intake form. Most of what you need should be on those pages."

"Sounds good," I said.

I went over and joined Sirius and Angie. They welcomed me with tail thumps. It was more than I deserved, but dogs are generous with their encouragement. Humans can be trained, although it's not easy.

CHAPTER TWO

SWEAR TO DOG

Heather accompanied Sirius and me to the front desk. I went behind the counter and waited while she made copies of Emily's paperwork. Sirius decided he wanted service and pushed up from the ground so that both his paws hung over the front desk.

The woman behind the desk began laughing. Her name tag said *Suzanne*; her button said, *Love Me, Love My Dog.*

"Why, yes, sir!" she said to Sirius. "I'll bet you'd like a treat."

I got paperwork; my partner got part of a rice cake and a massage. While Sirius was being told how handsome he was, I looked over the forms. Emily's medical treatment had been documented, but there were no contacts listed for animal control or the police. I hoped the vet listed at the top of the form would be able to provide me those names. I tried to make out the handwriting.

"Dr. Caitlin Misko treated Emily?" I asked.

Heather nodded. "She's the shelter's on-call vet."

Suzanne paused in the scratching of my partner's ears to ask, "Are you looking for Dr. Misko? She came through just a few minutes ago to examine the new puppies."

"I'll go introduce the two of you," said Heather.

My partner was given another piece of rice cake as a parting gift, and the two of us followed Heather over to what she called the quarantine area. Dr. Misko was in an enclosure with half a dozen puppies. Even vets aren't immune to such charms, and the doctor was enjoying their antics while she entered notes into her tablet.

"Kate," yelled Heather, "this is Michael Gideon. He's a volunteer here, but he wants to ask you some questions related to his day job."

"As long as he's not an IRS agent," the vet said, "that's fine."

Dr. Misko motioned for me to join her inside the enclosure. Sirius followed me in, and I went over to shake the vet's hand. "I'm Detective Michael Gideon," I said, "and this is my K-9 partner, Sirius. We're with LAPD."

"Kate Misko," she said. "We can talk after I finish up here. In fact, if you don't mind, I can use the extra hands."

"Glad to help," I said.

"I'm examining each pup, followed by picture taking. Would you mind corralling the three pups closest to you?"

I did as she asked, using my arms to make a puppy enclosure, or at least that was the idea. The clumsy puppies suddenly became seasoned escape artists. Luckily, I had a second line of defense; Sirius played middle linebacker and was able to push the escapees back toward me. Dr. Misko finished up with the first group, and we switched out the puppies. Two of my new charges were happy to stay within the confines of my arms and kiss me; the third kept close to Sirius, acting like his protégé. The little one had picked a good role model.

"Thank you, Detective Gideon," said Dr. Misko, finishing up her pictures and notes. The vet was around forty, small and slender, with short brown hair. On the tip of her nose, thick black glasses perched precariously.

"Gideon," she said, her voice suddenly thoughtful. She lifted her glasses up to her eyes and stared at me. "And Sirius," she added, turning her gaze to my partner.

At hearing his name, my partner's ears rose and he offered up his good side. The hambone enjoys any and all adoration.

Dr. Misko smiled triumphantly. "I remember now," she said. "It was the two of you who caught that awful killer."

Don't say his name, I thought. Like Voldemort, I was convinced, it was better to not say his name.

"Ellis Haines," she said.

I nodded, and then said, "He's an individual I don't like wasting my breath on."

Dr. Misko respected my wishes. Most people don't. With a smile she asked, "You said you had some questions for me?"

"I spent time with Emily today," I said, "and was told you were the one who performed emergency surgery on her."

"I did," she said. "Emily presented with some very serious injuries."

"When did this occur?"

Dr. Misko pursed her lips and tried to recall. "It must have been ten days ago. She was brought in early Monday morning. We suspect the dogs were dumped the night before."

"How is it that you were the one who treated Emily?"

"The animal control officer who called me knows I'm a soft touch. Officer Santana said I was the dog's only hope, but the truth is that Heather was her only hope. I had to call her to see if she would help with the cost of care, and whether Angie's Rescues had a spot for her.

"I made the call on the day the shelter officially opened. I'm sure it was absolute chaos here. I expected Heather to say no. That would have been the reasonable thing to do. And that would have been my out. There was no guarantee the dog would live, anyway, and I couldn't vouch for her temperament. It's difficult to place even the most docile of pit bulls, and I was asking Heather to take in a former bait dog that was going to be riddled with scars. At a shelter, space is always at a premium, which is what makes it so difficult to accept a dog into your care that might not be adopted for months or years, or maybe ever."

"It's a good thing you didn't settle on a career in sales," I said.

"I haven't even told you the worst thing I said. Heather asked me what I thought should be done with the dog. I said that judging from what I had been told, there was a good chance she'd survive the surgery, but despite that, it probably made more sense to euthanize her.

"Heather thought about that for maybe ten seconds and finally said, 'Do your best to save her.'"

"I don't think I've ever seen a dog with more stitches."

"Compared to how she looked when she came in," said Dr. Misko, "now she looks like an angel. When those monsters left her for dead, there was trauma to her head, open wounds everywhere, broken ribs, and a broken back leg that needed to be reset with pins."

That was the same dog who had licked my hand, and my face.

"Were all her wounds the result of bites?"

"I suspect a baseball bat or cudgel was also used."

"Did you take pictures of her prior to treatment?"

She nodded. "If you decide to look at them, I advise you not to eat beforehand."

"Did the police talk to you?"

The shake of her head was almost enough to displace her glasses. "That's why I'm glad you're talking to me."

"I assume animal control is investigating what happened?"

"I wouldn't assume anything," she said. "Animal control has to make do with a minuscule budget. They're stretched incredibly thin. But you should call Samson. He'd be able to tell you for sure."

"Samson?"

"That's what my staff calls Officer Santana. If you meet him, you'll see why. He has beautiful long, curly hair—almost to his shoulders. Would that I had his hair."

She touched her short hair and made a disparaging sound.

Once I was in the car, I grabbed for my lint roller. When you work and live with a German shedder, you need to buy lint rollers in bulk. Before I started in on my aerobic exercise, I went in search of the right music. The name Santana had been brought up earlier, and I took that as a portent. I scrolled through my sizable music library, and then turned up the sound. Anyone watching me might have thought I was holding a castanet instead of a lint roller; I did my shaking, rattling, rolling, and, most importantly, cleaning, to the song "Smooth."

I tuned in my musical time machine for a Santana encore, and the timeless music of "Oye Como Va" started playing over the speakers. Santana inspired me to more aerobic cleaning; I grabbed Sirius's brush and moved it through his coat to the beat of the music. My partner seemed to be moving to the same beat, or maybe he was just enjoying the grooming.

Each song seemed the perfect length for our respective cleanings. "I know you like to look good for the ladies," I said, finishing up.

I was tempted to play another Santana song but decided to call Officer Santana instead. When he picked up he identified himself by name, and I did the same.

"I'm following up on those dogs that were dumped," I said, "and the dog you brought in some ten days ago to Dr. Misko. Do you have a minute to talk?"

"I do," he said. "I never heard if the dog lived or not."

"She's alive," I said.

"I knew it," he said, sounding pleased. "I told the doc she was one tough dog who just needed a chance."

"You were right."

"She was on death's door," he said, "and yet she still wagged her tail when I came on the scene and she saw I was there to help her. That's why I pushed her on the doc. That's what I call game, even if those *pendejos* don't."

"'Game'?" I asked.

"The dogfighters say their dog is game if he has lots of fight in him. They think it's noble if their dog will fight to the death."

"Are you familiar with dogfighters in the area?"

"I've had to cross paths with them on the job."

"Dr. Misko said you were investigating the dumping of those four dogs."

"I left a message with the Animal Cruelty Task Force," Santana said. "And I'm investigating it by reminding people I meet on my route about the twenty-four-hour anonymous tip line and the reward money available."

"What kind of money is being offered?"

"Up to five thousand dollars," Santana said.

"Anything else being done to investigate the dumped dogs?"

"On our website we're soliciting information about the crime," he said, "and emphasizing the reward."

"I was told an LAPD officer was dispatched to the crime scene. Do you know if he reported his findings to the ACTF?"

"He left that to me," Santana said. To my ear, it sounded as if he was being diplomatic.

"What was the officer's name?"

"Brockington," he said.

"Hollenbeck division?"

"I assume so."

"He wiped his hands clean of the whole thing?"

"That's not for me to say."

"Does the dogfighting tip line ever lead to any arrests?"

"Now and again," said Santana. "Last year we were involved in taking down a ring. Usually our job is to collect the fighting dogs, while LAPD or LASD deals with the bad guys."

"If this is an ongoing problem, how come there aren't more arrests?"

"We're up against a secret society," Santana said, "and the bad guys have gotten sophisticated. They're able to organize last-minute fights in remote or secured spots."

"But you know who these bad guys are?"

"Most of them," said Santana. "Some of those dudes even operate out in the open by claiming they're training the dogs for guard service. But their equipment tells a different story."

"In what way?"

"It's like the difference between a regular gym and a boxing gym. Fighters need to have gloves, target mitts, headgear, heavy bags, punching bags, and a boxing ring. Dogfighting has specific training apparatus as well. They got these heavy ropes attached to trees that dogs swing from with their teeth. And typically you got flirt poles, dog weights, catmills, exercise turntables, spring poles, and treadmills."

"I hope a catmill isn't what I think it is."

"It probably was at one time," said Santana, "but now a nonliving lure is used. There's this central shaft in the ground that the dogs are harnessed to, and they run 'round and 'round after the lure. You know how dogs at racetracks run after the mechanical rabbit? It's sort of like that."

"What's a flirt pole?"

"It's this bamboo pole with an animal hide attached that the trainer swings. Imagine a fishing pole with a lure on the end. The dog goes crazy trying to attack it."

"Is it common for dead dogs to be dumped?"

"No," Santana said. "Dogfighters usually like to cover up what they're up to. I've heard of mass graves in the desert and carcasses left for coyotes to scavenge out in wilderness areas, but having four dogs dumped in an urban setting isn't the norm. Especially dogs that were shot."

"What happened to the three dogs that died?" I asked.

"They were cremated."

"And neither you nor Officer Brockington collected evidence?"

"I'm not trained to do that," said Officer Santana. "And to tell you the truth, no cop has ever been interested in a dead dog before. You're the first. Are you really planning to follow up on this?"

"Swear to Dog," I said.

CHAPTER THREE

END OF SHIFT

Officer LaVar Brockington was on patrol when I called him and left a message. Ten minutes later he called me back on his cell phone.

"Let's talk about four dogs dumped on the side of the road," I said.

Immediately, Brockington went on the defensive. "The animal control officer took charge of that situation."

"And you never considered contacting the Animal Cruelty Task Force?"

"Like I said, the animal control officer . . . "

"Are you aware that particular task force was created to act as a deterrent to dogfighting? The *crime* of dogfighting is something LAPD investigates. It's a felony."

"The dogs were dead . . . "

"One of the dogs lived. I saw her today."

"I didn't know . . . "

"You didn't care enough to know. You didn't do your job."

"With all due respect, Detective Gideon, that animal control officer assured me he was good to go. Was I supposed to question that?"

"Your job was to secure the crime scene."

"There wasn't any crime scene. The dogs were dumped."

"That wasn't your call to make," I said. "Evidence should have been collected."

"You're shitting me."

"No," I said, "but I will be shitting *on* you after I reopen this case and write up my report. The three dead dogs were all shot. A ballistics report could have told us what kind of gun was used and if the same gun was used on each of the dogs. And down the road when we finally arrest the bastard that did the shootings and we find him carrying, we could have matched those ballistics with his gun. But now we can't do that. Instead of getting serious jail time, the SOB skates. That's where we stand because you cut corners."

There was a part of me that knew I was overstepping my boundaries. Police officers put their lives on the line every day, and Brockington worked a particularly tough neighborhood. He was witness to all sorts of human tragedies playing out, and probably wondered where the hell I was coming from. These were dogs, he was thinking. If I wanted to get indignant, there was no shortage of human misfortune to comment upon.

I listened to the silence on the line. Brockington finally broke it when he said, "My bad," and then offered up an explanation. "I know it's not a good excuse, but the dog call came in at the end of my shift and I hadn't seen my wife in days. Both of us needed time together to work some things out."

I didn't want to let the incident completely slide, but at the same time, it was easy to sympathize with Brockington's position. I had been there, and I had probably done my share of kicking the can down the street instead of dealing with it. One of the reasons being a cop is so difficult is that there really is no end of shift. The cases never stop coming, and there is always carryover. End of career, I have decided, is when end of shift occurs.

"If you're wondering where I'm coming from," I said, "I was with Metropolitan K-9 for years. So I don't buy into the argument that because these were just dogs, and not humans, their deaths aren't important. The way we treat our animals speaks about us as a society."

There's a reason serial murderers invariably begin their awful predations by torturing animals, I thought. In their psychopathy they have no souls, and they want to learn their craft practicing on those who can't speak.

"You're right," Brockington said. "I screwed up. What can I do to make it right?"

I took a breath, let it out, and then said, "While you're patrolling, I want you to talk with the people on the streets, and get me a list of those suspects who work or live within the neighborhoods you work who are likeliest to be involved in dogfighting. Also, see if you can come up with any reason for those dogs being dumped where they were. Dogfighting is an activity that tends to stay in the shadows. Putting its victims on display makes no sense."

If Brockington was a good cop, he would have cultivated contacts who knew things, or heard things. It was likely he'd be able to pick up on information that might elude me.

"I'll get right on it," he said. Most officers aspire to a detective's shield. To that end, he added, "Are we good, Detective?"

No cop wants to be dinged in a report; one blackball could sabotage advancement, or at least slow it considerably.

"We'll be good," I said, "when you get back to me with some answers."

CHAPTER FOUR

EXPLAINING THE IMPOSSIBLE

Sirius and I stopped at an In-N-Out and ordered at the drive-through. I refrained from asking for my usual choices of a Double-Double, fries, onion rings, and a Neapolitan shake; Lisbet has been trying to get me to eat a more healthful diet, which means smaller portions and less fat. On the nights Lisbet cooks, Sirius and I get lots of fruits and vegetables and whole grains. Some of her dishes even border on being tasty.

I made my choices from the so-called secret menu. "I'll have my burger Animal Style with fried onions," I said, "and an order of fries. My hungry friend will have a Pup Patty."

Animal Style meant my burger would be cooked with mustard; a Pup Patty was a rare burger with no salt.

"And what would you like to drink, sir?" asked the cheerful female voice over the intercom.

"Just water, please," I said. "In fact, you'd better make it a double."

My partner has probably benefited the most from my new habits. He used to cadge half my fries and part of my burger. Now I carry a container of dried food in my car and he doesn't get my leftovers. Sirius has actually lost a few pounds from the arrangement. I wish I could say the same for myself.

I parked in the outer section of the lot, as far away from the street and car exhaust as possible. There was a light breeze, and I lowered all four windows. I pulled out Sirius's bowl, poured in a cup of dried food, and then crumbled up his Pup Patty. He watched the operation critically.

"Yeah, like you're Bobby Flay," I said, putting his bowl down in the back seat.

In less than ten seconds he'd finished everything, which meant I was only one bite into my burger when he took to staring at me.

Another change in my eating habits is Lisbet's encouraging me to eat slowly. More than a dozen years of interrupted Code 7s—the LAPD code for taking a meal break—had taught me to eat quickly. In fact, Sirius and I used to eat at about the same speed.

I took another bite of the burger. Brown eyes monitored every inch of the process.

"You're not going to get anything," I said.

Hope springs eternal, said his eyes.

"This isn't a Four-by-Four, or a Three-by-Three, or even a Double-Double. It's a solitary burger without any cheese. You should be feeling sorry for me, not trying to hypnotize me."

I took a sip of my water. He didn't find that as interesting. I put his cup of water in his cup holder and he started lapping. When I resumed my eating, he resumed his watching. I finished my burger, then started in on my fries. I looked in the rearview mirror; Sirius was all plaintive eyes, and something else.

"Quit drooling," I said.

What quit his drooling was my handing him two fries. I shoved the rest of the fries into my mouth so as to avoid any more guilt. Besides, we needed to get moving if we wanted to be on time for our monthly 187 Club meeting.

After Langston Walker was killed, I had warned the membership that there was no way I could ever fill the retired detective's sizable shoes. But in the months since his death, I had done my best to get to know club members. I had also read some books on grief therapy, which had mostly made me feel that much more inadequate in trying to deal with the group's collective loss. The dues to join the 187 Club are unimaginably steep: you have to lose a loved one to murder.

It's likely I would have thought that running the club was beyond me if not for Sirius. My partner would have made a great hospital or hospice dog. At the meetings, he seems to have a wet nose and a wag of the tail for everyone, even those who profess to being scared of dogs (and cops).

We arrived five minutes early at the Jim Gilliam Recreation Center. The lot was almost full. I knew I was in the right place when I saw all the bumper stickers on display that said, *Someone I Love Was Murdered.*

Luckily for me, Catalina Ceballos had agreed to continue in her role as club organizer. She fills gaps big and small, and I don't have to worry about the community room being set up or arranging for the monthly snacks. The previous month's speaker had talked about how poor nutrition accentuates depression; the membership must have listened, because as I stepped into the community room, I could see there were bowls with grapes, orange sections, and apple slices.

Our guest speaker was already there, and Catalina was introducing him to the club's members. We had never met, but over the years I had seen him profiled a number of times in the local media. Isaac Jordan made a point of being a loud voice for his flock, which he said was the same flock that Christ had tended to—namely, the poor, the meek, the disenfranchised, and most of all, the sinners. In addition to being a community organizer, Jordan was a prison chaplain.

My partner led the way into the room. Sirius somehow senses who is most in need of a meet and greet, so I let him do his version of search and rescue. Sirius coaxed reluctant hands to reach out, offering his muzzle and head to those in pain. "Good dog," most of them said. A look would pass between the afflicted and my partner, and I could see a real healer at work. Heather Moreland had referred to the oxytocin responses of humans and dogs. I was seeing it.

Sirius was the icebreaker; I had the easier job of shaking hands and offering a few words. Most of those I talked to I knew from other meetings, but there were several unfamiliar faces who identified themselves as irregular attendees. Only one person seemed to be new to the 187 Club. Marta Hernandez introduced me to Luciana Castillo, a diminutive young woman with big brown eyes. In broken English, Luciana explained that her fiancé, Mateo Ramos, had disappeared six weeks ago.

"He is dead," she told me, her big eyes filling with tears.

According to Luciana, the detective assigned to his case had done little to investigate his disappearance, and seemed inclined to believe that the undocumented Mateo had returned home to Mexico. Pointing to her heart, she said the detective didn't understand how much Mateo loved her.

In law enforcement there is a chain of command. There are supervisors whose job it is to oversee how cases are being handled. In a bureaucracy you're supposed to go by the book; in real life there are teary orbs and matters of the heart. Luciana continued to point at her heart as if that should explain everything. Maybe it did.

Normally, I take the night's speaker out to dine as way of thanks. Isaac Jordan had asked instead for a hundred-dollar contribution to the soup kitchen to which he ministered. That meant my evening was free.

"Do you have time to talk after the meeting?" I asked.

Luciana stopped pointing at her heart and nodded. Then she took her two small hands, wrapped them around my right hand, and said, "Yes, thank you."

"De nada," I answered, although I wished my Spanish were good enough for me to add, *You need to understand ahead of time I'm no miracle worker.*

"Let's go," I said to Sirius, steering him toward the speaker.

Isaac Jordan was of average height, but his exuberant presence made him appear bigger. He had a big gap between his front teeth, and a graying Afro. I could see he had the same talent my partner did of being able to put people at ease. Many club members have lost their joie de vivre as a result of a loved one being murdered. It's as if their true self has been replaced with a pale imitation, except for the occasional flashes of anger. Some revive with the passage of time; others seem forever tempered. I always seek out speakers that might offer club members a jump-start. The LAPD brass probably wouldn't have approved of my choice for our speaker of the month; Isaac was a regular critic of the force, especially if he thought LAPD was violating human rights. But even LAPD couldn't deny his passion.

"Reverend Jordan," I said, offering my hand, "I'm Michael Gideon. The two of us spoke on the phone. Thank you so much for being here."

"Call me Isaac," he said with a big smile. "And if you feel compelled to give me a title, call me Pastor Isaac."

I introduced Isaac to my partner. Pastor Isaac extended his hand for Sirius to smell and was rewarded with a lick.

"I won't take that as a comment on my hygiene, Sirius," he said, "but rather that I was helping in the kitchen before I came here."

I asked Isaac if he was ready to begin his talk, and at his nod and smile I made my way to the front of the room. Sirius didn't follow me; he still had rounds of his own and people to see. I waited while the room quieted and everyone took a seat. After reading a few announcements, I cleared my throat. Langston had liked to start and end each meeting with a poem. Of course, when he did his reading it sounded like a benediction. I didn't have his speaking voice, nor was I sure about the poem I had selected, but I knew better than to tamper with tradition.

"Tonight's poem," I said, "is Robert Frost's 'The Road Not Taken.' I picked it because I started thinking about how choosing different paths can take us on very different journeys. Because all of you experienced the untimely death of a loved one, I expect you were stopped in your tracks. What I hope, though, is that even with that terrible detour, you find a way to continue on with your intended journey."

The poem, luckily, was much shorter than my explanation. I read it slowly and did my best to make eye contact with the room at its conclusion:

> *Two roads diverged in a wood, and I—*
> *I took the one less traveled by,*
> *And that has made all the difference.*

Coming into the meeting, I wasn't sure how the words of a poet known for his rural New England sensibility of trees, farms, and snow would go over with a group of mostly nonwhite Southern California mourners, but I was glad to see heads nodding thoughtfully.

The poem allowed me to segue into our speaker's biography. "Pastor Isaac Jordan has made a point of taking the road less traveled," I said, "and I will let him tell you how it has made all the difference. I did some research on Pastor Isaac, and I found that his personal hero is Nelson Mandela. One of the reasons Pastor Isaac works as a prison chaplain is that Mandela was imprisoned in South Africa for twenty-seven long years. During that time, Mandela's native South Africa practiced apartheid—which means it favored the white minority ruling class and discriminated against all people of color. From behind bars Mandela managed to fight against apartheid. And while I wouldn't recommend going to prison, Mandela didn't let his many years there stop him from learning or becoming a better human being. He not only won the Nobel Peace Prize, but he became the president of South Africa.

"Pastor Isaac says he speaks for those who don't have voices, such as prisoners and the poor. Tonight he wants to minister to you. In the words of Nelson Mandela, 'A good head and a good heart are always a formidable combination.' Pastor Isaac is that formidable combination."

I gestured for him to come to the front of the room. The two of us shook hands, and then I took a seat.

"Thank you, Brother Gideon," he said, "and I thank everyone here for having me. As the good detective told you, my life's mission has been inspired by Nelson Mandela. In his lifetime Mandela accomplished what seemed to be the impossible. He explained his successes by saying, 'It always seems impossible until it's done.' I try to live by those seven words, and they are how I explain miracles."

Then, with his fingers, Pastor Isaac counted off the words as he spoke: "'It always seems impossible until it's done.'"

Everyone was already leaning forward in their chairs. It had taken Jordan less than a minute to capture the room's attention.

"As Detective Gideon mentioned," he said, "I am a prison chaplain. It is possible, and probably likely, that I have ministered to some of those who killed your loved ones. I'm sure that is not an easy thing for you to accept. Why provide solace to a murderer? Why give comfort to an individual who has caused so much pain in others?

"You are the ones who suffer. And I'm sure you believe those who murdered your loved ones should have your fate, but worse. An eye for an eye. I'm sure many of you believe that these killers should be offered no balm or succor.

"I understand your feelings of anger and abandonment. When Christ was crucified, he cried out: 'My God, my God, why hast thou forsaken me?' But what did Gandhi say of revenge? 'An eye for an eye, and soon the whole world is blind.'

"Nelson Mandela had many reasons to hate his oppressors. And for a time he did hate his oppressors. But then he realized that harboring such hate was pointless. Constantly feeding the hate, he realized, diminished him as a person. It kept him from *being*. I suspect it's the same with many of you. Hate is a full-time job. It was while he was in prison that Mandela came to a startling realization: 'If you want to make peace with your enemy,' he said, 'you have to work with your enemy. Then he becomes your partner.'

"That seems impossible, doesn't it? How on earth can your enemy become your partner? Let me repeat my favorite seven words: 'It always seems impossible until it's done.'

"You have good reason to hate. But you have better reason to forgive. Keeping hate alive takes great effort. You have to stoke its fires by reliving your pain. By directing your thoughts backward, you can't look to the future; you can't even live for today."

As Pastor Isaac spoke, I snuck glances around the room. There were wet cheeks and nodding heads. Most seemed receptive to his words, but some sat with crossed arms and rigid posture. Not all the membership was ready to give up their hate; its grip was too strong. Maybe they perceived hate as their only life preserver.

Still, when Pastor Isaac finished his talk, there was mostly warm applause. During the question-and-answer period that followed, though, some club members interrogated the pastor's lenient attitude toward "the monsters."

"I reject that label," Isaac said. "By calling these men and women monsters, what we are saying is that they are not human and are not deserving of human rights."

I thought about Ellis Haines. He had murdered Suzanne Epstein, the wife of 187 Club member Arthur Epstein. Arthur wasn't in attendance that night. Being a single parent now, he spent as much time as possible with his son, Joel. Judging by the messages he'd asked me to pass on to Haines, Arthur could neither forgive nor forget. I wasn't sure if I could either, but I was glad for people like Isaac Jordan. He made me think. What separated a prisoner's shackles from the spectral chains worn by the likes of Jacob Marley?

I walked to the front of the room, thanked our speaker for all his good work and insights, and then I paid homage to the late Detective Walker by reading his favorite poem, "Dreams," written by Langston Hughes. Many in the room knew the short poem by heart, and other voices bolstered mine as I recited the words.

My hope was the same as the poet's: I wanted the members of my club of woe to still dare to dream, and to find their wings.

CHAPTER FIVE

A FRIEND OF MINE

I helped break down the community room, putting away the chairs and making sure all the trash was picked up. A few of the club members stayed to chat, but before long the room was almost empty.

"Do you need anything else, Detective?" Catalina asked.

"Not a thing," I said. "Have I mentioned that I'd be lost without you?"

At her smile I said, "Let me walk you to your car."

She tried to wave me off, but I insisted, and stayed in the lot until her car started. Then I jogged back to the community room, where Marta and Luciana were waiting.

"Do you want to talk here," I asked them, "or would you prefer sitting down in a coffee shop?"

The two had a silent consultation of eyes and Marta answered for them: "Here is fine."

I turned to Luciana; her big eyes were tearing up again. "Take a few deep breaths," I said. "I promise I don't bite and I'll do my best to make this as painless as possible."

She nodded, but after taking the suggested breaths, she turned away from me, finding it easier to direct her eyes and words at Marta.

After hearing her out, Marta said, "Luciana say that something happen this week that tell her Mateo is dead. She no tell the other detective because she no trust him. She tell her priest, though, and he say to her she should talk to the police. But she want to know if what she say to you can be . . . "

Marta paused to speak to Luciana, and after getting clarification said, "She want it private."

"So she wants it off the record? She wants it unofficial?"

Marta nodded, and the women talked some more before I heard a translation. "She also want to know, if she got some money, if it is hers or if you take it. In Mexico you pay the *mordida* to the police. Do you know that word?"

I nodded. The official translation of *mordida* is *bite*, which is slang for a bribe. "Luciana doesn't have to worry about me demanding any money from her," I said. "However, there are laws about obtaining money from ill-gotten gains, which means you're not supposed to profit from an illegal activity."

Marta started to explain what I had said, but Luciana seemed to already understand and replied back.

"What if Luciana just got the money?" said Marta.

"If she didn't solicit it," I said, "I imagine she can keep it without penalty. But since I'm not a lawyer, it would probably make sense for Luciana to tell me what happened, but have her explain it to me as a hypothetical situation."

I could tell by Marta's confused expression that I needed to translate my own English. "What I mean by that," I said, "is she can say, 'What would happen to someone *else* if they were given money?' Or maybe she might ask, 'Is it illegal if a *person* was just given money by another *person*?' And instead of saying, 'This happened to me,' she could say, 'I heard this story about a *friend* of mine.'"

Both Marta and Luciana were nodding to show they understood. "*Sí, sí,*" said Luciana, who then started talking in rapid-fire Spanish.

"She know someone whose fiancé went missing," translated Marta. "This fiancé no have papers. He work as a day laborer. One day he get picked up for a job and never come back. Five weeks after he not come back, this lady she know get a letter with twenty-five hundred-dollar bills in it. Along with the money was a note. It say, 'So sorry for your loss.'"

"So Luciana's *friend* was mailed this money and it arrived at the address where that friend lives?"

Luciana nodded and said, "*Sí.*"

"Was anything in it besides the money and the note?"

Luciana's small body and large eyes made her look like one of the children in a Margaret Keane painting. Her answer came accompanied by tears.

"*Cartas amorosas,*" she said, "*y poesía del amor.*"

My Spanish was worse than Luciana's English, but I didn't need a translation. "Love letters and love poetry."

Both women nodded, and then Luciana spoke to Marta. When she finished, Marta said, "Her *friend* tell her this fiancé always write letters and poems to the *woman*. She say he have them in his wallet."

"Do you think the missing fiancé had the woman's address somewhere in his wallet?"

Marta translated for me, and then listened to Luciana before replying. "She sure of it. In fact, she *hear* the man get his mail sent to where this woman lives."

"So her address was his mailing address," I asked, "even though they didn't live together?"

Both women were nodding, and then Luciana offered a further explanation that Marta translated.

"This man move around. That why his wallet is full. He keep everything in it."

Luciana demonstrated for me the size of the wallet, extending her thumbs and fingers as far as possible.

I decided we'd done enough hypothetical buffering. "As far as I'm concerned," I said, "that money is Luciana's and she can do what she wants with it."

Luciana nodded to show she understood.

"You said Mateo was a day laborer," I said. "Did he work out of a particular location?"

Luciana didn't need a translation. "Home Depot Woodland Hills."

Then she added something to Marta, who said, "He always go early to work, no later than seven. And he work every day but Sunday."

"What are you doing tomorrow morning?" I asked Luciana.

Because of the 187 Club meeting, Lisbet and I had agreed it would be easier if we slept at our own places. From the road, I called to wish her a good night. It was clear from her tired voice that she was almost ready to sleep. We talked for a little while, and then I crooned, "'Happy trails to you.'"

The Roy Rogers–Dale Evans Museum used to be in Victorville; I went there a few times as a kid and was sorry when I heard it closed. I suppose nostalgia isn't what it used to be. Still, I sometimes sing Roy's saddle song to Lisbet as an homage to the past.

"The last singing cowboy," said Lisbet.

"The horse stopped with a jerk," I said, "and the jerk fell off."

She gave a little laugh, then whispered, "Night, pardner."

"Night, ma'am."

I didn't have any Roy Rogers or Gene Autry music on my playlist, but I wasn't totally out of cowboys to reference. In fact, given the circumstances of the night, I think I picked just the right cowboy. My musical time machine went back to the seventies with War's "The Cisco Kid."

The funk washed over me and I started moving my head to the rhythms of the sax, harmonica, flute, and guitar. Sirius perked up in the back seat as I sang the refrain, "'He drink whiskey, Pancho drink the wine.'"

And then it was Sirius offering up his own four-note phrase at the end of those lyrics, a series of little howls that made me laugh. I lowered the volume and timed my next call so that it included the refrain about whiskey and wine.

"Is your bar open?" I asked.

Seth Mann is not only my next-door neighbor, he's my best friend. In many ways it's a case of opposites attracting. Seth is a twenty-first-century shaman. He's also the smartest person I know.

"Let me guess," he said. "You'll be drinking whiskey and I'll be drinking wine."

"Oh, Pancho," I said.

"Oh, Cisco," he replied.

We were both laughing like loons as I ended the call.

My whiskey was served in a cold rocks glass. In keeping with the evening's motif, Seth had poured himself a merlot. Not to be outdone in the drinking department, Sirius was lapping up some brown rice served with chicken stock.

I looked at Seth expectantly, waiting for his toast before taking a sip. Usually he volunteers a funny or sage toast with our first drink.

"Here's to staying positive," he said, "and testing negative."

We clinked glasses, and I took an approving sip of my nectar. "How nice to partake of a drink," I said approvingly, "that is old enough to drink."

"Twenty years," agreed Seth. "Happy ongoing birthday."

I raised my glass to show my appreciation. On my last birthday Seth had bought me a bottle of Pappy Van Winkle twenty-year-old bourbon, which he kept at his house. The bottle was being parceled out to me one drink a visit. With sixteen drinks to a bottle, I now had a dozen libations left. It was a good way to spread out a birthday, not to mention it encouraged slow, thoughtful sips.

"I'm lucky you weren't entertaining," I said, "and were free to bartend."

Seth looks like a homely version of the Happy Buddha, with a big belly and shaved head, but that doesn't seem to deter the opposite sex. I'm convinced that during his South American travels a witch doctor must have taught him how to make a potent love potion/aphrodisiac.

"I settled in for a quiet night of music and reading," he said. "Just before you called, I was thinking a nightcap would be a welcome way to end the day."

"I can drink to that."

We both took another sip. Seth seemed to be enjoying his wine as much as I was enjoying my whiskey.

"I would say that this libation puts an exclamation point on the end of my day," I said, "but I've never liked that expression. In fact, I've never liked exclamation points."

"And how have they offended you?" asked Seth.

"They strike me as clumsy," I said. "They scream 'look at me.' How many situations truly merit an exclamation point?"

"You'd prefer an interrobang?"

"I don't know what an interrobang is."

"It's a glyph that combines a question mark and an exclamation point."

I thought about that and said, "I don't think that's any better. I'm wondering if some language employs a punctuation mark that isn't in your face as much as an exclamation point. I think I'd be happy for just half an exclamation point."

"You sound like F. Scott Fitzgerald," said Seth. "If I remember correctly, he said, 'An exclamation point is like laughing at your own joke.'"

"I wonder what Zelda thought."

"Of punctuation, I don't know. But I'm sure she would have approved of our finishing the day with a drink. And she might have been interested in the idea of your half exclamation point. There have been others who have proposed new punctuation marks, but I don't know of any that have been incorporated into our language for the last several hundred years."

"What kind of new punctuation marks?" I said.

"As I remember it, half a century ago a French author wrote a book where he proposed such things as a love point and an acclamation point. I find it ironic that he also suggested we have an irony mark."

"Maybe there should be a 'spoken under the influence of alcohol' mark, a symbol of a little bottle."

Seth shrugged. "It would explain much. Maybe there's an emoji for that. I suppose they could be considered the new punctuation marks."

I made a rude noise and said, "Emojis are considerably worse than exclamation points."

"You don't like pink unicorns?"

"I prefer to stick with pink elephants, thank you."

"You're getting to be a curmudgeon, Gideon."

"That's been a longtime goal of mine."

Sirius finished eating and came over to Seth for some scratching. "Am I still on for having Sirius over the day after tomorrow?"

I nodded. It was time for my monthly meeting with Ellis Haines. Seth pursed his lips in disapproval. He thought my meetings with Haines put a "contagion" upon my soul and brought jeopardy to my being. He was probably right about that; I was glad he cared, but I still planned to see Haines. The Weatherman refused to talk with anyone else, and the FBI's Behavioral Analysis Unit was counting on me to be the middleman between them and him so as to keep the lines of communication open.

My friend scratched under Sirius's ears and down his neck, and my partner began melting under his touch. I was reminded of how grateful Emily had been for the affection I'd offered her.

"Sirius and I visited Angie's Rescues today," I said. "One of the dogs I spent time with was a pit bull named Emily. I was told she was used as a bait dog, which explains the hundreds of stitches all over her. And today, not much more than a week after she was mauled and beaten, her tail was thumping while I scratched her. Emily is proving a lot more forgiving of the human race than I am."

"I've often wondered if Thomas Macaulay was right," said Seth. "He said that Puritans hated bearbaiting not because it gave pain to the bear, but because it gave pleasure to the spectators."

"And I worry about me being a cynic," I said.

"I'm afraid animal rights is a recent concept. Many of our institutions have roots in horrific spectacles. Think of the bulls and the bears of the stock market. Those two animals used to be pitted against one another. Usually it was the bear that won, but not always. That's why the stock market empathizes with the bull."

"Why are your history lessons always so depressing?"

"I'm actually hoping that when it comes to animals the depths of depravity are behind us," Seth said. "The opening ceremonies of the Roman Colosseum were about as horrific as could be imagined. Over the course of one hundred days, more than nine thousand animals were killed in spectacles of slaughter. I won't offer up tales from those so-called blood sports, for both our sakes."

"Almost all serial murderers start with the torturing of animals," I said. "What happened to Emily, I consider torture."

"I agree. I assume you're looking for whoever was responsible for inflicting those wounds?"

"I am."

"There are those who argue that there are cultural components to dogfighting and cockfighting, and because of that, some sort of dispensation should be afforded its participants. I've been in countries in Latin America and South America where cockfighting is legal. I suppose it's not surprising that immigrants from those countries continue with such practices."

"They're not going to get any slack from me. In many cultures slavery was once legal. That doesn't mean it was ever morally right. And not that long ago it was legal to beat your wife as long as you complied with the rule of thumb—whatever you were beating her with wasn't thicker than your thumb."

Seth extended his thumb, studying its length. He shook his head in disgust and sighed. Both of us returned to the sipping of our beverages.

"When you called me up playing music by War," Seth said, "I didn't expect you'd be in a pensive mood."

"I was looking for cowboy music," I said, "as an antidote to the 187 Club meeting."

"It's not easy being the ringmaster of grief," said the shaman.

I thought about that. Seth has a way with phrases. He was right—I was the ringmaster of grief.

"I met a new member tonight. She's convinced her fiancé is dead, and I'm inclined to agree with her. He went missing six weeks ago, and just last week someone sent her twenty-five hundred dollars along with a note that said, 'I'm sorry for your loss.' In the envelope they also included the fiancé's love poems. He was a day laborer. Tomorrow morning we're going to where he used to be picked up for work, so we can talk with other day laborers."

"Guilt money," said Seth.

"It sounds like it."

"My advice to you isn't original: Follow the money."

"That's what I'm going to try to do."

Seth got up from his seat. Wineglass in hand, he walked over to the living room. I watched as he started thumbing through his huge collection of vinyl albums.

"What are you doing?" I called.

"Enough introspection," he said. "We started tonight's conversation with cowboy music, and we need to continue in that motif. I'm looking for the ultimate expression in cowboy music."

"'The Streets of Laredo,'" I said, sounding overly confident.

Seth shook his head. "I don't think we want a ballad."

"Willie Nelson's 'Mammas Don't Let Your Babies Grow Up to Be Cowboys,'" I said, "or Bon Jovi's 'Wanted Dead or Alive.'"

"I'm not talking about an individual artist," said Seth, "but a musical score."

"The 'Paladin' song," I said. *Have Gun—Will Travel.*"

"Close," said Seth.

"'Rawhide,'" I said.

"Very close," said Seth.

I could see he'd found the album and was gently preparing it for play.

"Give me a clue," I said.

"Clint Eastwood," he said.

That was enough. I should have figured it out with "Rawhide." "*The Good, the Bad, and the Ugly*," I said.

Seth smiled and cued up the album. It was ironic that Italians had directed and written the score of one of the quintessential American western films, but that was the way with spaghetti westerns.

The music provided everything you'd want or expect in a western: gunfire, whistling, coyote calls, and yodeling. When the score came to a close, Seth said, "Pretty far removed from 'Home on the Range.'"

"About as far removed," I said, "as the once-upon-a-time land where buffalo roamed."

CHAPTER SIX

DANKE SCHOEN

I had a second drink. It wasn't Pappy but a sipping whiskey from Kentucky's neighboring state of Tennessee. As Seth poured himself another half glass of merlot, he mentioned that he would be presiding over a wedding that weekend. That seemed a good opportunity to do some ball busting, a time-honored male tradition.

"What kind of a couple," I asked, "picks a shaman to officiate their wedding, rather than clergy or a justice of the peace?"

"In most cases," said Seth, "an enlightened one."

"What will you be wearing? A loincloth?"

"I imagine a very nice suit."

"Will the music be the playing of didgeridoos?"

"I find that unlikely, since no one getting married is an Australian."

I pretended I had a stogie in my hand and did my best Groucho imitation: "'Marriage is a wonderful institution. But who wants to live in an institution?'"

Seth laughed. "Maybe I'll use that line in the ceremony. What better way to start life's journey together than through laughter?"

"So at your weddings there are no strange ceremonies, or tribal music, or ancient rituals?"

"Many rituals are ancient," he said, "even though we're not aware of it. The exchanging of rings is an ancient Egyptian custom that started thousands of years ago. Most couples want that in their ceremony."

I surreptitiously looked at my now-naked ring finger. It wasn't until several months after Jennifer's death that I'd finally removed my wedding ring.

"Why the interest in weddings?" asked Seth.

I avoided the question by saying, "It seemed like a cheerier topic than funerals."

Sirius had settled at my feet. At first it seemed as if he was listening to our conversation, twitching his ears when we spoke, but it hadn't taken him very long to settle into a deep sleep. Now he was actively dreaming, making small whining sounds and twitching his paws.

Seth and I both smiled. "I've heard the dream patterns in dogs," he said, "are very similar to the dream patterns in humans."

"I wonder if I'm in his dreams," I said.

"It only stands to reason. You're the leader of his pack. He's with you night and day."

"It would be interesting to see how he perceives me in his dreams," I said. "Am I this patriarchal figure? Am I a friendly big brother? In his mind, is my form distinctly human, or does he see me in a different image?"

"Do you dream of dogs?"

I nodded. "Sirius is in many of my dreams. Sometimes other dogs are there as well."

"Good."

"Why good?" I asked.

"Sirius is your spirit animal. He protects you when you're awake, and I imagine he protects you in your dreams."

Sirius was breathing harder now, and his noises were louder. The sounds were familiar.

"I actually think I know what he's dreaming about," I said. "He makes those sounds whenever I'm getting ready to throw a Frisbee. Sirius can hardly contain himself."

We watched his legs. They had gone from twitches to running in place, but the movements suddenly stopped.

"In his dream," I said, "he just made a great catch."

My visit with Seth was a short one, maybe forty-five minutes. I didn't want to stay up late, as I'd agreed to pick up Luciana at six thirty in the morning so that we could interview witnesses who might remember the last time they'd seen Mateo.

I turned in a little before 10:30. My hope was that I'd get at least seven hours' sleep.

Man proposes, God disposes.

The flames were everywhere. The fire was raging all around me, and the black smoke was making breathing impossible. Every breath felt like I was swallowing fire.

Over all the burning smells, one stood out. Cooking meat and hair. Our flesh was on fire.

I was holding a gun. I was also holding up my partner. Sirius was dying. He'd been shot by the scumbag who was helping me carry him. The murderer was assisting me for the simple reason that my gun was leveled at his gut.

"Please," said the man. "The dog's dead."

I considered shooting him. The fire had burned away my inhibitions. Murder was no longer something unthinkable. But the killer had a use: with two people it was easier carrying Sirius. Now we just had to find a way out of the fire.

"'He ain't heavy,' I sang, "'he's my brother.'" It came out as a raw whisper of pain.

The killer thought I'd lost it. I was singing in the middle of our immolation. My madness frightened him because he knew it liberated me. But I was aware enough to study the condition of my partner. When his rib cage infinitesimally expanded, my own breathing became easier. Sirius was still alive. I could feel the murderer tense, and knew he was about to throw Sirius my way.

"Time to die?" I rasped. I felt like the spokesperson for Death; I'm sure I looked it.

Embers showered down on us, burning our flesh. The killer screamed, while I pretended indifference to the pain. My eyes were focused on his; so was my gun. The killer reconsidered his escape plan.

"This way!" I said.

He followed my command, even though I didn't know where I was going, even though I didn't know if there was a way out of the flames.

Sirius helped me escape the inferno, nudging me with his muzzle and licking my face to wake me from the fire dream. Only two people know about my PTSD, Lisbet and Seth, and I'm not very forthcoming with them about it. The truth is I downplay what I go through, because I don't want them to be overly concerned. One day I might confess just how debilitating these dreams are. In fact, with each fire dream, I burn, and not only in my mind. Sometimes the welts show themselves; sometimes not.

It isn't easy to explain the pain. At one time or another, most people have awakened to a severe cramping in their legs. If they multiplied that pain by about a hundred, they'd have some idea of what occurs during a fire dream.

Whenever I escape from hell and experience the ecstasy that the sudden cessation of pain affords, my "third eye" opens. The insights come at a price; I burn for them. I suspect my visions reflect my preoccupations at the time, which are typically the cases I'm working.

With his back turned to me, a man played a guitar. Then he sang, "'Love is so short, forgetting is so long.'"

I knew that line. I had recited it at the previous month's 187 Club meeting. It came from Pablo Neruda's poem "Tonight I Can Write the Saddest Lines."

But I knew it wasn't Neruda who was singing his poetry. Even though I couldn't see his face, and even though I didn't know what he looked like, I was certain the singer was Mateo. His song was for his muse, Luciana.

Mateo continued playing the guitar, but the tune changed, morphing into Johnny Cash's "The Streets of Laredo." Mateo sang in English, "'I'm a young cowboy and I know I've done wrong.'"

And then I was in a crowd, but it was more like a mob. The faces were ugly and contorted. The stink of body odor filled the air; it was a primal smell. I was in stands that overlooked a pit. Two dogs were fighting; even louder than their snarls were the cries from their trainers exhorting them to "Kill, kill, kill."

My vision switched, and I found myself in a bigger arena, but I wasn't in the stands. I was at the Colosseum and was among the sacrificial victims being brought out. The crowd was cheering for carnage. They wanted blood. And then I saw Mateo and Emily also being forced into the pit. We were all lambs being delivered to the slaughter.

My third eye closed; the oracle stopped talking to me. I was back in my bed. My hot sweat was cooling. Perched protectively over me was my shepherd. "Good dog," I said to Sirius. And then Morpheus claimed me and told me lies, saying the fiery battle was behind me, which was enough for me to sleep.

The alarm went off too early. All I wanted to do was sleep away the morning, but I removed the sheets and began to slowly move around. As usual, I felt desiccated by my fire walk. I drank two glasses of ice water, and then started in on an iced coffee, downing two ibuprofen as chasers.

I put down some kibble for Sirius, and then shaved and dressed. Luciana lived in an apartment complex in south Van Nuys, which was less than five miles from my house. When Sirius and I set out for her place, it was still dark. It was a good reminder of what many people had to face every day just getting to work.

During the drive I thought about my vision from the night before. As usual, my oracle needed divining. There's never a priestess around when you need one, though. Some of my vision clearly had been inspired by my talk with Seth. He'd played the western music and brought up the wholesale slaughtering that had gone on at the Colosseum. Emily had clearly been in my thoughts as well. Of course, it made no sense that Emily and Mateo had both ended up in the pit. Come to think of it, I'd also been brought out as a blood offering. As was always the case, my oracular vision could be interpreted in all sorts of ways.

When I arrived at Luciana's apartment, I texted her that I was waiting out front. *OK*, she wrote back. Two minutes later she joined me and Sirius in the car. Marta had not been able to get time off of work, meaning Luciana would have to deal with my

Spanish and I would have to deal with her English. My secret weapons were Google Translate and an app I had downloaded that supposedly could translate my spoken English into Spanish.

With all the apps available on our cell phones, it seems to me we're getting closer and closer to Gene Roddenberry's vision of Starfleet tricorders. We can get information and readings on just about everything. I hope that proves to be a good thing.

The translation app seemed to work reasonably well, and the two of us "talked" during our seven-mile drive. Luciana told me Mateo had only lived in his latest residence for a few weeks before his disappearance. She said he had moved to Van Nuys to be closer to her, and had shared a two-bedroom, one-bathroom apartment with six other day laborers. On most days the roommates shared a ride to their favorite hiring halls, but because their car was out of service on the day Mateo went missing, he'd traveled with a vanload of other workers to Woodland Hills. On that day his roommates had decided to look for work closer to home and had gone to the Home Depot in Van Nuys. Mateo preferred the more affluent Woodland Hills, where he could usually demand up to twenty dollars an hour.

"But it's a big hassle," I said, "to have to travel from Van Nuys to Woodland Hills."

As the crow flies, it's only about six miles, but in LA those are often hard-fought miles.

The app had trouble with the word *hassle*, forcing me to rephrase my sentence to include the words *great difficulty*. At that, Luciana did some thoughtful nodding and looked like she was about to get weepy.

Mateo, she explained, was so anxious to get married that he was doing everything he could to make the most money in the fastest amount of time. In addition to sending money home, Mateo gave Luciana "marriage money" to bank. The two of them had agreed to save ten thousand dollars for their nuptials. Their plan was to return home to Mexico for the ceremony and a grand fiesta. According to Luciana, they had almost reached the half-way point in their goal when Mateo disappeared.

Woodland Hills is right off the 101 freeway corridor. It's an area that is mostly white and mostly well-off. During the summer months it is also usually the hottest area in LA. A few years back the *LA Times* ran a story explaining why that is. What it boils down to—*boils* being the operative word—is that Woodland Hill's location prevents it from getting any cooling ocean breezes.

I was glad it wasn't yet summer; I was also glad we were arriving early, before the heat of the day had had time to build.

Luciana agreed that it would probably be best if she did all the questioning. The presence of a white law enforcement officer might scare off the day laborers, most of whom were in the country illegally.

The Home Depot opened most days at six. At the moment there were around twenty-five day laborers assembled at the periphery of the parking lot. All the workers wore similar outfits: blue jeans, work boots, and layered shirts.

I used my phone and Google Translate to formulate the questions that I wanted Luciana to ask. The idea was for her to show Mateo's picture around, explain when he'd gone missing, and ask my questions.

Sirius and I went for a walk while Luciana took my phone and began her rounds. Even though we kept our distance, I could see most of the day laborers didn't want to engage with Luciana. This was especially true of the hierarchy that seemed to be running the labor pool. Most of the others seemed to take their cues from these unofficial jefes. Being a Good Samaritan is a luxury most people can no longer afford. Still, Luciana was persistent and managed to get a few of the workers to talk to her.

I leaned against a fence, trying to be unobtrusive. All throughout Los Angeles County there were day laborers like these looking for work. Though they are ubiquitous, they are also all but invisible. The longer I watched the goings-on in the parking lot, the more I made sense of their hiring system. There seemed to be several work organizers. One or two English speakers would ask questions about each job, learning what it entailed and how many hours the work was likely to take. They would ask if lunch was included and the number of workers needed. Then a big guy would pick which laborers got the job. It sort of reminded me of how organized crime functioned. At the end of the day, I was sure these organizers would get their own *mordida*, their cut of the laborers' wages.

Since I had time to watch the business of human trade going on, I was surprised at a number of things I saw. I would have thought that the average employer was some construction boss, but that wasn't the case. It was the citizens of Woodland Hills who were doing most of the hiring, and maybe twenty percent of those picking up the labor were women. Many of the women had their maids riding with them to translate. From a distance I could hear the negotiations; skilled work like electrical and plumbing commanded higher wages.

After half an hour Luciana came back to my car. She said no one could be sure if they had seen Mateo on the day he went missing, and no one was sure what job he had last worked. One of my questions, she said, had amused the workers. I had wanted to know: *Have you worked for anyone unusual?* I also had Luciana ask: *Has anyone ever asked you to do something strange on the job?*

The consensus, according to those she asked, was that all gringos are strange, but one older man in particular had quite the reputation. On a weekly basis he would pick up a worker, always one of the younger men, for what he described as "light gardening." There was never precisely a bait and switch, but after arriving at this man's house, the worker was always asked if he would prefer doing another task for more money—life modeling. The man would explain that he was an artist and was in need of a nude model. Some of the workers chose not to model, Luciana was told. And with much winking and ribald laughter, she was told that other workers did more than model.

Luciana also spoke to a worker who said he'd been hired to dig holes for a fence, but upon getting to the job had been asked if he'd like to act in a movie called *Macho Libre*. The young man who made the offer, he said, had told him that he would wear a mask like the *lucha libre* wrestlers, but that he would be fighting another man and the winner would get a purse of $350. That was more than double a typical day's wages. The worker said there was a boxing ring already set up in the backyard, and near the ring was a stable that housed a donkey painted with black stripes. The only other painted donkey the worker had ever seen was in Tijuana, where tourists liked to have their pictures taken with the "zonkey." For the fight, the laborer was asked to wear a zebra-striped outfit. His opponent, the worker was told, would be in a costume that looked like a banana peel. Because the whole situation didn't feel right, the worker had declined the fight, despite the persistent pitch of the young man to take his $350. Even if he lost, he was told, he would get a purse of $175.

"Did he tell you when this happened?" I asked.

"*Hace un mes*," she said, and then added, "*mas o menos.*"

A month, she said, more or less. According to Luciana, roughly one-third of the day laborers she'd talked to recognized Mateo from the pictures; a few had even worked with him and remembered him as a hard worker. Those who knew him recalled that Mateo had always been one of the first picked because he was skilled and strong and he could make himself understood in English. Luciana had remembered to follow through with my questions for those who had worked with Mateo. I had wanted to know if anything stood out about the work, and was curious if they knew of any other workers who had disappeared. No one seemed to remember anything out of the ordinary, and they weren't aware of any other workers going missing.

Luciana had also asked if Mateo had any "regulars" he worked for. There were a few contractors, the workers said, who requested Mateo whenever he was available. Luciana said the workers didn't really know those who hired them; they seemed to remember their trucks more than they did a bunch of middle-aged white men. One worker, nicknamed Indio, remembered there was a contractor known as "Hitler" who Mateo refused to work for. Hitler had gotten his nickname because of the bumper sticker on his truck that showed Hitler giving a Nazi salute. Indio said Mateo didn't like the man because he had refused to pay him the hourly wage that had been agreed upon.

It was a common story, unfortunately. The workers had no recourse. If they appealed to the law, they could potentially be deported. I liked it that Mateo had stood up to the man, but I wondered if his assertiveness had anything to do with his disappearance.

I complimented Luciana on all her work, and then asked her to go back for a second round of questioning. This time I wanted her to talk to the organizers and see if she could get names or addresses of the life-model artist, as well as the *Macho Libre* promoter, or at least get descriptions of the men and the general areas where they lived. While I was telling her this, I glanced up and saw a white Ford F-150 truck pulling up to where the laborers were waiting. There had been a lot of big trucks doing the same thing all morning, but what was different about this one was that Hitler was saluting me from a bumper sticker that read: *Raise Your Right Hand If You Believe in Gun Control.*

Der Führer was in the house.

Sirius and I started toward his truck. The driver didn't see us coming. He was too busy negotiating. "*Diez dólares* per hour," he said.

The man's accent was as bad as his Spanish. He was burly, with reddish porcine jowls and recessed, tiny black eyes. The two negotiators were shaking their heads.

"Easy work," he said. "Don't try and shake me down, muchachos."

"I understand that's your specialty," I said. "That and bait and switch."

All the workers took off. It's amazing how every nationality on this planet seems to have cop radar. Even the driver of the truck had it. Hitler rolled his piggy eyes to show his disdain toward me.

"How the hell was I to know these people were illegals?" he said. "You should be rousting them, not me. I'm a citizen."

"If you thought they were here legally," I said, "why were you trying to pay them less than the state's minimum wage?"

"I guess a cop with a cushy job that's chock full of perks wouldn't know the first thing about negotiating a price," he said. "The first rule is you start low."

"That's a wonderful tip, but I'm afraid I don't have time to hear any more. Early tee time at the club, you know?"

I showed Hitler the picture of Mateo. "Know this guy?"

"He done something?" The man's voice was hopeful. "He's a troublemaker."

"I understand you had an altercation with this man."

"It wasn't an altercation. It was more like a misunderstanding."

"What was the misunderstanding over?"

"He thought I shorted him some cash."

"And how did the situation resolve itself?"

"When he got pushy, I told him to go to hell."

"There was nothing physical?"

"He wasn't that stupid," Hitler said, patting a bulge under his Pendleton shirt.

"I assume you're licensed to carry?"

"I'm legal with Uncle *Scam*," he said, smiling at his clever-ness, "as long as he doesn't mess with my Second Amendment rights."

I asked to see his license, and he asked for my badge number. Both of us complied. Ken Ritter lived in Woodland Hills. I wrote down his address, handed back his license, and thanked him, then followed up with a few more questions. Ritter said he'd never seen Mateo anywhere besides this particular Home Depot parking lot, and after their disagreement they'd had no further interactions other than Mateo's occasionally hanging around in the background and "instigating against me like some kind of communist."

That was enough for me. It was time to take my leave. I was afraid in another minute Ritter might start singing the "Deutsch-landlied."

"Danke schoen," I said.

As Sirius and I walked away, I started singing the kitsch classic under my breath, crooning the words as if channeling Wayne Newton: "'My heart says danke schoen, danke schoen, auf Wiedersehen, danke schoen.'"

My partner knows bad German when he hears it and pre-tended he didn't know me. "It could have been worse," I told him. "I might have been wearing lederhosen."

CHAPTER SEVEN

A SONG FOR FERDINAND THE BULL

Sirius and I drove to the office, or at least what passes for my official office. SCU—the Special Cases Unit—was created by LAPD's chief of police, Gene Ehrlich, to keep Sirius and me on the force after we captured Ellis Haines and survived our fire walk. Officially, the two of us report to the chief. From the first, though, I knew better than to try and claim an office among all the suits in the Police Administration Building in downtown LA. In such an environment I would have needed a muzzle far more than my partner did. The solution was my cubicle at Central.

As the crow flies, the Central Police Station is probably not much more than a mile from the PAB. When Chief Ehrlich proposed my position, he likely reasoned that LAPD was playing with house money. Had I wanted to, I could have left the force on full disability, but the idea of being paid not to work wasn't what I wanted. Usually I'm happy with my decision, except when being forced to be a tin hero. On several occasions each year, the chief reminds me to polish my Medal of Valor and Sirius's Liberty Award, and he trots us out for some PR event.

Hearing the trumpet fanfare as Sirius and I entered Central's building made me feel as if I were attending one of those events. Sergeant Perez had obtained a recording of "La Virgen de la Macarena." In Seville, Spain, the matadors prayed to the Macarena prior to their entering the arena. Some people refer to the music as "The Bullfighter's Song." Older individuals remember it as the music that accompanied the appearance of Don Rickles on *The Tonight Show Starring Johnny Carson*.

I waved to the imaginary throngs. The sergeant's playing the music for as long and as loudly as he was doing meant the captain wasn't in. Perez tossed a plastic rose my way, which Sirius picked up and promptly returned to him. When Perez turned off the music, he said, "Speaking of bullshit."

Then he took the rose from Sirius and said, "I don't mean you, Officer Sirius." For whatever inexplicable reason, Sirius enjoys Perez's company. The sergeant scratched Sirius behind the ears and added, sotto voce, "And don't worry, I'm working on your request to get a new partner."

This was the third time I had been greeted by the same music upon arriving at Central. Up until now I hadn't asked the obvious question. Finally, I bit. "I know I shouldn't ask," I said, "but I'm curious as to what's behind your musical production."

"Our lord and master speaks to the peanut gallery," Perez said to Sirius. "We should be grateful. And we need to show this gratitude on those rare occasions when Detective Gideon graces us with his company. After all, his mere appearance deserves commemoration."

In a much less flowery tone, he said to me, "Of course, it was a tough choice between 'Bullshitter'—I mean 'Bullfighter'—and '(How Much Is) That Doggie in the Window?'"

Perez is openly skeptical of what he calls the "Strange Cases Unit." He also isn't a fan of my odd hours at Central.

"It's nice to be missed," I said.

As I walked to my cubicle, he started the music again. It might have been a touch grandiloquent, but it was also catchy. Hemingway loved his bullfights, and probably loved the music of "La Virgen de la Macarena." I preferred another bull story, that of Ferdinand the bull. *The Story of Ferdinand* had been a favorite picture book of mine as a boy, about a bull who preferred smelling the flowers to anything else. I doubted Hemingway had liked that story, but I also doubted he'd ever stopped to smell the flowers. Maybe they'll make a song for Ferdinand the bull one day. I think I'd like that as well.

I thumbed through my phone messages, and then the mail. What I couldn't figure out was why there were so many travel brochures about various locales around the world. I knew the likely culprit, though, and took the entire lot to Perez. He looked up from his work, acting surprised to see me standing there. His giveaway was an ill-concealed smirk.

"Any idea how these got on my desk?" I asked.

He stared at the brochures with feigned innocence. "Those?" Then he snapped his fingers as if suddenly remembering. "That's right," he said. "Since you're here so infrequently, Detective Dog, I assumed that, like me, you were contemplating the prospects of retirement."

"You're retiring?" I asked.

"In three hundred ninety-two days, three hours, and fourteen minutes."

I had been on stakeouts before where cops passed the time by calculating when they could retire and get the most bang for their buck. The calls between the unmarked cars weren't about the case we were working but about pensions and the factoring in of leave time and sick pay.

"I'm sure I speak for everyone here," I said, "when I say that your retirement can't come soon enough for us."

"Your words mean so much to me, Scooby-Doo," he said. Then an evil light shone in his eyes. "Note to self," he said. "Get the music for *Scooby-Doo*."

But of course, Perez couldn't wait for that. In the absence of the music, he made do with his voice: "'Scooby-Dooby-Doo, where are you? We got some work to do now.'"

Three hundred and ninety-two days, I thought.

I waited until Perez got tired of singing his ditty to call Detective Andrea Charles. Unfortunately, my call was delayed a few minutes because Perez found the *Scooby-Doo* theme song on YouTube and loudly played it two or three times. That was just enough for the song to get stuck in my head. In fact, I was humming it while calling Detective Charles.

She picked up on the third ring, after "We need some help from you now."

I had met Andrea the week before when I had gone to Las Vegas hoping to establish a relationship with a detective willing to work a case off the books. Andrea was in her early thirties; she was ambitious; and I didn't doubt that one day she would be the Las Vegas chief of police.

"This is your partner in crime, Michael Gideon," I said. "I'll be meeting with our friend tomorrow. You got anything for me?"

"You ever reopen cases other detectives have closed?" she asked.

"More times than I care to remember."

"Then I don't have to tell you about the bureaucratic stumbling blocks involved with getting information."

I had brought to Detective Charles all the dates Ellis Haines had stayed in Las Vegas during the five years prior to his apprehension. Haines was a skilled poker player; he'd even competed in the World Series of Poker on two occasions. I was able to document fifteen occasions when he'd traveled to Las Vegas, but there could have been more. It's only a four-hour drive, after all. Still, it was my contention that Haines couldn't have been such a frequent visitor without committing murder.

Once more I voiced the assertion that had gotten Andrea interested in the first place: "Haines was an extremely controlled killer on his home turf, but it's human nature to loosen up while on vacation."

"That's what you keep saying," she said.

"So you haven't found anything?"

"I didn't say that," she said. "What I'm telling you is that everything is taking time. I took the dates you provided and looked for homicides that occurred during the same period. Using your parameters, I've come up with four potential victims."

"That's great."

"In the next day or two, I'll send you the files at your private email address," she said. "Three of the women were white and one was Asian. The age range was twenty-nine to forty-three. Two women were from this area and two were from out of town."

I had asked Detective Charles to focus on women aged twenty-five to forty-five. The victims, I said, were more likely to be affluent than not. That was at odds with most female homicide victims, many of whom are prostitutes, are poor, and have drug problems. As far as was known, Haines had never preyed on the disadvantaged. His victims had been the suburban girls next door. That explained his reign of terror; so-called normal people had been scared.

"How were the victims dispatched?" I asked.

"They weren't strangled," she said, "just as you predicted."

Before his profession was revealed and Haines became known by most as the Weatherman, he had acquired the nickname the Santa Ana Strangler. The name was apt: Haines strangled his victims during Santa Ana conditions. Despite that, it would surprise me if Haines had strangled any of his Las Vegas victims. My guess was that he would have wanted to deviate from his MO. People on vacation like to do new and different things. And Haines wouldn't have wanted any of his crimes in Las Vegas to be linked to the California killings.

"Two died from knife wounds that were almost surgical in nature," she said, "one overdosed on a cocktail that included Rohypnol, and another had drugs in her system and was probably unconscious when she died of blunt-force trauma."

"Everything is detailed in the reports you're sending?"

"Every gruesome bit."

"Any questions you want me to ask him tomorrow?"

She thought about that. "If you can get him on the topic of Las Vegas," she said, "you might ask him about his favorite entertainment and dining spots. That might give me a point of connection between him and his victims."

"Will do," I said, "and please keep digging. Linking Haines with these homicides will put the nails in his coffin. I want to blindside him. Right now, his lawyers are challenging everything that happened in California. They're not looking beyond the cases that have already been made against him. But there is no way he confined his killings to Los Angeles County."

"You know him better than anybody," she said.

"Unfortunately, you're right about that."

"The crime scenes weren't completely clean," she said. "I've got a full plate right now, but in the next few days I'll be filling out paperwork to run tests."

"No shortcuts," I said.

The unsaid was that I didn't want Haines's lawyers to be able to challenge any of the new results.

We agreed to keep in touch and I hung up, heartened by the possibilities.

In the quiet of my cubicle, I organized my notes from the morning. Afterward, I checked the system and read the missing-person report on Mateo Ramos. From there I looked at arrest reports involving day laborers. In most cases they were the victims of crimes rather than the perpetrators of them. I checked police reports and called the coroner's office; no bodies matching Mateo's description had turned up.

My cell phone rang; the display told me Officer LaVar Brockington was calling. "Gideon," I said.

"This is Brockington," he said, "following up on our last call."

"Thanks for getting back to me."

His begrudging "uh-huh" reminded me that I hadn't given him a choice in the matter. "Anyway, I got some leads for you. Multiple informants offered up the name of the man they think dumped the dogs. They're pretty sure your guy is Humberto Rivera, called Tito by most. This Tito isn't a gangbanger or a meth head. He's a local businessman who runs a salvage yard and also trains and sells guard dogs. His legitimate businesses allow him to hide his real passion in plain sight. He works out his fighting dogs in the salvage yard. That means if he's ever questioned, he can always say he's training guard dogs."

"Has he always been so slick? What's his rap sheet look like?"

"A few misdemeanors," said Brockington, "but none in the last decade. When Tito was in his twenties, he was found with some dead roosters and got pinned with a charge of animal cruelty. Another time, he was caught holding a controlled substance. Tito started in cockfighting. It's a family thing going back to his days growing up in eastern Honduras. Back then, his street name was El Gallo Negro."

"The Black Rooster," I translated.

"The word is he still does cockfighting, but he found dogfighting was much more lucrative."

"You figure out why our rooster dumped the dogs out in the open?"

"I've got a theory on that," Brockington said. "I don't think he had a choice. There was a shootout between the Big Hazard gang and some bangers from MS-13, not far from Tito's salvage yard. The Criminal Gang and Homicide Division set up checkpoints throughout the area and were stopping cars, looking for the shooters. My guess is that Tito got caught up in the dragnet when he was coming back to his business from one of his dogfights. Maybe he saw what was going on, or was listening to a police scanner, or one of his confederates warned him. I'm sure the salvage yard is his usual spot for disposing of the dogs' bodies, but he couldn't chance getting caught with the goods, so he dumped them."

"You ever have any dealings with Tito?"

"None," said Brockington. "But people who know him say don't be fooled by his pretend Caribbean smile and easygoing ways. They say he's a shark."

"Got a business name and address for me?"

When Sirius and I left Central, Perez once again turned on "The Bullfighter's Song." I couldn't help but think of the irony. The world of animal fighting seemed to be following me.

Being a recovering Catholic, I'm not exactly sure where I fall on the religious scale. I love dogs, but I'm not sure about dogma. Two of the men I most respect, Seth and Father Pat Garrity, live their faith as a vocation. Although I might be a C&E Catholic (Christmas and Easter), I am always alert to synchronicity in my life. A dog left for dead had miraculously survived and prompted discussions of bearbaiting and animal fighting. In my dreams I had felt as if I were in that loathsome pit.

My destination was in an unincorporated industrial area to the east of Boyle Heights. Within its six and a half square miles, the Boyle Heights neighborhood houses 100,000 residents. It's a gritty area, made more so by the three freeways and the railroad tracks that run through it. The LA County coroner's department is located in Boyle Heights, as is the USC Medical Center. Attached to the hospital is the Navy Trauma Training Center. The military wanted to ready their doctors for battlefield medicine, and for many years the vying gangs in and around Boyle Heights have provided those doctors with plenty of war-zone-type injuries.

The small houses and apartment units gradually gave way to an industrial triangle filled with warehouses, heavy industry, auto wrecking, impound lots, and salvage and recycling. Concertina wire abounded, as did spiked metal gates and security cameras. Two signs confirmed that I was in the right place. One said, *Best Scrap*. The other sign had a graphic of a slathering Rottweiler and the words *Junkyard Dog Services*. Smaller signs warned against trespassers, promising an armed response and attack dogs.

I drove through the open gate up to a trailer that looked as if it was serving as the office. When I got out of my car, dogs in distant kennels began barking. I wasn't being scrutinized only by those with four legs. From inside the trailer two men stared at me. One was small and squat and wore an eye patch over his right eye. He had the face and physique common to many with Mayan ancestry. The other man wore a panama hat and cowboy garb—blue jeans, boots, denim shirt, and bandanna. He had the darker look of what some people refer to as Caribbean Hispanics or Afro-Hispanics. A toothpick moved from one side of his mouth to the other.

As I entered the office, the man I suspected was Humberto "Tito" Rivera smiled at me, showing a gold cap on one of his front teeth. "What you want, Mr. Lawman?" he asked in an island accent.

The toothpick made a contemplative loop of his mouth while he studied Sirius. From inside the car my partner eyeballed him right back.

"You come here to sell me your dog, is that it?" Tito shook his head. "He be a bit long in the tooth. And shepherds don't make great guard dogs. They're too passive, and they get bored too easily. I'd rather have a Maligator."

Because of their aggressiveness, the Belgian Malinois is often called Maligator.

Tito removed the toothpick from his mouth. "Twenty bucks," he said. "That's the top price I can pay for your dog."

"Is that the going rate for bait dogs?" I asked. "Is that what you paid for the pit bull you dumped not too far from here last week? The vet who treated her said she had been used as a sacrifice to a fighting dog."

"Don't know what you're talking about, man," he said. "My dogs are well taken care of. Junkyard Dogs supplies businesses and households all over LA with guard dogs trained by me and Fausto here."

The man with the eye patch nodded.

"Since that's the case, I assume you won't mind if I walk around your junkyard and look around?"

"Salvage yard," said Tito. "Haven't you heard I'm an environmentalist? I buy metal and recycle it."

"Then you have nothing to hide, right, Tito?"

"I wish I could help you out, Mr. Lawman, but my insurance company is touchy about unauthorized individuals walking on these grounds. There are a lot of sharp objects that could hurt you. I'd hate for that to happen and then have you turn around and sue me."

"On your rap sheet I'm told you have the street name El Gallo Negro. How did that come about?"

"I'm not sure," he said. "Probably because I love to eat chicken, and I think the dark meat is best."

"As I understand it, you were big into cockfights."

"That was a long time ago," he said. "That was before I became a respectable businessman."

"I was told that the lowlifes that train dogs to fight have a lot of specialized equipment. Is that what you don't want me to see?"

"I already told you how strict my insurance company is."

"Or are you afraid you didn't tidy up well enough after one of your kills? I got to admit this is a perfect setup to rid yourself of bodies, with all your loaders and crushers and heavy machinery. And do you have one of those smelting furnaces on the property? That would make cremations a breeze, wouldn't it?"

"Are you selling scrap metal, Detective? If you're not, then we don't have nothing else to talk about unless you're unloading that dog of yours. But now that I can see him better, I'm thinking twenty bucks is too generous an offer. He's old, and he doesn't look like he's got much game. What do you say we settle on ten bucks, *man*?"

I did my best to swallow my anger. Tito was watching me with that big smile of his.

"Is it true what they say about the men who fight dogs to the death?" I asked.

"What is it they say?"

"I wouldn't worry about it," I said. "You ever hear the word *overcompensate*? I'm sure you have."

"All right, all right," he said, as if conceding something. "I'll pay you fifteen bucks for that dog of yours. There's an English mastiff I'd like to introduce him to."

He wanted me to take a swing at him. I was all but certain his trailer was set up with CCTV.

"You own a gun, Tito?"

"The State of California isn't very forgiving about youthful indiscretions," he said.

"Is that a yes or a no?"

"As you are aware, I have a record. And because of that, California says I can't own a handgun."

I turned to the man with the eye patch. "What about you?" I asked.

Instead of answering, the man turned to his boss.

"Fausto's English isn't very good," said Tito.

"California citizen?" I asked.

"He has a green card," said Tito.

"I'd like to see it."

The man produced his permanent resident card. Fausto Alvarez had been born in Mexico in 1972 and was admitted as a permanent resident to the US in 1995.

"How long have you worked here, Fausto?" I asked.

He shrugged. "Ten years?" he said, making it sound more like a question than an answer.

"We're kind of busy, Mr. Lawman," said Tito. "We need to get back to work unless there's something else you want to discuss."

"Four dogs were dumped less than a mile from here," I said. "The dogs were beaten and shot."

I didn't bother to tell him that no ballistic tests could be run anyway because all of the forensic evidence had gone up in smoke.

"Is that so?"

"I am going to do my best to link you with those dogs," I said. "There will be commercials aired on TV offering a five-thousand-dollar reward for information pertaining to that animal abuse. Someone is bound to come forward. And what do you think your insurance company is going to do when they learn about your side business?"

Tito's smile was no longer quite so pronounced. "You going to eat a steak tonight, Detective?"

"I'm not sure what I'll be eating."

"But I'll bet you like a good steak."

I didn't answer.

"I find it amusing that a meat eater like you acts so righteous about a blood sport, but you're okay with legalized killing."

"I don't think any meat eaters get joy from the killing of their protein. Only sick assholes derive enjoyment from seeing animals rip each other apart."

"What you call sick, I call natural. You can't change the way of the world, Detective. Roosters naturally fight other roosters. Male dogs want to fight other males."

"And you engineer it so that the fight is to the death."

"Nature's gene pool is designed to reward the winners and punish the losers. It's survival of the fittest, *man*."

"In nature the loser can run away and come back to fight another day. You don't allow that. You set up your pens so that there is no escape."

Tito smiled and shook his head. "All over the world animals get pitted against one another, and everywhere you go there is an audience cheering them on. It don't matter if they're fish or fowl, animal or insect. If it crawls, swims, or flies, people want to watch a fight to the death. Will the praying mantis beat the black widow? Who will come out alive, the wolf or the pit bull? Shrews happily fight to the death, and you can't keep Siamese fighting fish apart. Lots of people see nothing wrong with showcasing what comes naturally to animals. So who made you the judge?"

"I enforce the laws that society has determined," I said. "Society drew that line in the sand. You might say that line is hypocritical or arbitrary, but I say that line is necessary. Without lines like it, without boundaries, society implodes."

Tito shook his head. "Do you really think the world is less violent than it was? If it's bloody, they will come. Mixed martial arts bouts stop just short of death matches, and no sport has ever grown so fast."

"Two wrongs don't make a right," I said.

"Are you sure about that, *man*?" he said, his Caribbean accent and his smile mocking me.

Just because the slope is slippery, it doesn't mean right and wrong have become interchangeable.

"I'm sure, *man*," I said.

CHAPTER EIGHT

LET SLEEPING DOGS LIE

After leaving the Junkyard Dogs lot, I felt in sore need of a friendly voice and offered up Lisbet's name to my car's hands-free Bluetooth system.

My entreaty got me the mechanical response of "Calling Lisbet on her cell phone."

She picked up after two rings, and I said, "I called out your name and you appeared."

"That'll teach me to not screen my calls," she said.

"When I shouted 'Lisbet' to my car's electronic genie, I sort of sounded like Stanley Kowalski shouting, 'Stella!'"

"Doesn't sound like you've had a good day."

"It's suddenly better now," I said.

"Who is this sweet stranger?"

"I'll introduce you. When will you be receiving callers?"

"Come over anytime," she said. "I was just about to start dinner. Have you given any thought as to what you want to eat?"

I thought about my food conversation with Tito. "I was thinking bean-and-cheese burritos."

"That sounds like a dinner I would have suggested," she said, "and that you would have vetoed."

"That was the old me," I said. "If you want, I can pick up the burritos."

"No," said Lisbet. "If you'd given me advance warning, I could have soaked the beans overnight, but there's a nearby *mercado* that has wonderful frijoles. They also have homemade tortillas and make the best guacamole."

"I'm drooling."

"Pretty soon, I'm not going to be able to tell you and Sirius apart."

"I'm the one who doesn't drink from your toilet."

"Sirius doesn't do that either."

"Yeah, but he's the one who leaves the toilet seat up."

"I was wondering who the guilty party was."

"Let me talk with him about it. It's a male thing."

"I'll happily leave you to it."

"See you in a few."

"Ciao and then chow," she said.

Both Lisbet and I have a drawer at the other's place. Of course, Lisbet also happens to have most of my walk-in closet, but I don't mention that. Sirius isn't forgotten in the equation; Lisbet keeps provisions for him. In fact, after Seth gave her his recipe for the Sirius Burger (ground turkey, cooked and grated yam, cooked oatmeal, and egg as a binder), Lisbet took to cooking them ahead of time and freezing them. There have even been occasions, Lisbet says, when a Mother Hubbard cupboard necessitated her eating one of Sirius's burgers. According to her, they are delicious and should be marketed to the public as the first human/canine cuisine.

Lisbet has a lot of good ideas; I have my doubts about that being one of them.

I drove toward West LA. Lisbet's apartment is about a mile from the Loyola Marymount campus; a number of graduate students live in her complex. Because her apartment doesn't allow pets, whenever we're in common areas my partner goes by the formal name of "K-9 Sirius." So far, management hasn't busted us.

Lisbet's apartment is only eight hundred square feet; it's not only her residence, but her business address. One of the two bedrooms is devoted to her graphic arts business; the smaller bedroom is for sleeping. The apartment is cozy and well thought out, sort of the opposite of my house. When it comes to furnishings, I act out of necessity, not aesthetics.

As Lisbet opened the door, all the aromas from her cooking came rushing at me. I took a deep and appreciative breath but wasn't alone in the heavy-breathing department. Sirius was doing some major nostril twitching.

"Go ahead, Sirius," said Lisbet, "your dinner is ready."

My partner went running inside. In my whiniest voice I said, "What about me?"

"You can start with sugar," she said, tilting her head back. The two of us kissed.

"And now you can proceed to your appetizer plate," she said, "which consists of tortilla chips, salsa, guacamole, and some black bean dip. Dinner will be served in about twenty minutes. Right now I'm putting together the finishing touches for some Mexican rice."

"I want a second helping of sugar," I said, and got a second kiss.

"There's also cold beer in the fridge," she said.

That was encouragement enough for me to follow Lisbet into the kitchen. On her moveable butcher's block, I could see she'd already sliced and diced onions, tomatoes, cabbage, radishes, and limes for our burrito garnishments. She had also filled bowls with crumbled queso fresco, alfalfa sprouts, and sour cream. The vegetables and herbs she was chopping—cilantro, epazote, jalapeños, onions, and garlic—looked destined for her Mexican rice. We did a tango around one another as I made my way to the refrigerator. Finding a six-pack of Modelo Negra in bottles made me a very happy man. I flipped a cap, got my plate of chips and fixings, and by inhaling and moving sideways was able to ease my way out of the galley kitchen.

Once I was safely out of Lisbet's way, I took a seat on the sofa. "Dorothy Parker once shared a very tiny office with Robert Benchley," I said, "and Parker said that if the office were an inch smaller, it would have constituted adultery."

Lisbet laughed, but then realized I was impugning the size of her kitchen. "My kitchen is small but mighty," she said.

"I am in awe of what you and your small but mighty kitchen are able to accomplish."

I took a long pull of my beer. "Imagine," I said, "two of the world's greatest wits sharing that small office. I would have loved to be a fly on the wall. Whenever the chief forces me to give a talk, I almost always steal Benchley's line about why dogs are so important in a boy's life: 'A dog teaches a boy fidelity, perseverance, and to turn around three times before lying down.'"

Lisbet thought that was funny enough to laugh, but my comment also made her curious. "Why do you think dogs do that?" she asked.

Sirius must have decided his bowl was not going to magically fill up with another burger; he joined me at the sofa.

"Good timing," I said to him. "Why do you make circles before lying down?"

When Sirius didn't answer, I said, "I'll Google it." And then I spoke my question into the phone.

Lady Google didn't want to directly answer either. "Here is an article that deals with that," she said.

I expanded the phone screen but still had trouble reading, so I put on my reading glasses. "This anthropologist theorized that wild dogs had to tamp down grass and underbrush for bedding. She then went on to say that the circling might have been done for safety reasons, to make sure the space was clear of critters."

"A scientist used the word *critters*?"

"I might have paraphrased," I admitted.

"Your *vittles* are ready, Bubba," she said.

"Well, butter my butt and call me a biscuit."

I went through the burrito buffet line, filling my tortilla until it looked like an overinflated balloon. After I'd finished what was on my plate, it was my stomach that felt like an overinflated balloon.

"My compliments to the chef," I said.

"No room for seconds?"

"'I'm absolutely stuffed,'" I said, doing my best Mr. Creosote imitation.

"But, monsieur," said Lisbet, paraphrasing the John Cleese waiter line, "a wafer-thin mint."

We both started laughing. How many times had the two of us acted out the same silly scene? Lisbet enjoyed playing the unctuous waiter as much as I enjoyed playing the slovenly glutton. As she pantomimed the incredibly thin mint, I began to lose it, which prompted her to redouble her entreaties that I eat the mint.

Everyone has their definition of true love. I say if you and your partner can do the same Monty Python skit together over and over, and laugh as hard each time, then that's true love.

"I needed that," I said.

"Oh?"

"The day started early," I said. "I was at the Woodland Hills Home Depot at dawn, trying to get a lead on a missing day laborer. It's believed he was picked up for a job, but no one knows by who, or where he went."

"That doesn't sound like your usual case," Lisbet said.

"You mean it's not strange enough?"

"Something like that," she said.

"Luciana Castillo, the missing man's fiancée, came to last night's 187 Club meeting," I said. "She told me her fiancé has been missing for six weeks. Because Mateo came to this country illegally, it doesn't sound as if much has been done to find him. From what Luciana told me, the detective assigned the case seems to think it likely that Mateo just went back to Mexico. But I know that's not it."

"How do you know?" asked Lisbet.

"Love poetry," I said. "Mateo wrote reams of it to Luciana."

"Is that all?"

"Luciana said that he was working very hard to earn money for their wedding in Mexico. She was holding that money, and said they were halfway to their goal of ten thousand dollars."

"I hate to be cynical," said Lisbet, "but could there be some other woman?"

I shook my head. "I'd bet dollars to pesos against that. And I didn't tell you about a key piece of evidence. Last week Luciana received an envelope with twenty-five Benjamins in it. In the envelope were a few personal items that Luciana said were lifted from Mateo's wallet. There was also an unsigned note with the words *So sorry for your loss*."

"Guilt money," said Lisbet.

"That's what I've been thinking. Mateo was hired for work, but he never made it home alive. Something happened. Maybe he was working with electricity. It's possible he was on a ladder, or up on the roof, and fell down. Last year, I remember reading about this undocumented worker who was doing some gardening at a residence, and he upset a hive of bees or hornets and got stung all over, causing him to go into anaphylactic shock and die. There was some talk that the homeowner might have delayed taking the worker to the hospital because he was afraid of being liable for the death."

Lisbet shook her head and made a disgusted sound. "I hope that's not true. I hope someone didn't hesitate to treat a human with a medical emergency because of money."

"Whoever wrote the letter and sent the money showed some compassion," I said. "He or she sent along items that I believe were meant to comfort Luciana. I think the words of sympathy were also meant to offer closure. Luciana suspected Mateo was dead but still had doubts. After receiving the envelope and its contents, she's now convinced he's dead."

"Poor woman."

With a sigh and a shake of my head, I said, "She wants to have his body shipped home."

"But she just needs you to find it first."

"Just?" I said. "I have an essentially anonymous population that's doing unregulated work, and my potential witnesses are reluctant or uncooperative."

"No clues?"

"It's too early to even know what might be a clue," I said, but then realized I sounded testy. "You're hearing my tiredness, too. I had one of my dreams last night."

"Did you dream about the missing man?" she asked.

I nodded, but knew that wouldn't be enough for Lisbet. She thinks that our talking about my fire dreams is therapeutic. Of course, Lisbet also thinks my visions are a blessing from God. I haven't asked her who I can "thank" for the recurring fires.

"My after-dream was actually a mishmash of two cases I'm working."

"If you want to talk about that mishmash, I'd like to hear about it."

"In my dream I had this sense Mateo was dead," I said, "and that was before I went out and did the interviews this morning. Mateo was strumming a guitar and singing in the dream, but he kept his back turned to me and Luciana. He sang a love poem to her, and then the tune changed to 'Streets of Laredo.' He stopped playing after the line 'I'm a young cowboy and I know I've done wrong.' But what wrong could Mateo have done? What did he do that he paid with his life? Then Mateo was gone, and I found myself with Emily."

I stopped talking for a few moments, ostensibly to gather my thoughts; the truth is, I didn't want my voice to break.

"I wasn't going to tell you about Emily. She's a sweet pit bull that I met yesterday when I went in for my volunteer shift at Angie's Rescues." I told her what a miracle it was that Emily had survived, even though the vet had to essentially stitch up her whole body, as well as set a broken hind leg.

"Anyway, Emily and I met up with Mateo, and in my dream I sensed that all of us were being forced to fight for our lives. I don't think we were in a pit; it was more like we were in an open arena. It might have even been the Colosseum, because earlier in the evening Seth had offered up some of its gruesome history."

To me, that seemed like confession enough, especially the way Lisbet takes things to heart. Every week she puts in sweat equity volunteering for several causes that are important to her. She is one of those people who try to shore up the frayed fabric of society. I hoped my unburdening didn't have the consequence of burdening her.

"It sounds like you've had some tough days—and nights," she said.

"I'm sure it sounds worse than it really was."

"I'm sure it doesn't," she said. "In fact, I'm certain more went unsaid than said. For example, I'm all but sure you're looking into Emily's situation."

I nodded. She knew me well. There was no way I could let that sleeping dog lie.

"You've probably even talked to a suspect or two."

"You're probably right."

"Do you want to tell me about it?"

I shrugged. "It was a frustrating field interview," I admitted. "The suspect's street name is the Black Rooster. He's not your usual felon. In fact, he operates two legitimate businesses. Our interview was just a game to him. We both know he's guilty, but he acts as if the only thing he's doing is providing a service. He suggested that in a so-called natural state, male dogs would be fighting, and that all he was doing was facilitating what comes naturally to them."

"He admitted this?" she asked.

"He admitted nothing," I said, "but he didn't try to disguise what he believed."

I ran my hand along Sirius's back. "I let the bastard get under my skin," I said. "At first he pretended that he believed the reason I was there was to sell him Sirius as a bait dog. He said there was a mastiff he wanted to introduce him to. And he kept offering these paltry sums, all designed to get me to react. I'm sure he wanted me to take a swing at him. That would have given him a free pass to continue with his dog carnage."

Once more I stopped talking, not trusting my voice. Sirius was more than my partner; he was family. The idea that I would reward his love and friendship by selling him made me feel sick. Sirius could tell I was upset and nudged my hand. His prompt got me to start scratching him again.

"Please be careful in your dealings with this man, Michael," Lisbet said. "If an individual is so depraved that he forces dogs to fight to the death, it's clear he has no scruples or ethics."

"No argument here," I said. "But his business needs to be shut down. And I can't wait to put him in a cage."

Lisbet's voice was as deadly serious as my own: "I'm counting on it," she said.

CHAPTER NINE

TAKING A TRIP TO TRINIDAD

Trinidad, Colorado
1,035 miles from Los Angeles
April 1

John Crabbe wasn't the oldest resident of Trinidad, Colorado, but no one had lived in the city for as long as he had. The eight-four-year-old Crabbe had moved to Trinidad when he was a boy of only eight. There had been times in Crabbe's life when he hadn't lived in Trinidad, such as the years he'd been deployed in the military, but his roots were deep there.

As an adult, Crabbe had worked for the post office. All three of his children had been raised in Trinidad, and that was where Evelyn, his wife of almost sixty years, was buried. She had died two years earlier. Crabbe had never imagined that he would be considered an eligible bachelor, but hard as it was to believe, there were a few women in town who thought so.

Because it was a beautiful spring day, Crabbe decided to take a drive and do some shopping. You never knew if the weather was going to change. April was one of those months that could go either way. Some years it was cold and dreary. This year the month was starting out sunny and warm. Crabbe hoped that wouldn't prove to be just another April Fool's prank.

Crabbe expected there would be lots of tourists enjoying Trinidad's downtown Victorian charms. Interstate 25 is the most traveled route between Colorado and New Mexico, and Trinidad's fortunes could long be attributed to its location; in the 19th century it had been part of the Santa Fe Trail.

It's too bad I wasn't around then, Crabbe thought, imagining all the characters who had ridden the trail. Crabbe was Trinidad's unofficial historian. It's because I'm old, he thought. What was ancient history to others, he knew, was merely his own history. That was part of it, of course, but it was also true that Crabbe had enjoyed learning all he could about the area.

Most of the locals, for example, had no idea that Butch Cassidy and the Sundance Kid, along with their Hole-in-the-Wall Gang, had hidden out in the canyons and hills south of town. Black Jack Ketchum's criminal career had come to an abrupt end in Trinidad back in 1899, when his right arm was shot off as he attempted to rob a train. What remained of his arm had been amputated at Trinidad's Mount San Rafael Hospital, before the Hole-in-the-Wall Gang desperado was transported to New Mexico, where he was hung.

Our criminal past, thought Crabbe, and known by so few. Even more recent history seemed to have been forgotten. Why, Crabbe would bet that most of Trinidad's current populace didn't even know the history of the town's onetime catchphrase, "taking a trip to Trinidad."

In 1969, Trinidad surgeon Dr. Stanley Biber was asked by a local social worker if he would perform a sex-change operation to make the man a woman. After reading up on the procedure, Biber consented, and it wasn't long before he was performing, on average, four sex-reassignment surgeries a day. Those seeking a sex change began referring to the procedure as "taking a trip to Trinidad." Biber performed more than 4,000 gender-reassignment surgeries, and Trinidad became known as the sex-change capital of the world.

Biber's Trinidad legacy came to an end in 2003, when the surgeon who took over his practice moved it to San Mateo, California. Crabbe was sorry that had happened. To his thinking, Trinidad had been a more interesting place back then.

Crabbe parked in Trinidad's downtown, walking over the red bricks with TRINIDAD stamped on each; tourists thought they looked so quaint. At least the town hadn't withered up and blown away. Lots of residents had thought that would happen when the area's coal mines had started shutting down. There had been a time when coal was king in Trinidad.

John Crabbe got his groceries. He didn't need much, just some canned goods, along with some beer to wash it down. It wasn't any fun cooking for one; most of Crabbe's meals came out of the microwave. He missed Evelyn's cooking, but even more than that, he missed their conversations.

I've lived too long, Crabbe thought, not for the first time.

He drove home. At the age of eighty-four, Crabbe liked to think he was still a good driver, but he knew better than to drive at night. It was hard for him to see in the darkness. His house was on the outskirts of Trinidad, past the town golf course. He and Evelyn had decided to move to a spot farther out in the country when the kids were young. Back then there had been very few houses in the area, but that had changed.

Crabbe parked in the garage. The brick and stucco home was neat and tidy. It was out of respect for Evelyn that Crabbe tried to keep the place up. That's how she had liked it.

As he was putting away the groceries, Crabbe was surprised to hear someone ringing his doorbell.

He walked through his living room, and without checking to see who was at the door, opened it wide.

"April Fool!"

It wasn't the words that made Crabbe step back; it was the axe. Seeing it, Crabbe regretted having been so trusting. And then another thought came to him that fiercely contradicted what he'd been musing about earlier: I haven't lived too long.

But it was too late for Crabbe to take back that thought. It was too late for him to do anything.

CHAPTER TEN

WHAT DO THE CARDS SAY?

In the distance I could hear Ellis Haines singing "Jailhouse Rock." He was always one for making an entrance. The singing grew louder as he neared the meeting room where I was waiting. Elvis's version of the song was better, but not by much. Haines has great pipes; that's probably why the correctional officers were letting him belt out the lyrics.

"'Let's rock, everybody, let's rock,'" he sang, "'everybody in the whole cell block.'"

Maybe for some, Haines and his singing livened up the prison; to me, it was like putting perfume on a corpse. I don't like spending time in prisons, especially San Quentin. It's a place where over 400 inmates have been legally killed. When I visit, it's not as if I see ghosts or hear the wailing of poltergeists, but the despair of the place has soaked deep into its concrete walls, and the miasma it exudes feels contagious.

The FBI seems to think they can learn a lot from Ellis Haines. Their hope is that he will facilitate a dialogue with other serial murderers, a project that is now in its early stages. I have warned the Feds to be careful what they wish for. Haines only cooperates if it's in his best interest. His price for initially helping the FBI in this endeavor wasn't special rations or prison favors. Instead, he gets a monthly delivery of crime scene photos compiled by the FBI. The pictures show homicides believed to have been committed by serial murderers. To his credit, Haines seems to have a talent at profiling. In several instances he has identified clues that law enforcement missed. But Haines hasn't suddenly become a Good Samaritan. The crime scene photos are his fix; it's like giving heroin to a junkie.

For me, the worst thing about this bloody show-and-tell is that I am the middleman in the process. Haines refuses to talk to the Feds. They give me the photos, along with any questions they have, and I'm expected to make note of Haines's impressions. Taking dictation from a killer is not something I like doing. That, I am sure, only adds to his enjoyment.

Today, though, I had my own agenda.

"Enough singing, inmate," said one of the correctional officers.

Haines shut up.

Every month I visit San Quentin; every month a shackled Haines is brought to see me in a conference room that is referred to as the "lawyers' room." The correctional officers are used to the routine by now; one guides Haines inside the room while the other waits outside to remove his handcuffs.

As usual, Haines acts oblivious to his constraints and pretends to be as insouciant as an incumbent Congressman in a gerrymandered district. From across the room he called to me: "Good morning, Detective Gideon. If you'll just excuse me for a moment, I'll be right with you."

Turning his back to the wall and pushing his hands through a slot, Haines waited while his handcuffs were removed.

"Abracadabra," he said, showing me his bare hands.

"Shucks," I said. "You didn't disappear."

"That would have been rude," he said, "seeing as we haven't even had a chance to talk."

"Believe me, I wouldn't have taken any offense."

Haines took a seat across from me at the table. I waved off the CO, telling him there was "no need" to tether Haines.

The CO shrugged as if to say, *It's your funeral*, and then turned around. Before closing the door behind him, he said, "I'll be outside the door if you need me."

The sound of the door locking behind him was overloud, or maybe it just seemed that way because I was now sharing a room with a notorious serial murderer.

"How nice of you to visit," Haines said.

"I'm a glutton for punishment."

Haines tilted his head slightly, extending his left ear my way, as if by doing so he could pick up my every nuance. His keloid scarring is on the left side of his face; mine is on the right. Together they tell the tale of our fire walk, and our flesh that burned away while carrying Sirius out of the inferno.

"You look tired," he said. "Are you still *burning* the midnight oil?"

From what Haines has intimated, he experiences fire dreams much as I do.

"Business is too good," I said.

"How is Sirius?" he asked. "And how are things with the little woman? What's her name again? Liz Beth? No, that's not it. Now I remember: Lisbet. That sounds so old-fashioned, almost like a Louisa May Alcott kind of name."

I stared at Haines without saying anything. There are certain subjects I won't respond to, and he knows that. I let my displeasure sink in for a few moments, and then said, "If you cross that line again, I'm out of here. Understood?"

He lost his smile for long enough to nod, before showing me his teeth again. "You have the advantage of me, of course," he said.

I tossed the folder of crime scene photos between us, and Haines began flipping through what he called the "last kill and testament." Most of the pictures only drew his disdain. The vast majority of victims lived on the fringes of society, prostitutes or drug addicts. They had put themselves in bad positions where bad things often happened. Haines is invariably scornful of these kinds of murders, with most of his vitriol aimed at the killers. He thinks the murderers "unimaginative," especially if they only take the "low-hanging fruit." For Haines, those types of homicides are the "lowest common denominator."

The act of murder is repugnant to most of us. Ellis Haines doesn't seem to see the horror in a grisly crime scene.

"How very banal," said Haines; he turned the picture over and went on to the next.

By now he'd gone through more than two-thirds of the pile. "Let me consult my notes," I said, looking at my blank notebook. "So far, the pictures you've seen have inspired you to say, 'boring,' 'derivative,' 'uninspired,' and 'insipid.'"

"Let's not forget 'soporific' and 'ennui inducing,'" he said, turning over another photo. Then he added, "There are two Ns in *ennui*."

"Oui, oui, oui," I said, "all the way home."

Haines didn't call me out for being so puerile, but only because one of the pictures suddenly had all his attention. He was preternaturally still; only his eyes moved. Haines usually likes to lecture me about what he sees, especially if he thinks he's offering insights that have been missed by others, but for a minute or more, he was silent while taking in all the details of the picture.

Finally, he put aside the picture and read the write-up of the case. The synopsis of events was met with a disdainful snort and Haines saying, "They have eyes but cannot see."

Whenever Haines quotes scripture, I am reminded of the Bard's line: *The devil can cite Scripture for his purpose.*

"It took them all this time," he said, "to decide that this homicide was *likely* the work of a serial murderer. Likely."

Haines shook his head before continuing: "And even now there is some speculation that the man's death was the result of a hunting accident."

He passed me the pictures and I looked through them. The victim was a white male, age fifty-eight. He had been duck hunting and died of a bullet wound to his eye.

I decided to play devil's advocate. The best way to get Haines talking is to take up a position contrary to his own. "The man was hunting," I said, "in an area that draws hunters. I can understand how it would be reasonable, then, to wonder if the death might not have been accidental."

"There was nothing accidental in this," Haines said. "Even the Feds were aware enough to realize the body was moved. And that made them question whether that might have been done in order to stage the crime scene."

"You believe it was staged?"

"Without a doubt," he said.

"And what do you see that others have missed?"

"Bullets and ducks," he said.

I looked at the pictures, and then at Haines. "Bullets and ducks," I said.

"Yes, yes," he said impatiently.

"Both of those things seem to have been taken into account. The report tells us the hunter field dressed the duck he shot, and the picture shows the hunter was shot in the eye."

"You're missing the point."

"If it looks like a duck, swims like a duck, and quacks like a duck, then it probably is a duck."

"What does the duck tell you? What do you think when you look at it?"

"Duck a l'orange," I said.

He waved away my humor as if it were offensive gas. "Both bullets and ducks are symbolic," he said. "Both stand for something. In poker, bullets refer to aces, and ducks refer to twos. The crime scene was staged to show a hand of ace-two. The killer has announced that hunting season has begun."

"Hunting season?" I questioned.

"If you played poker," he said, "you would know the reference. Players refer to an ace-two hand as hunting season."

"If you're duck hunting," I said, "then it stands to reason that you're dealing with bullets and ducks."

"Not bullets," he said, "pellet shots."

"Maybe the second hunter was going after deer."

"This wasn't a hunting accident so much as it was an assassination," he said. "The killer wasn't trying to bag Bambi. And even if you're being purposely slow on accepting the announcement of hunting season, there is another obvious clue that shows that the crime scene was staged."

I didn't ask Haines what that clue was. Had I done that, he might have withheld the information. He likes others to be in awe of his perspicacity. So I said, "I'll tell the FBI that, according to the smartest boy wearing prison orange, they need to look for another clue."

"Or you might stop being intellectually lazy and look for that clue yourself. It's about as inconspicuous as a tarantula on a slice of angel food."

"That, I recognize," I said. "You're stealing a line from Raymond Chandler."

"I'll give you a *sporting* chance to figure out the obvious," said Haines, emphasizing his taunt.

I picked up the crime scene photos, and then looked at the write-up. The victim had been out hunting in Colorado in the middle of November. It was believed the hunter became the hunted in the very early morning.

It would have been cold, I thought. So why had the hunter removed his coat and his sweater? The man's Pendleton shirt was also unbuttoned. He was wearing a white T-shirt with a red L enclosed by a black oval. The L was situated almost like a bull's-eye, and there was something familiar about it. My first consideration was that it was the first letter of a college or professional team, much like a red N represents Nebraska, and a blue M stands for Michigan. Louisville, I thought, but I was pretty sure the Cardinals didn't advertise themselves in such a way. I considered and also rejected Louisiana.

Haines was watching my struggles. "Tell me what you're thinking," he said.

"Why would you remove several layers of clothing on a cold day," I said, "and what does the red L on the hunter's T-shirt stand for?"

"If only you had an interest in meteorology," he said.

"If only you didn't," I said.

Haines was a meteorologist. For years he'd been the weekend weatherman on an LA television station. Because he'd strangled his victims during Santa Ana conditions, his lawyers were now trying to claim that Haines was susceptible to wild mood swings during certain weather events. It was an ailment they said was like seasonal affective disorder, or SAD. The media had picked up on the claim and were referring to Haines's supposed condition as SAD Mad.

Belatedly, I made sense of the hint he'd offered. "That red L is the meteorological shorthand for a low-pressure system."

Half politely, half mockingly, Haines clapped his hands.

"So, as you see it," I said, "a crime scene was staged with poker and weather clues. That hardly seems coincidental."

"As you say."

"You seem to have been the target audience for this communication. Any idea who did this?"

"I suspect this was the first letter sent to me, but it is clear there will be more."

"How is that clear?"

"There is another meteorological clue. I believe it is both an homage offered up to me and a cautionary piece of advice to those doing the investigating."

"And what is that?"

"On the ground near the victim's right hand is an umbrella. I find it unlikely that the dead hunter would have brought an umbrella on a hunting trip. You can't hold an umbrella and shoot a shotgun at the same time. And his camo outfit is designed for inclement weather. If my eyes aren't mistaken, on the casing of the umbrella there is what looks to be an imprint, or a decal, of dark clouds with a lightning bolt. That is not a brand or a logo I know; instead, it is a weather image that is used nowadays to indicate thunder and lightning. *Donner und Blitz*, Detective. I think you'll find the killer somehow applied that image to the casing so as to announce stormy weather. You might remember at my first trial I made much the same announcement, but in a more memorable fashion."

At his trial, Haines had interrupted court proceedings by singing the song "Stormy Weather." I have heard that Haines's creepy courtroom serenade has resulted in a few hundred million YouTube views, a number that far exceeds the views of the brilliant renditions recorded by Billie Holiday and Lena Horne. Go figure.

I began asking questions and taking notes. "Any idea when you'll next hear from the killer?"

"More than four months have passed since the hunter was murdered," he said. "I need you to emphasize to the FBI that I require timely information. In fact, it wouldn't surprise me if our killer had already struck again."

"But how would the killer know you've seen his handiwork?"

"The news that I am assisting the FBI in looking at crime scene photos isn't exactly secret. And good poker players understand the necessity of a long game. Even had I missed the initial murder, the killer knew it would only be a matter of time before his note reached me."

"If another murder has already occurred," I said, "can we expect the killer will be trying to communicate with you through the languages of poker and weather?"

"That's exactly what I'd expect," said Haines.

"Any predictions as to the next killing?" I asked. "Is there anything the FBI should be looking for?"

"I'm not ready to make any rash predictions."

"Do you expect another shooting death?"

"I would think not. Aces have already been played. If I am correct in that assumption, the killer might be proceeding in a numerical progression. That would mean a cowboy would be up next."

"Which is what?"

"King Kong," he said with a knowing smile, "or Elvis. There is no shortage of poker nicknames for a king."

I remembered the questions Detective Andrea Charles had wanted me to ask Haines and thought this was a good time to broach them.

"The only thing I know about poker," I said, "is that if I don't want to lose my shirt, I better not play the game."

"I would think it would be right up your alley, Detective. Poker is as much about psychology as it is mathematics. And I know how you love to play mind games."

"The pot just called the kettle black."

"I imagine if you put your mind to it, you could be a good player. Your work requires you to bluff and call bluffs. And from personal experience, I know you are always looking for tells."

"I guess I'm cheap," I said. "I don't like the idea of losing money."

"If you play the game right, you will win more than lose. And you can play poker online on some no-charge sites, but don't expect much in the way of competition."

"Did you play online?"

"On occasion I did," he said, "although I much preferred playing at tables where I could gauge the competition."

"You liked to see the whites of their eyes?"

"Some players wear shades to prevent that. But they can't hide their body language."

"I'm surprised you didn't buy a condo in Las Vegas. It was your second home for years."

"The hotels sometimes comped me a room. At the worst, I'd get a major discount."

"Where'd you like to stay?"

He named a few spots on the Strip and a few off. Showing up the FBI, and showing how smart he was by interpreting crime scene photos, had put Haines in an unusually good mood. I tried to take advantage of that and get him talking even more.

"I heard you played in the World Series of Poker," I said.

"Twice," he said. "I did it the old-fashioned way, though. I won enough in satellite tournaments to cover my buy-in. To enter the tournament, there's no rule that you have to be a good player. You can be a fish if you have the ten-thousand-dollar entry fee."

"How'd you do in your two tournaments?"

"I ended up in the money, and in the top five hundred players, in both of them."

"And how many players entered?"

"Between six and seven thousand."

"You beat the odds."

"I never made it to the finals table. That's still a goal of mine."

His eyes challenged mine, and I said, "Don't expect me to wish you good luck."

"I know better," he said.

"I'm going to have to spend three days in Vegas next week," I said. "But I think I'll stick to blackjack."

"Why will you be there?"

"An assistant DA wants my testimony in an LVPD case. Got some good restaurant tips for me? I'd prefer to be away from the glitz."

Haines played the seasoned tour guide, rattling off half a dozen restaurants and lounges that he said only the locals frequented. I wrote down the names. When I looked up, Haines had stopped talking. It might have been my imagination, but he seemed to be regarding me differently, perhaps even suspiciously.

"This is the first time we've ever talked poker," he said.

"This is the first time a murderer has shown us his cards, so to speak."

"This is also the first time we've talked about Las Vegas."

"Poker and Las Vegas go hand in hand."

Haines offered an almost imperceptible nod, but he didn't look convinced.

"I have a flight to catch," I told him, "and calls to make. The FBI is going to want to hear about hunting season, a low-pressure network, and stormy weather."

Reminding him that he had seen what the FBI had missed seemed to mollify Haines, but his guard was still up. He had sensed there was more to my questioning than I had let on. I wondered what tell had alerted him.

I called to the correctional officer and said our session was done.

"Enjoy your time in Las Vegas," Haines said as he stood up. He turned around, slid his hands through the slot, and was handcuffed once more. When the correctional officers unlocked the door, Haines had one last piece of advice for me.

"Tell the FBI to look for a recent homicide where a sword or an axe was used. And I want them to get me the pictures as soon as possible."

"A sword or an axe?"

He heard my puzzlement and saw it in my expression, and that seemed to please him.

"You heard correctly," he said.

And then he started down the hallway, clanking like Jacob Marley's ghost. Marley had offered up the sins of his past as an example to Scrooge. I was hoping that Ellis Haines had inadvertently done the same for me.

CHAPTER ELEVEN

NOT YOUR USUAL AXE MURDERER

The murder weapon turned out to be an axe. The son of a bitch had called it correctly.

If I'd been smart, I would have made the card and weapon connection on my own. In a typical pack of playing cards, three of the kings brandish swords. The king of diamonds is the odd man out. He wields an axe. Card players refer to him as the "man with an axe."

An axe murderer had cleaved the skull of John Crabbe in Trinidad, Colorado, last week. Mr. Crabbe, an eighty-four-year-old widower, had the misfortune of being the only Crabbe in town.

As part of my belated poker education, I learned that a king-three hand is often referred to as King Crab. Card players apparently think the number three looks like a sideways crab. I guess the killer was now saying it wasn't only hunting season; it was also crab season, or at least poor–Mr. Crabbe season.

Unfortunately for me, poker players have a lot of nicknames for two-card hands, which meant I had a lot of memorizing to do if I wanted to try and predict the actions of the killer. There were also meteorological symbols to acquaint myself with. Weather symbols had been left at the Crabbe crime scene, but they hadn't been noticed until after the fact, when investigators were advised as to what they should be looking for. It's easier to look smart when you're given the answers to the test.

It was my FBI contact who told me about the investigation into Mr. Crabbe's death the day after my visit with Haines. Special Agent Ben Corning seemed unusually deferential and friendly when he called, but then people often are when they want a favor. The Feds wanted me to visit Haines for a second time that month and deliver him a packet relating to Mr. Crabbe's murder. I politely declined. Seeing Haines once a month was penance enough.

The special agent tried to keep me on the line in the hopes of winning me over through sustained conversation. "Our serial killer is being referred to by two nicknames," he said. "Maybe we have another Ellis Haines on our hands."

"Maybe," I said.

"There are two vying camps," Corning said. "The weather geeks want to call him the Stormy Weather Killer; the card sharps are lobbying for the All-In Killer.

"I'm in the card-sharp camp," Corning said. "Which do you like?"

"I like Nail the SOB."

"That's not a name we could release to the public."

"I've never figured out why serial murderers are given nicknames. Is it some rule in the Bureau?"

Ted Bundy had been the Lady Killer; David Berkowitz went by the Son of Sam. And there had been the Grim Sleeper, the

BTK Killer, the Night Stalker, and the Killer Clown, just to name a few.

"I think it's a carryover from the military," Corning said. "There's a long tradition of giving nicknames to the enemy."

It was a good way to depersonalize the enemy, I thought. And it was a good tool to get the media to report on the killer. In that, it served its purpose.

"I'll leave you to your name game," I said. "I have to run."

Corning hurriedly spoke before I could end the call. "If you reconsider going to see Haines," he said, but that was as far as he got.

What I hadn't told Special Agent Corning, or anyone at the FBI, was that I was working on putting a permanent end to my visiting Haines in San Quentin. That would only come about, though, if I got the goods on him in Nevada and he was extradited. There were a variety of reasons I wanted him to be convicted in Nevada; primary among them was the appeal his lawyers were working on in California. I had lied under oath when I said that I had read Haines his rights before arresting him, and I didn't want that lie to haunt me. The hard truth was that I wasn't sure if I could lie under oath a second time. There were also some LAPD procedural issues his lawyers were questioning. If I recanted, Haines might have grounds for a successful appeal.

I couldn't let that happen. Since his conviction I had spent a lot of time with the families of his victims. I didn't want to be responsible for reopening their wounds. They needed the assurance that Haines would forever pay for his crimes. It didn't matter to me that Haines liked to believe we were irrevocably bonded by our fire walk. The cop in me, the human in me, couldn't forgive Haines for his lack of remorse. His stalking and killing, even his remembering, seemed like a game to him. Haines being in prison provided at least a little solace to the loved ones of his victims. I couldn't deny them that.

It had been a dozen years since California had executed an inmate. Nevada was much more inclined to carry out the sentence on its death row inmates. If Detective Charles and I succeeded in linking Haines to one or more Las Vegas killings, he'd likely be transferred to death row at Ely State Prison. There, Haines would either die behind bars or eventually be legally executed. I could much more easily live with either of those possibilities than I could with the possibility of his release.

Detective Charles and I had been playing phone tag. I tried her number once more. This time I succeeded in reaching her.

"I was just calling you," she said.

"That must mean our investigation is in sync."

"How was your visit with Haines?"

"I am not sure if I *aced* it," I said, "or if I got *jack* shit."

"Were you questioning him or playing cards with him?"

"I'm thinking both," I said. "In the batch of crime scene photos that I brought him, he was able to decipher some messages the killer had left for him in the form of meteorological symbols and poker hands. From that, Haines was able to accurately predict what kind of murder weapon the killer would be using in his next homicide."

"There already was a next murder?"

"As it turns out, it happened just a few days ago. The crime scene photos that Haines interpreted were from mid-November of last year. By the way, the weapon used in the second murder was an axe."

"An axe?"

"It's a king thing. Haines predicted the coup de grâce would be delivered by an axe or a sword."

"Old school, as in medieval."

"You said it."

"As interesting as that development was, you still haven't told me how you made out."

"I got what I went for, or I think I did. Haines offered up the names of hotels where he stayed, along with his favorite restaurants and nightspots. I got this feeling, though, that he realized I was up to something, even if he wasn't sure what that was. That's when he suddenly got wary, or at least that's how it felt to me."

"Hopefully, he gave you what you wanted before he got suspicious."

"My thoughts exactly," I said.

I referred to my notes and began repeating the names of Haines's favorite haunts to Andrea. When I finished, she said, "I don't think I'll even call on the hotels. They're too big and impersonal. And the casino hotels have cameras everywhere. We know from other murders he's committed that Haines has a sixth sense about cameras and has always been good at avoiding them. That's why the restaurants and lounges are our best chance to find a killer on vacation. Some of them I'm familiar with. They're intimate little places, good spots to take a date."

"Haines became infamous during his trial," I said. "I'd be surprised if witnesses didn't notice that he'd dined at some of those restaurants."

"I've never heard of any local restaurant advertising 'The Weatherman Ate Here.'"

"Let's not give them any ideas, then. The more low profile you can keep your investigation, the better. Haines might be on death row, but he seems to have lots of eyes and ears working on his behalf."

"Mum's the word," she promised.

The Los Angeles Animal Cruelty Task Force had been formed more than a dozen years ago. According to what I read on the

LAPD informational website, the task force combatted animal cruelty in all forms and worked to educate diverse communities.

It was depressing looking at the ACTF Facebook page; I flipped through the pictures of animals that had been tortured and maimed and found myself muttering and growing angrier. The number of mistreated animals far exceeded convictions. Since the inception of the ACTF, there had been fewer than fifty convictions for animal cruelty.

As horrific as any form of animal cruelty is, I thought it even more horrific to profit from it. Tito had seemed incredibly insouciant, confident that he couldn't be touched. It was only when I'd talked about offering up a reward that he grew uneasy. Someone could have seen something on the day he dumped the dogs. Tito's Achilles' heel needed to be exposed.

I tried to figure out the best way to proceed, and looked to see if I knew anyone assigned to ACTF. One name stood out: Detective Porter Bennet. I remembered Bennet as a fellow officer at Metro K-9. Although I didn't know him very well, from what I remembered of him he was a good guy. During the time we worked together, I'd had trouble keeping up with all his nicknames. If you're a cop with the first name Porter, you had better expect a lot of different monikers. I remembered hearing him called Suds, Brew, Ale, Pint, Bud, and others.

Naturally, he answered with his surname: "Bennet."

"Detective Bennet," I said, "this is Michael Gideon."

"You mean Michael Gideon who will forever be the pride of Metro K-9? You mean Medal of Valor recipient Michael Gideon?"

"Feel free to call me Sir Michael, Porter."

"Porter? I haven't heard my real first name in years. You better call me Bud. Even my wife calls me that now, but then again, she is my third wife."

"Bud," I said.

"And I wasn't shitting you about being glad you got that hardware, Gideon. You're no phony. I know that because we live in the world capital of phonies. Because you did your job well, a lot of cops were able to bask in your glory. It was a good thing for LAPD."

"Sirius and I got lucky," I said. "The expression 'blind pig finds acorn' pretty much sums up what happened."

"Is your four-legged partner still alive?"

"Sirius is doing great. Both of us were supposed to get Medicals, but then the chief offered me a position where I could still work with Sirius."

"I heard something about that," he said. "It must be two, three years since you left Metro."

"Almost five years," I said.

"Shit," he said. "We're getting old."

"Tell me about it."

"So I got a report on my desk today," he said, "that says you're poaching our business."

"It's more like I was minding my own business," I said, "when I got acquainted with this poor dog who was dumped and left for dead. That's when I started investigating what happened."

"I can't believe LAPD let animal control take the lead," he said, "and that animal control thought leaving us a message about those dumped dogs was adequate notice. That's not acceptable."

"I'm not excusing what happened," I said, "but I do know the animal control officer who was called out to the scene was shocked when he found one of the dogs was still alive. That's when trying to get her help became his priority."

Bud's growled "yeah" sounded begrudging.

"As for Officer Brockington," I said, "he was able to identify a potential suspect for me. In addition to that, he determined that on the day the dogs were dumped, the Gang Task Force had set up checkpoints and was stopping cars looking for a suspected

MS-13 shooter. He did me a solid, and I'd hate thinking his jacket would get tagged over this."

"Snafu," said Bud. The sanitized translation is "situation normal all fouled up."

"Snafu," I agreed.

"I'll try to keep any shade from being thrown at that cop," Bud promised.

"That's good to hear. Officer Brockington put me onto a suspect named Humberto 'Tito' Rivera. Tito's street name is El Gallo Negro, or the Black Rooster. Rivera is believed to have dumped the four dogs that were in his truck."

"I am well acquainted with Rivera," said Bud. "In fact, he's been on the ACTF radar ever since he was into cockfighting, and that goes back a number of years."

"Why haven't you nailed him?"

"He's slippery. And the dogfighting circuit, as you have probably heard, is notoriously closemouthed. Most fights aren't announced until the day of, and they're usually held at some remote ranch, which makes surveillance all but impossible. That, combined with Rivera's veneer of respectability, makes him a tough target. He paints himself as the poor kid who's made good with his businesses. Of course, it's those businesses that allow him to hide in plain sight."

"I visited Tito at his junkyard," I said. "Or as he calls it, his recycling center."

"Yeah, he and Kermit like to sing about how tough it is to be green."

"He's got lots of heavy equipment at the junkyard. I would bet that's where he intended to dispose of those four dogs, just as he has other dogs in the past."

"I'm sure of it," Bud said.

"You ever try and get a search warrant to look there?"

"Rivera isn't dumb. That's why his guard dog business operates out of his junkyard. You know how tough it would be to try and isolate evidence in that environment?"

"When I questioned our rooster," I said, "he lived up to his street name. He acted like the confident cock of the walk. The only time his self-assuredness seemed to slip was when I mentioned that I was going to try and get an ACTF reward commercial aired. He has to be worried that someone might blow the whistle on him and his dogfighting for the right price."

"I like that idea," said Bud. "In fact, we might be able to make it a coproduction of ACTF, Crime Stoppers, and an organization like the Humane Society."

"Perfect," I said. "If we bring Crime Stoppers in, they can film a reenactment in the exact spot where the dogs were dumped. Someone had to have seen something."

"And there's nothing like the offer of money to sharpen memories."

"I've even got the perfect star for the commercial," I said, and told him about Emily.

"I'm not sure about using a pit bull," Bud said. "The breed doesn't come across as very sympathetic."

"With all of Emily's stitches, right now she sort of looks like a Frankenstein dog. If ever there's been a sympathetic pit bull, she's it. Emily definitely looks vulnerable."

"That would make her story all the more compelling," he said. "But I'll have to run it by the team. Usually we avoid showing the ugly face of animal abuse because that makes it too easy for people to just look away."

"Emily can personalize the story," I said. "And her image might help us get something on our sick prick."

"That's what I used to call Michael Vick," said Bud, referring to the former NFL quarterback who pleaded guilty to a federal dogfighting charge. "Sick Prick Michael Vick."

"Our rooster is as bad as Sick Prick Vick," I said. "That's why I want to nail him on felony charges, and I want him to do jail time. I expect his lawyers will use the same tactics as did Vick's. They'll say Tito grew up with cockfighting, and that dog-fighting was just a natural extension of that. We'll hear how he didn't know right from wrong, and that it was part of his South American heritage. Then they'll bring out his good-businessman card and probably find out that he's supported local youth sports, the chamber of commerce, B'nai B'rith, and the ACLU."

"If we get the goods on him," Bud said, "he won't skate. He'll do jail time."

"That's what I needed to hear."

CHAPTER TWELVE

ONCE MORE UNTO THE BREACH

Ever since interpreting Sirius's Frisbee dream at Seth's home, I had felt guilty about not spending more time with him. Sirius is a working dog, and it's up to me to keep him at the top of his game. I also need to work on my handler skills. Communication goes both ways.

Repetition and consistency are necessary components for any good K-9 team. Just as people block out time to go to the gym, I needed to see to our team's workout.

There are several Metro K-9 training fields around Los Angeles, but the primary site is in Glendale. People are always surprised at its location. The facility is on the east side of the LA River, an on-again, off-again body of water that flows along a mostly concrete channel through the heart of Los Angeles. The eleven-mile section called the Glendale Narrows actually has an earthen bottom. It's a popular spot for fisherman and birdwatchers, an oasis in the middle of an urban jungle.

As Sirius and I drove through a mostly industrial area, he began to get increasingly excited.

"Yeah, we're going home," I said.

Home might overstate it, but not by much. My partner and I had bonded on these fields along with the rest of our K-9 platoon. Sirius had been the A student. Because I have never liked showing up others, I have always been more of the Gentleman C type, or at least that's been my explanation over the years.

We turned into a small parking lot, which was deserted save for one car. As I had hoped, the large field would be all ours. The mostly grass park was surrounded by a tall chain-link fence; hedges shielded the expanse from prying eyes.

Sirius was making all kinds of happy noises as I sprang him from the car. He ran up the path, back to me, and then up the path again, while I gathered our bag of tricks. We walked by the cinderblock building that serves as a conference room for Metro K-9; in the outlying kennels a few of the housed dogs barked at our appearance, but without much conviction.

There was an obstacle course on the field, but before taking it on, Sirius and I did our stretches. Our encounter with fire, and our burns, had compromised our ranges of motion. Each of us had gone through intense physical therapy; the post-therapy was supposed to be a lifetime of specific stretches for the two of us. I stretched Sirius's hip flexors and shoulder flexors. Then I had him do an abduction stretch and a back stretch. Between all his stretching, he got a massage and a rubdown. He always likes those best. I'm the same.

Then I did my own stretching. My coach impatiently barked a few times. It didn't take a dog whisperer to know he was shouting, "Hurry it up, slowpoke."

Since the obstacle course was already set up, I decided to send Sirius through his paces. We started with the weave poles. I motioned to them and said, "Let's see what you got."

In and out he snaked, his wagging tail hitting every pole.

"That was simple," I said, "and you're already breathing hard. Time for some low hurdles for conditioning."

I directed him to the obstacles, and he easily cleared the lot of them.

"Okay, walk the dog," I said.

In some drawer at my house is a dusty yo-yo. About the only trick I can do with that yo-yo is a maneuver called "walk the dog." The yo-yo seems to propel itself along the floor. Sirius doesn't have a yo-yo; his "walk the dog" is traversing a fourteen-foot aluminum dog walk. When he made it over, I yelled, "Back," and motioned for him to return from where he'd come. He did as directed.

"Time for the A-frames," I told him, and both of us jogged over to the structure, even though only one of us went up it, and then down it.

I noticed Sirius was breathing hard, so I announced, "Water break!" Then I broke out his bowl and the water. One of us began to slurp.

It was a perfect spring day, warm and sunny. The skies were almost a deep Dodgers blue, with no sign of smog. Sirius finished drinking and came over to my side. Instead of continuing with the obstacle course, I told him to sit and stay. For several minutes I mostly kept my back to Sirius, walking the field and making sure it was clear of glass or anything sharp. What I was really doing, though, was forcing Sirius to wait for my next command.

"Sirius, come," I called.

He ran to my side. "Heel," I said, although the command was unnecessary. My partner stayed by my side until I motioned him to go through the agility tunnel. In the field, handler and K-9 have to be able to work independently of one another. There are situations that sometimes require me to be absent from Sirius's line of sight. The fabric-covered tunnel didn't allow him to see me, but he easily navigated his way through it.

After that, I reacquainted Sirius with the teeter-totter. It had been quite some time since he'd done the old up and down on his own, so I had only myself to blame for his early missteps. It didn't take him long, though, until he found his legs and was climbing up and scrambling down.

One of the favorite obstacles for handlers and dogs is the tire jump. Handlers like to toss around a football and try to throw it through the opening in the tire. Dogs are expected to vault through the tire.

"Once more unto the breach, dear friend," I yelled. Luckily, my hand signal was more instructive as to what I wanted. Sirius ran to the tire, vaulted, and made it through.

"One of us has still got it," I said.

We had a second water break. I would have been content to call it a day, but not Sirius. He knew the special toys I had in my bag and couldn't wait for me to bring them out.

It was Frisbee time.

Sirius thinks that sticks and balls are a waste of his talents. I started him off easy, tossing the discs so that he didn't have to move far for the catch. In my bag are a variety of discs, all different sizes and weights. I went through my repertoire of throws, trying to remember all the names, along with the proper hand and arm positioning. I don't know who came up with the names, but Frisbee throws includes such tosses as "the hammer," "the scoober," "the thumber," "the duck," and "the chicken wing."

Before we started, I had Sirius do a few more exercises. It was the beginning of snake season, with young rattlesnakes hatching. I tossed a ball on the ground, and with Sirius heeling at my side we walked toward it. As Sirius was about to pick up the ball, I yelled, "Leave it!" He immediately jumped back.

"Good dog," I said.

He'd earned his Frisbee time; maybe we both had. My best throw is the overhand, which somewhat resembles a discus toss. My high release consistently sends the disc fifty yards or more, and the hang time allows Sirius enough time to get under it. Today there was little wind, so Sirius wasn't having to make any drastic last-second lunges. We were like a dad and son playing a game of catch.

For fifteen minutes I threw and Sirius mostly retrieved. It's always easy to tell when he's tiring. He still wants to catch, but he's not so keen on providing the retrieving.

I waited until he made a particularly good catch, cheered and clapped for him, and then yelled, "Winner, winner, chicken dinner!"

Then I called him in. Both of us sat next to one another and had a long water break. My partner was panting but happy. He was delighted to be sharing the perfect moment with me. I tapped into his contentment and we let the sun warm us and the slight breeze cool us. His eyes closed, and so did mine. We shifted a little, finding that sweet spot in the universe.

Usually, I'm too preoccupied with cases to dwell on the past, but a memory of another dog and another time came to me. I must have been nine or ten. Earlier that day I'd had a falling out with Donald Baldwin, my sometimes friend and sometimes enemy. We'd been squabbling when Donald pronounced, "Well, at least I have a *real* family. Your *real* mother didn't even want you. You're *adopted*, Gideon."

He said the word like it was something ugly; hearing it spoken like that made me feel dirty. When I went home, the only thing that made me feel not quite so miserable was Roxy, our family dog. She knew I was upset from the moment I entered our house and stayed with me, doing what she could to make me feel better, but even her licks and nudges weren't quite enough to stave off the blues. My mom eventually noticed my doldrums and got out of me the story of what had happened. I repeated Donald's words about my "real" mother not wanting me.

"It's true I'm not your birth mother," she said, "but I love being your mother more than anything."

That took some of the sting out of what Donald had said, but not all. My mom took notice of Roxy's repeated attempts to jolly me out of my mood.

"Do you think Roxy is a part of our family?" she asked.

"Roxy, foxy, moxie, boxy," I said. I was going through a phase where it was rare that I didn't refer to Roxy by multiple rhyming names. "Of course she is."

"Well, if you think about it," my mother said, "Roxy was adopted as well."

Hearing that resonated with me. In my mind there was no doubt that Roxy was part of our family. If that was the case, then I was also part of the family. I wasn't the only one who had been adopted.

Those were the thoughts of a long-ago boy. They were also my thoughts as a man. Some things don't change.

Almost four million people live in the city of Los Angeles. On most days that's something I am only too aware of. But for a few moments at least, it felt as if Sirius and I had the whole city to ourselves, and all was well in the world.

Detective "Bud" Bennet called me while Sirius and I were walking toward the car. "Good timing," I said. "Sirius and I just finished our workout at the K-9 field in Glendale."

"I miss those times," he said, "but my joints don't."

"I'll be popping two ibuprofen as soon as I hit the car."

"You want me to call back in a few?"

"Now is fine."

"Our discussion yesterday has generated a lot of excitement," he said. "The two Lous were all for doing the commercials."

The two Lous were the two lieutenants under which Bud worked.

"There's only one thing, though. They think Sirius should be part of the casting."

"What about Emily?"

"We'll still use her in the context of animal abuse. But the Lous are all for using the resource at hand. Did you know your partner's Q-Rating is still off the charts in the LA area?"

I turned to Sirius and said, "Did you know your Q-Rating is off the charts?" Then I said to Bud, "What the hell is a Q-Rating?"

"It's what marketers use to rank the appeal of celebrities and products. If you have a high Q-Rating, it means people know and like you."

"How did Sirius even get a Q-Rating, seeing as I nixed either one of us doing any commercials?"

"The two of you did that one LAPD promo," said Bud, "and lots of people still remember the time when the chief draped the Liberty Award over Sirius, and he stuck out his paw and the chief shook it."

For a few days it had been a ubiquitous image replayed by the media.

"In fact," said Bud, "we were thinking it would be best if Sirius could do the commercial wearing his Liberty Award. Selena Gomez has already expressed interest in doing the spot with him. We're thinking a great ending is having Sirius shake her hand."

"And how will that help us nail Tito?"

"This commercial is the PR piece for ACTF. It will be running for the next year. We'll also be doing a second commercial specific to what occurred and where it occurred. It will be made for Crime Stoppers."

"That needs to be the priority; not some commercial with Selena Lopez and Sirius."

"Selena Gomez," he corrected me. "And I can understand your thinking, but since the stars seem to be aligning for us to get her, we have to act now."

"You'll get Sirius and his medal," I said, "after the Crime Stoppers commercial begins airing."

"I agree with you that's the way to go," Bud said, "but the two Lous aren't going to be happy. I think both of them have a crush on Gomez."

"Tough," I said. "Emily might not have your star's Q-Rating, but I know her survivor story will get a lot of attention. And people will want to nail the sick prick who left Emily for dead."

"Especially with a five-thousand-dollar reward," Bud said. "We've got a dog food company that's agreed to sponsor the reward."

"Money talks," I said, "and in this case that's just what we need."

I decided to visit Angie's Rescues. Heather Moreland needed to be told what I was plotting for Emily, and for her shelter. There was also the matter of my keeping up with my volunteer hours.

When I told Heather I needed a few minutes of her time, she suggested we combine our talk with our walk. I walked with a shepherd mix named Waldo, and Heather had a chow/retriever named Oprah. Along the way we coached the animals to heel and sit, and rewarded good behavior with Charlee Bear treats.

I expected Heather to be taken with the idea of publicizing Emily's survivor story, but she surprised me by having qualms.

"I don't want it to look like the shelter is benefiting from Emily's tragedy," she said.

"If you hadn't footed her bill, she would be dead," I said. "That's our job."

"Fundraising is also part of your job," I said. "You have a lot of animals counting on you, not to mention staff."

Heather was still shaking her head. "I told my own story in the hopes that I wouldn't have to exploit the animals."

That was the core of her reluctance, I thought. Heather's tell-all had required one painful recollection after another. The brutality of Emily's situation was probably bringing up hurtful memories.

"Emily's survival story isn't yours," I said. "Four dogs were dumped. It's likely someone saw something. If we can get someone to come forward and identify our suspect, we might be able to substantially reduce dogfighting in Southern California."

That possibility, more than anything else, brought Heather around. "Okay, then," she said. "I'd prefer not to be interviewed for this commercial. If they need a human, perhaps Dr. Misko might consent to talk about Emily's condition when she was brought in. As you pointed out, though, it's hard to imagine a more poignant story than Emily's."

"I'll tell them that," I said.

"And I'd prefer the shelter not be mentioned by name," Heather said, "even though I'm not above product placement. They can shoot our sign if they want."

"Are the St. Francis statues okay to shoot?"

"Just as long as no one is expecting a miracle."

I put in a few hours' work at the shelter, although once again I spent a disproportionate amount of time with Emily. She was wearing her Elizabethan collar, better known as a cone-head or pet cone.

When I entered her cage I asked her, "How is the reception with that thing?"

Luckily, Emily was a mellow dog. A Pekingese probably would have bitten me if I'd asked that question.

All of Emily's stitches were driving her crazy. The cone on her head and the cast on her leg were preventing her from scratching or biting. That tough love was necessary, but it made for one miserable dog.

I ministered to Emily's itchy skin, scratching around her wounds and stitching. She made a series of appreciative sounds and shifted her body to make sure I found one sweet spot after another. After a time, she grunted contentedly, and even seemed to fall asleep. I kept up my finger massage, and her breathing became deeper and more settled.

There was a bandage covering the side of her head, and I wondered if her wound was still bothering her. The last time I'd visited, Emily's temperature had been on the high side. I felt her ears and paws; it might have been my imagination, but both seemed warm.

"Sweet dreams," I said to Emily, and I tried to move away as quietly as possible.

She opened one eye at my escape. Even the poor dog's docked tail had suffered bites during her ordeal, but that didn't stop her stub from wagging at my departure.

If a dog could bestow a blessing, she had.

CHAPTER THIRTEEN

THE OPPOSITE OF WHAT WE NOW KNOW TO BE TRUE

I had warned Lisbet I needed to get up early. When my alarm sounded I crept around in the darkness, trying to not awaken her.

The night before, she'd prepared a breakfast to go for me: Greek yogurt with blueberries, topped with wheat germ. The other choice she had offered me was steel-cut oatmeal with bananas. *None of the above* hadn't been an option.

I ate the yogurt because a woman who cared about my welfare said the food was good for me. Her love was my spoonful of sugar. Of course, I hadn't been as amenable the night before when she had offered me my morning menu choices. At the time I had paraphrased from Woody Allen's *Sleeper*: "Wheat germ? Why yes, years ago it was thought to contain life-preserving properties."

In a different voice, I responded in surprise: "But what about deep fat, and steak, and cream pies, and fudge?"

And then I returned to my voice of medical reason, and not a little condescension, and concluded: "Oh, those were thought to be unhealthy, which is the opposite of what we now know to be true."

Lisbet had listened to my little show, smiled, and said, "Keep talking and I'll add castor oil to your breakfast."

I don't think I've ever had castor oil, but the threat was enough to shut me up.

It was also enough for me to redirect my first spoonful of yogurt Sirius's way. He sniffed it, and then licked the spoon clean.

When he didn't start frothing at the mouth, I said, "Thanks for being my taster."

I finished the rest of my breakfast, and then the two of us jogged out to the car. My goal was to make it to Woodland Hills at six thirty, while the day laborers were still showing up. Having already observed how the operation functioned, I knew who I wanted to question and what I wanted to ask. My targets were the de facto labor bosses.

It wasn't quite dawn when we set out. We had left early enough to beat the morning commute traffic, but there were still plenty of cars on the road. Every driver seemed to have one hand on the wheel and one hand on a coffee cup.

"A day in the life," I said to Sirius.

My day in the life, I thought, was to try and investigate the last day of Mateo Ramos's life.

I didn't want to stop for coffee, so I chose music as my caffeine. My earlier pronouncement dictated my selection, and I called up "A Day in the Life." The piece runs for about five and a half minutes, and every time I listen to it I'm grabbed in its spell. The last piano chord is like a long cry of "Om." The sound continues until you're not sure if you still hear it. It's like one of those vibrating tuning forks.

The music started, transporting me in time. When the last piano chord finally played itself out, I said, "'Trust thyself: every heart vibrates to that iron string.'"

Sirius wagged his tail. I didn't credit the quote to Ralph Waldo Emerson, and there was no tip of my hat to the philosophy of transcendentalism. I'm okay with letting my partner think I'm a genius.

"If you're good," I told Sirius, "later I'll play you 'Martha My Dear.'"

McCartney's ode to his English sheepdog Martha isn't much of a song, but the words are sung with love, and that's what a dog wants to hear more than anything else. Come to think of it, everyone wants to hear that more than anything else.

I pulled into the Home Depot parking lot and drove toward the back of the lot, where the day laborers were congregating. Just like the last time I visited, two men seemed to be running the work pool.

The smaller man, who had a mustache and slicked-back hair, was the one who engaged the gringo drivers. His bigger compadre had a square face, sturdy frame, and hard, piercing eyes that shut down conversations with just a glance. It was his job to identify which workers went with which driver.

My window was rolled down. The facilitator came over to me and, with a raised hand, asked, "How many?"

He showed me one finger and said, "One?" When I didn't respond right away, he raised a second finger and asked, "Two?"

I signaled a goose egg and turned off my ignition. Suddenly, everyone was alert. As I stepped out of my car, most of the day laborers began walking away, including Mustache and his muscle.

"Relax," I announced. "I'm LAPD, not immigration. And I'm just here to ask a few questions."

My reassurances didn't stop the exodus.

"You and you!" I yelled, pointing to the two organizers. "If you don't get back here right now, I'll send my dog after you, and then I'll arrest you."

Number One and his henchman slowed, but it looked as if they weren't sure whether to run or come back. Sirius had his head out of the car and was watching them. Luckily, they couldn't see his wagging tail.

"*Perro vicioso*," I said in my pidgin Spanish. "Don't make me send him after you."

After a meeting of eyes, the two men began walking back toward me. Their return stopped the flight of the other day laborers. From a safe distance everyone gathered to see what was going on.

With one eye on Sirius and one eye on me, the two men waited to hear what I wanted. I showed them my wallet badge, gave my name, and asked them their names.

After a moment's hesitation, Slicked-Back Hair said, "Rafe Hernandez."

"Hugo Reyes," said the muscle.

Both names sounded familiar, and I didn't doubt that they had been lifted from somewhere.

"Those are bullshit names," I said.

The two of them made momentary eye contact and seemed to accept that they had been busted.

"But I really don't care what you want to call yourselves," I said. "That's the only lie you get, though. If I catch you in another one, I am going to arrest you."

"On what charge?" asked Rafe, speaking with very little accent.

"I'll start with public loitering. Does that work for you, counselor?"

Rafe had the good sense to look at his shoes and say nothing.

"I was here earlier this week. Do you remember seeing me?"

My presence had been noted by all the day laborers in the parking lot, even though as long as I kept my distance they had pretended not to notice me. "We remember," said Rafe.

"I let the woman who I was with ask the questions. Her name was Luciana and she was the fiancée of a day laborer named Mateo Ramos. This woman asked you questions about Mateo."

"We answered her," said Rafe.

"Actually, you didn't answer her. You and Hugo here told her to get lost."

"We were busy," he said.

A truck drove up. I lifted up my wallet badge and the truck drove away.

"If you want to get rid of me," I said, "answer my questions and I'll let you get back to work. Here's my warning, though: if you don't answer them to my satisfaction, I promise you I won't be good for business."

"What do you want to know?" he asked.

"Did you know Mateo Ramos?"

Rafe shrugged. "I knew him from around here."

I turned to huge Hugo. "What about you?"

"Same," he said.

"You ever talk to him?"

"Here and there," he said. "He wanted the money jobs."

"Why do you think that was?"

Hugo shrugged. He looked at Rafe, who also shrugged. I already knew the answer to my question but wondered if they did.

Mateo had been keen on making money so that he could marry the woman of his dreams.

"You pick out the workers for the jobs, right?" I asked.

Hugo nodded.

"And if they have certain skills—for example, if they can do plumbing or carpentry—they get paid more. Is that right?"

"Right," he agreed.

"And Mateo had those skills, didn't he? So he was able to get higher-paying work?"

Rafe decided he should answer that question. "Sometimes," he said. "But there are days when everyone wants the Indians and no one wants the chiefs."

It was easy to understand why Rafe was the spokesperson for the day laborers: his English was good enough for him to even use gringo slang.

"Did any of the day laborers here resent Mateo for always trying to get the highest-paying jobs?"

Rafe and Hugo shook their heads. "You got the skills, you get the money," said Rafe. "That's the rule."

"And you and Hugo get your cut from that money?"

Neither man said anything.

"Did that, or does that, cause any problems?"

They shook their heads. "Someone's got to organize," said Rafe.

"Tell me about the client known as Hitler," I said. "I understand Mateo thought he shortchanged him."

"There was a misunderstanding on one job he was hired for," said Rafe. "Hitler thought everyone was getting the same hourly rate, and Mateo thought he should have gotten more."

"From what I heard, Mateo held a grudge."

"He was sure Hitler knew about the different rates. Because of that, he wouldn't work for him again."

"That was the extent of it?"

I got nods.

"Mateo was dispatched on a job from which he never came back. Do you remember Mateo's last client?"

Both men looked at each other, and then shook their heads.

"Nothing stands out? Seeing as Mateo had construction skills, maybe someone was looking for a specialized kind of worker? Something like that ring any bells?"

A big Suburban drove toward us, and once more I waved my wallet badge. The vehicle made an abrupt turn and drove away.

"C'mon, man," said Rafe. "That guy in the Suburban always wants at least four workers."

"I'm glad you know your regulars," I said. "I need you to talk about a few of them."

Rafe sighed. "What do you want to know?" he asked.

"I need to hear about your odd clients. I want to know about anyone who behaves in a strange way around your workers or asks them to do strange things."

The two men started talking to one another in Spanish, and I was only able to pick up every third or fourth word. They said the word *desnudo* a few times, and both started laughing.

"What's so funny?" I asked.

"There's a dude we call 'the naked guy,'" said Rafe. "He doesn't wear any clothes once he gets to his house."

"Does he make advances on your workers?"

"He's not like that," said Rafe. "But we like to send new guys to his house. It's sort of a . . . "

He tried to think of the word and I said, "Initiation?"

"Yeah," said Rafe.

They started talking in Spanish again; there seemed to be some debate about "the mamacita."

"Everyone wants to work for one lady we call 'the mamacita,'" explained Rafe. "She isn't young, but she's had a lot of surgery."

He raised his hands and cupped them near his chest. "Every time our guys work at her place she goes out in the sun with just a towel. Whenever she puts on sun block or moves around, the towel mostly falls off. Everyone watches more than works."

It sounded like the scene from *Cool Hand Luke* of a scantily clad woman washing her car to an audience of chain gang prisoners, with the same expected results.

Then Rafe said something about "Diego Rivera" to Hugo, whose reply made both men laugh. I tried to translate the words and was pretty sure they were something to the effect of "His stomach is so fat he can't see his penis."

"Who is this Diego?" I asked.

"That's not his real name," said Rafe. "He's a heavy man, a painter. That's why we call him Diego Rivera. He picks up a worker here once or twice a week."

"'Home and garden work,'" said Hugo, mimicking the man's words with a smirk. "That's what he asks for. But that's not what he wants."

"He offers more money if the men take off their clothes and let him paint them," Rafe said, "than if they do landscaping."

"That's why he wants the young and pretty ones," Hugo said, gesturing with a limp wrist.

Machismo still reigns in most of Mexico. There are as many gay people there as anywhere, but the culture still forces most to be closeted.

The two men spoke in their native tongue, and Hugo replied in the affirmative. Then he said to me, "Mateo work for him sometimes."

That surprised me. "Mateo posed for him?"

Both men nodded, but without the mock mincing that had accompanied their earlier words. "He do it for the money," said Hugo.

"Recently?" I asked.

"*Creo que sí*," said Hugo.

I think so, I translated. "Do you know Diego's real name and do you have his address?" I asked.

Hugo called to a few of the bystanders. His question resulted in some laughs and jeers. Although I didn't get either a name or an address, the workers were able to supply some landmarks, as well as the *concurso de meando* that set the house apart from its neighbors.

"Look for the pissing contest," Hugo explained, adding that out in front of the house were statues of a boy, a girl, and a dog, all engaged in the act of peeing.

I wrote down some notes while Rafe and Hugo talked about other crazy gringos. There was a client they called *el doctor*, not because he was an MD but because he was apparently afraid of germs and wore a mask and plastic gloves around the workers. I also heard about *gringo culo*, an older man who would get frustrated when the workers couldn't speak English to his satisfaction, and would raise the volume of his voice as if that would help them understand better.

By that time half a dozen cars were waiting in line, and everyone but me was ready to get on with their business. I looked at my notes and saw where I had starred one entry.

"*Macho Libre*," I said. "One of your workers said something about being recruited for a film project based on *luchadores* and *lucha libre*, but that the guys filming it referred to it as *Macho Libre*. Evidently, there was a fighting ring set up in a backyard and an outdoor set with oversized sombreros and props. There was even a painted donkey. I need to know if that sounds familiar to anyone."

Hugo called out to the crowd. I couldn't follow what was going on, but a few of the workers referenced someone named Javier. Hugo called out to a man in a muscle shirt, but everything he asked was met with a shake of the man's head.

"What's the problem?" I said.

"The others say Javier talked of being in such a place," said Rafe, "but now he doesn't want to say nothing."

"Tell him to come over here," I said.

Hugo made the pronouncement; he was about the only man there bigger than Javier. Scowling, Javier came forward.

I was the obvious reason for his reluctance. Mexican nationals don't trust cops in Mexico or in the US.

"Tell him I'm not here to hassle him," I said. "Tell him that I just want to know where this house is located."

Javier responded before any words were translated. "I don't know no street names," he said. "But the house you want is up there."

He pointed east.

"In the hills," he added.

"How about I pay you a hundred bucks for a few hours work?" I asked. "I'd like you to help me find that house."

He still looked unsure, so I decided to seal the deal. I took out my wallet and extended five Jacksons his way. He reached for the money, tucking the bills deep in the right front pocket of his jeans.

"Once we find that house," I said, "I'll bring you right back here. Okay?"

"Okay," he said.

CHAPTER FOURTEEN

WAR AND PEACE

Javier Moreno sat in the passenger seat. He smelled of work, and his living conditions, and fear of me, and fear of Sirius. I opened both our windows, and I'm not sure which of us was happier at that. Javier stuck his nose out the window, as did I.

Richard Pryor once did a comedy skit that's usually referred to as "the African hitchhiker." After picking up a hitchhiker on an African road, Pryor described being hit by the man's body odor. "He had that *odor*," Pryor said, showing how strong it was with his face and body. Pryor described doing everything he could to avoid the stench; his physical comedy made the piece. His body gyrated and his face shifted anywhere and everywhere to try and escape the odor. And then Pryor said he happened to look in his rearview mirror at where the hitchhiker was sitting, and it was clear the other man was in as much olfactory distress as was Pryor. Two different cultures had collided, each with its own unique scents. Pryor's antiperspirant was as offensive to the other man as his lack of antiperspirant was to Pryor.

It was probably that way in my front seat. I had aftershave on, and body wash borrowed from Lisbet, whose scent I seemed to remember was called Alpine Lavender. Javier was apparently not as fond of it as Lisbet was.

After a few stops and starts while Javier oriented himself, we drove in a mostly easterly direction, heading toward the foothills of the Santa Monica Mountains. The route we took went through an upscale area, with most of the houses north of a million dollars.

During the drive, my passengers got acquainted with one another. Javier didn't have much of a choice, as Sirius kept sniffing him appreciatively. At first Javier tried to shrink away from my partner's probing nose, but before long a rapprochement was reached and he began running his fingers through Sirius's fur.

"What his name?" he asked.

"Sirius," I said.

"Serious?"

I pointed upwards and said, *"Perro estrella."*

"Ah," he said, "Sirio."

That sounded right to me, so I nodded.

Javier had a sense of direction that I envied. Some people always seem to be able to orient themselves. You can spin them around until they're dizzy, but when they come to a stop they can still tell you what direction they're facing. I am one of those people who are extremely glad that GPS surfaced in my lifetime.

Every so often, Javier would lift his index finger, and then, compass-like, point it in a direction. It was my job to find the right asphalt surface to get us to where he was pointing.

"Who hired you for this job?" I asked. "Did he tell you his name?"

Javier nodded. "He tell me to call him Hitch." He thought about it. "Yes, Hitch."

"Describe Hitch for me."

"He young. I think he my age, *mas o menos*. But he pick me up in a new Lexus."

Millennials in luxury cars are ubiquitous in LA. "And how old are you?"

"Twenty-three."

"Was Hitch clean-shaven?"

He nodded.

"Physically, was he fat, regular, or skinny?"

"He is *flaco*—skinny."

"What kind of clothes was he wearing?"

"He have nice boots," Javier said, sounding a little envious. "And I think his watch a real Rolex."

"Did Hitch talk a lot?"

Javier nodded. "He talk fast. And he keep saying, 'Right? Right?' He like a *loro*."

"*Loro*?"

"Bird," he said, and then came up with "Parrot."

"What was Hitch talking about?"

"He ask me if I like boxing. I tell him yes. And he ask if I ever fight."

"What did you tell him?"

Javier shrugged. "I say I fight a few times when I young."

My passenger opened his mouth to say something else, and then closed it. His mouth stayed closed. I wondered about his sudden clamming up, and figured my profession was the cause. It's tough opening up to a stranger, and even tougher opening up to a cop. I wanted to make it easier for him.

"You don't have to be afraid that anything you say might get you in trouble," I said. "I want to find out what happened to Mateo, so I need you to be honest with me. Whatever you tell me, I won't use against you."

Javier nodded to show he'd heard, but I could tell he was still uncertain as to whether he should believe me. Finally, he must have decided to take a chance.

"Hitch laugh a lot. He say I too serious. While we drive, he ask me if I want to smoke some *mota*."

He stopped talking, probably gauging my reaction. *Mota* is Spanish for *weed*.

"So you and Hitch did some smoking during the drive," I said.

"'Loosen'—is that the word?—'Loosen up,' he keep saying."

I nodded and smiled, doing my best to make him feel at ease. Like Hitch, I wanted him to loosen up.

"During the drive he ask me if I ever go to see *lucha libre*, and I tell him I had. That make him happy. We talk about the wrestlers, and he get very excited. Hitch say they making a movie with masks and fighting. Then he say I would make a good Frito Bandito. I ask him what that is."

I only knew about the Frito Bandito because I took a course on racism in advertising during one of my six years matriculating at Cal State Northridge. The Frito Bandito ad campaign ran for four years and wasn't pulled until the early seventies. If a mustachioed, pistol-toting Fritos thief wasn't stereotypical enough, the commercials had their own jingle, sung in heavily accented English to the tune of the classic folk song "Cielito Lindo."

"Hitch say I can be like a *luchador* and wear a mask of the Frito Bandito. I act like I understand what he's saying, but he talk too fast. When we get to the house, I begin to see what he mean."

In the backyard of the house, Javier told me, he met Hitch's two friends, along with another day laborer, named Octavio. A boxing ring was set up in the yard. Beneath it were pens with chickens and a pig, and a donkey painted with stripes. A converted Tuff Shed served as the costume and mask room. The outfits weren't like what *luchadores* wore, but were getups exploiting Mexican stereotypes. Javier said there were huge sombreros, bullfighter outfits, and iconography featuring questionable-looking saints, including one who was pregnant. There were also masks featuring chili peppers, frijoles, and hot sauce. And, of course, there was the Frito Bandito.

Octavio was glad to see Javier, because he didn't speak any English and Hitch's two friends spoke very little Spanish. It fell to Javier to do most of the translating. The three friends, who referred to themselves as "tres amigos," explained to their workers that they were moviemakers.

"They say they want to film us fighting. And they want each of us to wear costume. At first we say, 'No, no.' But then they say they pay us good money."

"So you put on the costumes and got in the ring?"

Javier nodded. "And they make us up with paint and hair. I got this long mustache, and Octavio's face was painted red like the devil. They said that when we fight we need to yell things like, 'Time for a siesta,' and 'I am a bad hombre.' And during the fight they keep spraying the back of our shirts with water. And when the pig walk across the ring, we are told to yell, 'señorita' and '*mi amore*.' And they tell us to pound our hearts and pretend the pig is our true love and that we fight over her."

"Did you catch the names of the other two men?" I asked.

"One tell me he Quentin, and the other say he Martin. But that's not the names they call each other."

Hitch, I thought, short for Hitchcock, and then there was Quentin Tarantino and Martin Scorsese. The young filmmakers had quite the egos. They'd also proved adept at the bait and switch. While Javier and Octavio continued to drink and smoke, the filmmakers said they wanted their action film to "look realistic." To that end, they proposed that Javier and Octavio do more than play fight—they asked them to fight for real.

The two men declined at first, but the offer was sweetened, and sweetened some more. They agreed to the fight and a purse of eight hundred and fifty dollars. The winner was to get five hundred dollars, and the loser three hundred and fifty dollars. But the match would continue until only one of the men was standing. They were told anything was legal. They could kick or head-butt; they could pile-drive and rabbit punch. The only thing they couldn't do was cry uncle, or at least not without their pound of flesh. One man would win by beating the other man into submission.

Martin did the announcing, while Hitch and Quentin worked the cameras. Before the actual fight, Javier said, there was lots of starting and stopping for such stunts as the chickens walking through the ring, Martin dressing up as a mariachi and pretending to play "El Torero" on a trumpet, and the pig parading around in a *folklórico* dress while the two contestants threw roses her way. Javier admitted his memories of much of the day were hazy, clouded in drink and smoke and blows to the head. The fight, he said, was bloody and long.

Javier couldn't remember how many rounds they fought. He and Octavio were evenly matched; after a time they didn't have the strength to run around the ring. They ended up toe to toe, each having to muster the strength to throw a punch. Their arms became weights that could only be raised with effort. Late in the fight neither of them could even raise their hands to try and deflect the other man's blows.

Their staggered swinging at one another was the last thing Javier remembered while being in the ring. He wasn't sure whether he was knocked out or whether he passed out, but he recalled that he fell in a bloody heap. When he awakened, he found himself lying on a pool chaise. On a chaise next to him was Octavio. Both men were given ice bags, Advil, and Band-Aids. Over the course of about an hour, they recovered—and sobered up. And then Hitch drove Javier back, and Quentin took Octavio. Both were given the money they had been promised, although in retrospect Javier didn't think his three hundred and fifty dollars was worth it.

He was okay with his black eye and the bruises, Javier told me, but not his broken nose.

"It still hurt," he said, reaching a hand up to touch it.

Luckily, he didn't need to use that nose to sniff out the house. Javier's sense of direction never faltered, and we were finally able to reach what he referred to as *el casa de boxeo.*

Like the other homes in the neighborhood, *el casa de boxeo* was situated on about half an acre. All the residences in the area had been built in the early sixties, and almost all had been rebuilt and added on to since that time. The homes felt as if they were out in the country, even though they weren't very far from Ventura Boulevard and the 101 freeway.

Most of the houses on the street had backyards that extended up into the hills. Italian cypress trees bordered both sides of *el casa de boxeo,* effectively blocking off the neighbors from being able to see into the backyard.

I left Javier and Sirius in the car and walked up a flagstone pathway to the front door. After ringing the doorbell, I waited for half a minute before ringing it again. The second ring also went unanswered. Turning around, I motioned for Javier to join me; Sirius crashed the party by slipping out of the car before Javier closed his door.

Javier made his way up the flagstone pathway, and I said to him, "I want to make absolutely sure this is the right house."

He looked around. "I think so," he said, "but I was inside. We take the path to the back."

Javier pointed out a gate to the right of the garage. We walked over to it and found it was locked. On tippy-toes the two of us looked over the gate and fencing. Sirius wanted to see what we were staring at and got up on his back legs for his own look. He wasn't tall enough to see over the fence, but maybe he had another purpose in mind. Sirius tried working the lock mechanism with his nose. During the past six months, my partner had learned all on his own how to turn door handles with his teeth and open windows with his nose.

"That's not going to work, Houdini," I told him. "It's locked from the inside."

"He open doors?" asked an amazed Javier.

The first time I'd seen Sirius work a knob with his teeth and open the door, I had been round eyed as well. But now I was used to the manipulations of my escape artist. I had thought to document my Houdini's efforts, but when I went to YouTube I saw that dozens of people had already posted videos of their dogs opening everything from front doors to windows to car doors.

Who really needs opposable thumbs?

"He's a police dog," I said, as if that should explain it.

The pathway extended along the side of the house; flanking it was fencing. As an additional privacy measure there was a canopy of mature cypresses.

"Look familiar to you?" I asked.

Javier nodded, but not emphatically enough for me. "Let's see if we can get a better look at the backyard by walking next door," I said.

We made our way along the border between the two houses, following the line of trees until we were stopped by the neighbor's fence. Javier pushed aside foliage and we were able to get a partial view of the backyard. There was no boxing ring, no animals, and no costumes to be seen. Despite the absence of all those things, Javier now seemed certain that this was the right place.

Since we were already well into the neighbor's yard, I decided to trespass a little more. I told Javier to take Sirius back to the car, and then I cut across the lawn and made my way up to the neighbor's house. I pushed the doorbell, but instead of hearing it ring, I saw the reflection of lights turning on and off in the house.

Those who are hearing impaired often eschew a doorbell in favor of lights turning on and off. I heard movement from inside the house and held up my wallet badge so that it could be seen through the peephole. It must have passed inspection, because a few seconds later a woman opened the door. Before I could identify myself, she raised her hand in a gesture that told me to stop. Then she handed me a card that read: *Today is a nonverbal day for me. Please do not invade my silent world. If you feel that communication is necessary, apply pen to paper.*

In her hands were a notepad and pen. I reached for them, and then considered my words before writing.

What is your name?

She took the pen and notepad back and wrote, *Jillian Booker.*

It was my turn. *TY, Jillian. I am Detective Gideon. Please tell me the name(s) of your neighbors.* I pointed to the house I'd come from.

She took the pad and wrote, *Dory Cunningham.*

It was my turn with the stylus: *Does Dory have a son who lives with her?*

I studied Jillian while she wrote her answer. She was attractive, probably mid-fifties, with long, pulled-back hair that was mostly gray. Her garb was plain but stylish: an untucked men's button-down white oxford shirt, blue jeans, and sandals.

Jason has his own place, she wrote, *but occasionally spends time at his mother's house.*

Jason Cunningham? I wrote, and she nodded. Then I wrote, *Do you happen to have Jason's or Dory's telephone number?*

Jillian continued with our Quaker meeting, tapping her finger on Dory's name. Then she raised a finger and retreated into the house. Half a minute later she returned and wrote down Dory's home phone number.

I wrote down another question: *Good neighbors?*

Jillian took the pad and jotted: *We live in different worlds with little contact.*

I had the feeling my silent friend lived in a world different than most, but I didn't write that. Instead I took the pen and inked, *Thank you.*

Jillian concluded our Carmelite interaction by bringing her hands together above her chest, nodding slightly, and then writing the word *namaste*, making little hearts out of both A's.

I nodded back and made my silent escape.

CHAPTER FIFTEEN

IT IS NOT ALWAYS THE BULL WHO LOSES

I dropped Javier off at the Home Depot. He was happy with our arrangement, telling me that it shouldn't be hard to pick up a second shift that day. If he could be that motivated to work, so could I. Instead of driving away, I went into the home improvement store. There were plenty of items I should have picked up for my house, but instead I bought a few handfuls of copper piping.

Before leaving Woodland Hills, I decided to search for the artist known as Diego Rivera. I had been told his house wasn't far from the Woodland Hills Country Club, and that it had a view of the golf course, but that didn't prove to be much help. As I drove around, I found a number of residential streets with homes overlooking the course.

I was just about ready to give up on my search when I saw a middle-aged woman with a ponytail threaded through her Dodgers cap walking her female Australian shepherd. Judging by the woman's pace and the defined musculature of her legs, she was a serious walker. Sirius suddenly perked up as I pulled up next to her and lowered my window. Before I could say anything, he extended his muzzle and offered a little "woof," which got their attention. My partner is an incorrigible flirt.

"Excuse me," I said, showing the woman my badge. "I'm sure this sounds strange, but I'm looking for a house that's supposed to be nearby."

"What's the address?" she asked.

"That's the rub," I said. "I have a description of the house, but no address."

"Good luck with that," she said.

"I was told there were some unique statues out front. If my information is accurate, there's a statue of a little boy, a little girl, and a dog."

That didn't spark any sign of recognition.

I had to continue, even though I was afraid the woman might think I was some kind of pervert. "I was told all of them are peeing."

"Oh," she said, "of course. That's the peeing family. They all have names, I think, but I don't remember any of them except for Toto. He's the peeing dog, and he's the nearest to the sidewalk, so you can imagine he's a favorite target for all the dogs around here."

"Where can I find this peeing family?" I asked.

"Two blocks over," she said. "Just continue up this street, and then make your first left and go to the end of the cul-de-sac."

"Thank you so much," I said.

"Thank you for what you did," she said.

By that time Sirius and I were sharing the window space. He woofed again, and the woman said, "Yes, thank you, too." She looked at me and said, "Is he friendly?"

"To the point of being forward," I said.

She stroked the side of his head, and then in a quieter voice asked, "Is this the same dog that went into the fire with you?"

Even though it happens with less frequency now, the people of LA still surprise me by remembering our encounter with Ellis Haines.

"Same old dog," I said, "same old human." And same old story.

She must have detected my reluctance to talk about the subject, and stepped back to the sidewalk. "I just want you to know that everyone around here slept a lot easier because of the two of you."

I nodded and said, "Thanks again for the directions."

The peeing family wasn't the only garden statuary; there were pink flamingos and garden gnomes, including a gnome mooning the world, a cat eating a gnome, and a gnome with a cleaver standing over a beheaded pink flamingo.

"Gnome, sweet gnome," I told Sirius.

He ignored me, as he was busy peeing on the peeing dog. I couldn't help but think the locals should have come up with a better name than Toto; the statue dog definitely looked more like a retriever than a terrier.

I followed pavers up to the front door, passing fountains and wind chimes and planters full of colorful sages that I wasn't alone in appreciating; humming bees were going from flower to flower.

Pressing the doorbell brought on the four notes from the Westminster Chimes; all that was missing was the clanging of the hour. The door opened just as the chimes concluded, and the painter known as Diego Rivera greeted me with a cautious "Hello." Other than being heavy, the painter bore no resemblance to Rivera. He was an older man, probably late sixties, who wore white linen pants and an expansive Aloha shirt.

I displayed my wallet badge and identified myself. "I'd like to ask you a few questions," I said. "I'm investigating the disappearance of Mateo Ramos."

The man started shaking his head. "I don't know any Mateo Ramos."

"He's a day laborer," I said. "I'm told you painted him more than once."

The artist began wiping his chin with a nervous hand and regarded me with an ambushed expression. "I—I'm not—"

I interrupted him before he expressed any qualms about talking with me or decided he needed a lawyer. "The only reason I'm here," I said, "is to see if you can tell me anything about Mateo."

He thought about that and finally said, "I'll help if I can, but I can't be certain I even know who he is."

"I have some pictures of him," I said. "Would you mind looking at them to see if he's familiar to you?"

The artist nodded, and I handed him my cell phone. After studying the two pictures Luciana had given me, he said, "I think he modeled for me two times, possibly three."

"Nude?" I asked.

He let out some air and did a series of small, nervous nods.

"As I said," I told him, "I am only interested in what happened to Mateo Ramos. I'm not here trying to roust you."

"I'm glad to hear that," he said. "When I was younger the police were not kind to people like me."

"Both of us can be glad those days are in the past. How well did you know Mateo?"

He shook his head and said, "To be honest, I didn't even know his name."

"Speaking of names, I'd appreciate you providing me with yours."

For a moment he looked too surprised to respond. Finally, he said, "If you didn't know my name—which is Scott Harrelson, but everyone calls me Hal—how did you find me?"

"Those who have been to your property remembered your statuary," I said.

He flipped up his hand, shook a finger, and said, "Of course."

"I'm told the locals even have names for them."

"They do," he said, "even though they aren't the names you'd hear in Brussels, where the original statues can be found. *Manneken Pis* was the first and most famous of the Brussels statues; its translation is *Little Boy Pissing*. But then the world became more egalitarian, and along came *Jeanneke Pis*, the little girl squatting. So I suppose *Het Zinneke*, the statue of the urinating dog, was inevitable."

"What prompted you to put those statues, and your other pieces, out front?"

"I don't have any kind of twisted fetish, if that's what you're asking. But I've always had what you might call a warped sense of humor. There are plenty of replicas of *Manneken Pis* around the world, but I think I'm the first to unite all three pieces in one spot."

"Maybe if you get tired of the three statues, you can sell the lot to a urological practice."

"I know they're tacky," he said, "but they're also good fun. People are always pulling over to the curb to see the pissing family. Little kids of all ages stop and laugh. And like the original statues, people are always dressing them up in costumes.

"Every Valentine's Day, Little Dickie Leak—that's what I call the boy—is dressed up as Cupid," he said. "And he's been a leprechaun, and a jolly elf, and dozens of other characters."

"So you're the fun house on the block."

"I've always believed it's better to be over-the-top than boring."

It all felt friendly enough, I thought, but so had John Wayne Gacy when he dressed up as a clown. Still, Sirius seemed to like Hal, and my partner is usually a good judge of character.

"How about we go inside where it's more comfortable, and you can ask your questions there?" said Hal.

"Thank you," I said, and then turned to Sirius and said, "*Sitz und bleib.*"

Sirius complied with my commands to sit and stay, but not without pouting. His acting ability didn't go unnoticed, or unrewarded.

"Oh, your dog doesn't have to stay outside," Hal said. "He's welcome in the house."

Sirius understood the invitation and didn't need to be told twice; he hurried inside. "*Geh voraus,*" I said to his disappearing tail, which means "go ahead."

Hal motioned for me to enter. Sirius rejoined me at my side and expertly heeled as we walked down the hall. He was good at making others believe I was in charge.

We were directed into the living room, where I took a seat on a comfortable leather chair. The walls were covered with at least twenty canvases. "Your paintings?" I asked.

"Mostly," he said.

The majority of Hal's paintings were colorful abstracts, althhough there was the occasional landscape or portrait.

"Not many nude day laborers portrayed," I observed.

"No nudes at all," he said. "Some people aren't comfortable looking at the human body, so my living room is sans nudes."

It was an interesting prohibition for a man who had the peeing family on display. Without any further preamble I asked, "What do you remember of Mateo Ramos?"

"I thought of him as 'the *guerrero.*' Do you know the word?"

I shook my head and he said, "It's Spanish for *warrior.* He was always tense when he modeled, and I used to have to ask him to unclench his fists. I guess his body language was supposed to ward me off from making advances."

"Did it work?"

"I have never forced myself on any of my models."

He hedged his answer, but I didn't want to back him into a corner, at least not yet. "Do you sell paintings of the nude males who model for you?"

"The gallery I paint for has had some success with them," he said, "but in most cases the subjects end up clothed, although sometimes just barely. Last year I did a series of paintings showing different facets of Aztec culture. The slaves wore only loincloths, as I tried to be accurate in portraying the clothing of my subject matter."

"Not to be rude," I said, "but I'm more interested in Mateo than the subjects of your paintings. And I specifically need to know if the two of you had any kind of sexual relationship."

He shook his head and said, "No, we didn't."

"What do you imagine was his motivation to be your model?" I asked.

"He had the same motivation as do most of my models: money. Would you rather be doing backbreaking work in the hot sun or striking a few poses in an air-conditioned room?"

"I checked with Mateo's fiancée: she never knew about his modeling for you."

Hal smiled. "Should I be surprised? Machismo is part of the Mexican culture. Who's going to want to talk about posing naked for a gay artist? Even a gay model would be unlikely to talk about it, as most gay Mexicans I know are closeted. It was clear that the *guerrero* was never exactly comfortable with my sexuality."

"But he still posed without clothes?"

"He was well aware that I pay an extra ten dollars an hour to my models if they agree to be unclothed."

"When was the last time he modeled for you?"

"I would guess at least three months ago."

"Did the two of you talk much?"

He shook his head. "Very little. I don't think he approved of my lifestyle. That's why I typically put in requests for models who aren't so judgmental. I had enough disapproval and guilt growing up. Can you understand that?"

"I was raised Catholic," I said.

He laughed, and then said, "I should have offered you and your dog something to drink, Detective."

"We're both fine, thanks," I said, "and we'll be leaving shortly. I'm not sure how to broach this question, so I'll just come out with it. I was told that sometimes the guys running the workforce like to do a kind of initiation prank on the newer and younger workers. Their main target is a nudist, but I wonder if you've also been singled out."

Hal nodded. "On a few occasions they've sent naïve newcomers," he said. "Those boys always react with shock when the fat, gay, sixty-something gringo artist asks them if they would like to pose nude instead of work."

"I imagine that's awkward."

"Not as much as you'd think," he says. "Many of them are happy to model, especially for the extra money, and those who prefer to keep their clothes on get assigned to weeding or pruning or digging. I have a big yard and there's always lots of work that needs doing."

. . . .

I made my way over to Boyle Heights and parked on the street in a spot that allowed me to look into the lot that advertised *Best Scrap* and *Junkyard Dog Services*. For almost an hour I studied what was going on inside of Tito's businesses. The dogs were securely chained around the property. When the chains were pulled out to their maximum length, no more than eighteen inches separated one dog from another. Their proximity to each other seemed to stoke their animosity.

The recycling business was busy with a constant flow of customers. Most came into the lot by truck or car, but a few homeless people pushed in shopping carts mainly filled with crushed aluminum cans. Both Tito and his one-eyed assistant, Fausto, could be seen inside and outside of their trailer. A third employee, a middle-aged Hispanic man, stayed mostly in the back, working the heavy equipment. On those occasions that required his presence in the trailer, the man took care to travel along a specific path that kept him clear of all the chained dogs.

Finally, I decided I'd seen enough and drove into the recycling center and parked. Sirius's window was open, and the other dogs must have caught his scent. They rose en masse and began barking. As much as they didn't like each other, they became united in their animosity toward the newcomer.

Tito started in as soon as I stepped into the trailer. He pulled out a very thick billfold, plucked out a Hamilton, and extended it my way.

"I figured you'd reconsider about your dog," he said, flashing me that fake smile of his.

"I thought we'd agreed on twenty," I said. "Is bait and switch how you operate your business?"

"Got an A rating from the BBB," Tito said, giving me another dose of his pearly whites.

"Best Crap got an A rating?" I said. "That surprises me. I would have guessed the BBB wouldn't want anything to do with a business named Best Crap."

"Best Scrap," said Tito.

"My mistake," I said. "I mean, the word *best* is easy enough to make out on your sign, but then you've got the dollar sign in front of *crap*. I guess lots of people have made that mistake before."

"No one else has been that stupid," said Tito. "Isn't that right, Fausto?"

The small, quiet man with the eye patch nodded. One eye was enough to give me a look that could kill.

"So you don't buy crap," I said. "You buy scrap."

"I am glad you finally understood that."

"As it so happens," I said, "I have some copper piping in my car. Do you buy copper?"

"Cash on the barrel," said Tito.

"Let me get it, then."

I went out to the car and came back with an armful of copper pipes, which I laid on the counter.

"Where did you get the copper?" Tito asked.

"From a plumbing project I did at my house," I said.

"Lots of copper gets stolen from construction sites and remodels," said Tito. "How do I know you didn't steal this stuff?"

"I guess you'll just have to trust me."

Tito looked at Fausto and nodded. The smaller man took my copper and weighed it.

"Would you like a receipt?" asked Tito.

"That would be nice," I said.

He wrote out a receipt. "We pay a dollar sixty a pound for good copper. You don't have quite three pounds' worth, which comes to four dollars and twenty-three cents."

I had paid about three times that at Home Depot. Like most of my investments, I bought high and sold low.

Tito went to the safe and opened it. There were plenty of greenbacks inside. He pulled out a few dollars and put the money on the counter.

"I'm glad I didn't sell you my dog," I said. "He's going to be a star. These producers want him to do an animal cruelty commercial with Selena Gomez. The two of them are going to promote awareness for the LA Animal Cruelty Task Force. But I'm getting ahead of myself. That's the second commercial. This week they'll be shooting the first commercial. Crime Stoppers and ACTF will be teaming up to do a piece on those dogs that were dumped nearby. And you'll be happy to hear a pet-food manufacturer has agreed to ante up a five-thousand-dollar reward for information leading to the arrest and conviction of whoever dumped those poor dogs. That kind of money ought to get lots of people calling in, don't you think?"

Tito shrugged. "It's been my experience that people don't stick out their necks like chickens do when they are on the chopping block. What a strange behavior that is. It makes it so easy to chop off their heads. Then again, I have known one or two people who are like those chickens. It's almost as if they ask to be hurt."

He looked at me, made a slashing motion with his hand, and smiled.

His threat didn't go unnoticed. "Whenever I hear some lowlife say, 'They asked for it,' you can be sure they didn't."

"Have you ever gone to a bullfight, Detective?"

"I have."

"You surprise me."

"I was with friends in Mexico," I said. "The excursion had already been planned."

"What did you think?"

"It wasn't to my taste."

"And yet Hemingway—a writer some say is the greatest of all time—loved going to bullfights. In the arena, he saw the artistry, and the skill, and the bravery. He immortalized the sport."

"So Hemingway is right and I'm wrong?"

"My point is that some issues are not so black-and-white."

"Hemingway shot himself in the head. Does that speak to his judgment?"

"Maybe it speaks to his cojones."

"I try not to think with those."

He smiled at me and said, "I heard a story about Hemingway, but I do not know whether it's true or not. It's said he went to a restaurant in Spain where he'd never dined before, and as he sat at his table he heard this—how do you say it?—this celebration going on. Hemingway watched as three waiters made their way to a nearby table, struggling with the weight of their tray. They lowered the tray to the table, and then the cover was taken off of the plate and a great bowl of soup was revealed. In the midst of this bowl were two huge balls. As the steam rose into the air, everyone in the restaurant cheered.

"Hemingway was puzzled. He called over one of the waiters and said, 'What's going on?' And the waiter said, 'Oh, Señor Hemingway, today there was a bullfight and we are serving up the balls of the bull who lost. It is a great delicacy that is called the Grand Victory.'

"After thinking about this, Hemingway said, 'I would like to have a serving of the Grand Victory.' And the waiter said, 'Oh, I am sorry, Señor Hemingway, we only offer one serving of it a night. Because of that, the Grand Victory is booked far in advance.' That news only encouraged Hemingway all the more, and he asked for the first date when he could partake of the Grand Victory.

"Three months later Hemingway returned to the restaurant, sat at his table, and waited with great expectation for his dinner to be served. Then the moment arrived, with all the waiters coming to his table. But when the cover was taken off the huge soup bowl, there was no cheering from the patrons in restaurant. Instead of two huge balls in the bowl, there were only what looked like two small eggs.

"Hemingway did not understand what was going on. He looked at his soup and asked, 'What is this?'

"And the waiter shook his head sadly and said, 'Alas, Señor Hemingway, it is not always the bull who loses.'"

CHAPTER SIXTEEN

THE EVIL THAT LURKS WITHIN

I let the rooster do his crowing while I walked to the car. Cops are used to getting attitude, but it usually stops short of threats. Tito's threats had been veiled, but I knew it wouldn't do to underestimate him. He had been born poor and escaped poverty. I was a potential threat to the lifestyle to which he had become accustomed, and I imagined he would fiercely resist any possibility of returning to the poorhouse. I also had to be mindful of his character—anyone who could kill dogs without compunction was not likely to be much more charitable when it came to humans.

From inside his trailer, Tito was still waving goodbye to me, hoping he could provoke me into doing something. In my time in his trailer, I had identified two hidden cameras.

Mindful of those cameras, I stifled my impulse to give him a one-finger salute, and instead waved back. Then I said to Sirius, "Just remember, you can be a preening, strutting rooster one day and a feather duster the next."

Sirius lent me one upraised ear, heard my rant out, and then dropped that ear and went back to sleep. I couldn't really blame him. I started up the car and exited Best Scrap.

"Let sleeping dogs lie," I said.

I thought of the dogs that Tito had dumped. Using Bluetooth, I said, "Call Bud Bennet."

Bud picked up on the second ring and said, "I was just about to call you."

"And what were you about to say?"

"That I need the name and number of that vet who treated the surviving pit bull A-SAP," he said.

"The vet's name is Kate Misko. She has her own practice, but I don't remember its name. If you need her business number right away, you could call up Angie's Rescues. She's their on-call vet. Or I can text her number to you the next time I pull over."

"That works for me, as long as you don't forget, and as long as I get it within the hour."

"No problem," I said. "But what's the urgency?"

"Crime Stoppers and ACTF want to start filming our commercial early next week and we need to find times that work for Dr. Misko."

"I'm glad you're doing that spot sooner rather than later," I said. "I just left Tito Rivera's business, and I happened to mention the Crime Stoppers commercial. That's the one intangible he can't control. Tomorrow I think I'll return to Best Scrap and ask him if he wants to audition for the role of the animal-killing asshole."

"Sounds like the two of you are getting real chummy."

"Yeah, we're close," I said, "but I want to take it to that next level of closeness and slap some irons around his wrists. When I was at his junkyard, I couldn't help but notice it was a cash business. Given the neighborhood, I'm certain Tito has a gun handy, even though he claimed to me that because of his record he doesn't have one."

"Capone went to the Big House for his unpaid taxes; maybe you'll get the opportunity to nail Tito for his unlicensed gun."

"By now he probably knows the dogs were cremated and that we don't have anything to connect him with the shootings. Since that's the case, he might have held on to the handgun he used."

"Assuming there is a handgun."

"There is," I said, certain of it. "And I can't imagine he hasn't used that gun to put down other dogs in the past. I'm told Tito's dog ring runs throughout Southern California. What if he shot dogs in a county other than Los Angeles? What if one of the nearby counties, like Riverside or San Diego or Imperial, collected ballistic evidence from the dead dogs? There's a lot of remote desert area in those counties, places where dogfights and cockfights could be conducted without much chance of prying eyes. Tito might not have been as careful in those isolated locations."

"I don't remember hearing about any fighting dogs turning up with bullets in them in those other counties," said Bud, "but it's something I'll look into."

"Maybe we'll get lucky," I said.

Just like I hoped I had gotten lucky with Ellis Haines in Las Vegas.

A funny thing happened on the drive home. I became so preoccupied thinking about my cases that I didn't consider my route and essentially let autopilot take over. When I awoke from my fugue state about ten minutes later, I found myself driving toward Angie's Rescues.

"Damn it," I said.

I began recalibrating my route, but then I reconsidered. There had to be some reason my subconscious was directing me to Angie's Rescues. For most of my life I haven't listened to my subconscious, but I am no longer totally deaf to it. Maybe there was a reason my right foot had been commandeered. After my conversation with Bud Bennet, I remembered playing the longer version of the Temptations' "Smiling Faces Sometimes," and then followed up with the shorter version recorded by the Undisputed Truth. The instrumentals were exceptional on the original recording, but the words jumped out more on the song's cover version. I kept thinking about Tito Rivera's smile while the music played. The lyrics seemed made for him, and I had found myself singing along:

"'Smiling faces, smiling faces tell lies, and I got proof.'"

But I didn't have proof, or at least not yet. Was the proof to be found at Angie's Rescues? Or was I mistaking poor navigation for mystical guidance?

I pulled into the shelter's parking lot. Before going inside, though, there were some promises to keep and calls to make. I tapped into a search engine and looked up the contact details for Dr. Kate Misko. After laboriously retyping the information, I texted everything to Bud Bennet.

Then I pulled out my notes and dialed the number that silent Jillian had given me. Dory Cunningham picked up on the third ring.

"Hi, Mrs. Cunningham," I said, speaking in a higher-pitched voice than was usual. "This is Michael. I'm wondering if Jason is around."

As I hoped, Dory didn't ask, "Michael who?" She also didn't ask me the purpose of my call.

"Hi, Michael," she said. "I'm afraid Jason isn't here."

"Ummm," I said, "I seem to have misplaced the number for his cell. Could you please give it to me?"

"Sure," she said, and rattled off a number.

I repeated the digits to her, and Dory confirmed them back. "Thanks so much!" I said.

"No problem," she said. "Bye-bye, Michael."

It was possible Jason had a friend named Michael; it was also possible Mrs. Cunningham didn't know the names of most of her adult son's friends. Either way, I dialed the number. When Jason picked up he said, "Yes?" He sounded much more suspicious than his mother, but then again, he knew who his friends were, and their names.

"Jason," I said, "this is Detective Michael Gideon of the Los Angeles Police Department. I was hoping you could answer a few of my questions."

"What kind of questions?"

"Questions that have to do with *Macho Libre*."

"I'm kind of busy now," he said.

"This won't take long," I said.

"I really don't have anything to say. That project has been shut down."

"Why is that?"

"Among other things, it was a casualty of lack of funding."

"Can you tell me about the shooting you did before shutting it down?"

"Like I said, it never really took off."

"I know it lasted long enough for you to hire some day laborers as actors."

"It was the least expensive way to get some extras."

I decided to push harder for answers. "You supplied them with pot and booze," I said, "and then you asked the workers to whale on each other."

"None of that sounds familiar," he said.

"Do you really think it would take me more than five minutes to track down where you rented your donkey and other livestock from? Your boxing ring was probably also rented. I sure hope you returned everything undamaged. You didn't use permanent dye when you painted on those zebra stripes, did you?"

"Look, man," Jason said. "The truth of the matter is that we didn't have film permits. I thought we could get by without them, but then I learned that I could be subject to some hefty fines if anyone found out about our illegal shoot. That's why we had to shut everything down. And that's why I don't want to talk about it."

Everything he was saying sounded logical. But my rational mind wasn't in charge at the moment. I was still navigating with my subconscious.

"I'd like to see the rough footage of your film," I said.

"It's been destroyed."

"I find that unlikely. I've been told filmmakers always keep the footage of whatever they've worked on."

"Like I told you, we didn't have permits, and I didn't want to chance getting sued after the fact."

"In that case, can you provide me with a working script?"

"What good would that do you?"

"I'm curious about what kind of film you were shooting," I said, "and wondering if it could tie in with a woman's fiancé who's gone missing. This individual worked as a day laborer at the same parking lot where you picked up another day laborer, a fellow named Javier. If you don't remember his name, you might recall you cast him in your production as the Frito Bandito."

Static noise came over the phone. As it grew louder Jason said, "I think we're breaking up."

"How about you meet with me today?" I asked.

The static was louder now. " . . . can't . . . you." Then our call was terminated.

I was suspicious at the convenient timing of the static and remembered a trick I'd been told about. If you wanted to get out of a conversation, you could create your own static and pretend the call was breaking up. All you needed to do was run your finger along the phone's speaker.

When I hit redial I wasn't surprised to hear a busy tone. Jason was likely calling his friends to make sure all their stories aligned.

Maybe my fingers could move faster than his. I used my phone to look up Jason Cunningham on various social media sites. In five minutes I had the names of his two friends: Brad Steinberg and Chase Durand. The former, I was pretty sure, was "Hitch," and the latter was "Marty." That meant Jason Cunningham was "Quentin."

All three of the friends made references to the "short" they were filming. In various entries it was called a "farce," a "spectacle," and "action packed." There were even shots of some of the costumes and some of the animals (chickens and the pig). I couldn't find any references to the title *Macho Libre*, nor to the subject matter. Were they trying to keep their short under wraps, I wondered, or were they afraid there were those who might find the subject matter offensive? The closest thing I could find was a proposed production called *WW*. I found those initials in three posts, but no explanation of what they stood for. *World War*? *Weight Watchers*? I was pretty sure they didn't stand for *Wonder Woman*.

Of course, I had no real evidence to link Mateo Ramos with the three filmmakers. I was working on a gut feeling and not much else. No one could yet say for sure that Mateo had been hired by one of the three young men. And there were no witnesses that could put Mateo at the Woodland Hills address. Even if I were able to locate a witness that could do that, it wouldn't prove Mateo participated in the movie, or that he got hurt.

My best chance of getting to the truth, I thought, would be to go through Steinberg or Durand. One of them, I hoped, had a conscience. One of them, I believed, had sent Luciana the $2,500 and the love poems of a dead man, and had allowed her a chance for closure.

I just needed to keep following the money, and maybe my muse.

CHAPTER SEVENTEEN

IN SEARCH OF LIGHT

Something had brought me to Angie's Rescues, but now that I was there I didn't know what it was or what I should be doing. There's never a burning bush and a voice speaking from within it when you need one.

I checked into the shelter's front desk area, asked if Heather was available, and was told she was in a meeting. Then I inquired if Dr. Misko was on the property and was told she wasn't there. It didn't seem as if my stars were exactly aligning.

"Let's go see a friend," I said to Sirius.

We walked over to the dog compound, passing St. Francis along the way. I pretended that the good saint was talking to me and that I couldn't quite hear him.

"What's that you say? 'For it is in giving that we receive'? Didn't you know that's not in keeping with today's mores? There are those who insist that it's only by taking that we receive."

And then I remembered another St. Francis of Assisi quote, or maybe I heard it in the wind: *All the darkness in the world cannot extinguish the light of a single candle.*

Was I looking for that candle? Diogenes the Cynic had walked around ancient Greece during the daylight hours carrying a lantern and proclaiming that he was looking for an honest man. Accompanying Diogenes on his search was his canine companion, Rataplan. Neither man nor dog ever found that honest individual. Diogenes seemed to believe that dogs were much more innately virtuous than humans. Indeed, the word *cynic* derives from the Greek and originally meant *doglike.* After Diogenes died, his connection with dogs was remembered by the Corinthians. They erected a statue of a resting dog made from Parian marble, a white, semitranslucent stone that was the most sought-after marble of its day.

"At least our casework doesn't involve us having to try and find an honest man," I said.

It's always good to have a dog at your side. You can chatter away and people will just assume you're talking to your dog. Today my dog and I were having a philosophical discussion, even though I doubted seriously that we'd be mistaken for Diogenes and Rataplan.

Maybe Emily had heard me talking out in the courtyard. As we turned the corner, she could be seen standing at the entrance to her cage. It looked as if she expected us.

"Go ahead," I said to Sirius, and he ran to her.

For a moment I was afraid the Frankenstein dog might retreat in fear. She had been used as a chew toy by fighting dogs. The abuse she had suffered offered her every reason to be afraid, but her nub of a tail wagged furiously at Sirius's arrival. She was wearing her cone, and her broken back leg forced her to move awkwardly, but that didn't stop her from shadowing Sirius's movements and shuffling from side to side in her cage.

I offered Emily my hand to sniff, and her docked tail signaled her joy. This time I didn't exclude Sirius from coming inside the cage. Both of us entered the enclosure, and Emily reacted with delight, rubbing her stitched and scarred body up against us.

"Good girl," I said to her.

When I began to scratch Emily's coat, she didn't want me to stop. Her body contorted, twisting one way and then the other, allowing me to get to the spots that itched the most. After a few minutes I decided her entire body was one big itch. I did what I could to offer her relief; Emily's cone was not such an obstacle that she couldn't lick my fingers, and occasionally my face, with her tongue. Sirius also got his share of affection, if not a bath.

"Hey!"

The three of us had been enjoying our lovefest so much that none of us had noticed Heather's approach to the cage.

"Hey," I said.

She squatted down; Emily had more than enough love to accommodate Heather, too. Seconding that motion was Sirius. Heather used one hand for each dog.

"Where's Angie?" I asked. "Of course, if she were here, she'd probably insist that you scratch her with your foot."

"She'd probably insist on both feet," laughed Heather. "Her royal nibs is taking her late-afternoon snooze. She's found a spot not far from here that gets the last rays of the afternoon sun. Angie doesn't like to miss the opportunity for a sunbath."

"Smart dog," I said.

"What are you doing here?" asked Heather. "I thought you did all your volunteer hours earlier in the week."

It wasn't until Heather asked her question that I knew the answer. Suddenly, it was obvious to me why I was there.

"We're here to adopt Emily," I said.

"Are you sure about that?"

Sirius was looking back and forth at the two of us, as if he was following the conversation.

"*We're* sure," I said.

CHAPTER EIGHTEEN

DEAD MAN'S HAND

While I was in the middle of signing paperwork to make the adoption official, Lisbet called. I wasn't sure if her timing was providential or couldn't have been worse, and I excused myself to take her call.

"Lisbet," I said, prepared to offer an apology and an explanation, but she beat me to it.

"I'm sorry," she said. "I'm going to have to cancel on our evening. Deborah is down in the dumps. I told her I'd bring her some dinner, and then if she felt like it we'd play a few games of Scrabble."

Deborah is Lisbet's good friend who is fighting breast cancer. She'd recently had a double mastectomy. Shitty thing, cancer.

"I'm the one who should be apologizing to you," I said. "Let me remind you, though, that you're always saying I need to be more spontaneous."

"Uh-oh," she said. "I hate it when you quote me to me. What did you do?"

"Consider this my begging forgiveness rather than asking permission," I said. "I know I should consult you on any big decision, and I hope you won't be upset at what I've done, but I've gone ahead and adopted Emily."

There was silence on the line. The longer it lasted, the more sure I was of Lisbet's disapproval at what I'd done.

"Lisbet?" I said.

"That's the dog that was left for dead, right?" she said.

"Correct."

"And she's a pit bull?"

"She's an American Staffordshire terrier," I said, "but yes, her breed is commonly referred to as the pit bull."

Lisbet sighed and said, "I wish I could be enthusiastic, Michael, but I've always thought that anyone who owned a pit bull was asking for trouble."

"She's a sweet, sweet dog," I said. "From the moment I met her, that was apparent. And she almost died because of that sweetness. The reason Emily was used as a bait dog was that she wouldn't fight in the pit."

"Didn't you say she's horribly scarred?"

"She won't be winning any beauty contests," I said, "but then again, neither will I."

"After what she's gone through, aren't you afraid something might set her off?" asked Lisbet. "What if she just snaps?"

"I'd say my PTSD is much more pronounced than hers," I said.

Lisbet was quiet again for a few moments. Finally, she said, "I hope you selected her for the right reasons, and not just because you sympathize with her plight."

"I wouldn't have picked a dog that didn't feel absolutely right to me. Everyone I've talked to who has dealt with Emily

ALAN RUSSELL

has sung her praises, and that includes an animal control officer, a vet, and Heather Moreland. If there's a mean bone in her body, it's well hidden."

"Expect your home insurance rates to go up," said Lisbet, "that is, if you can get insurance."

"You're not making me feel very good about this."

"I'm sorry," she said, "but I'd be lying if I didn't admit to having some reservations."

"I'm still at the shelter. If you're completely opposed to this, I'll cancel the adoption."

"No," said Lisbet. "I know you wouldn't be doing this if you didn't believe it was the right thing to do."

"I know it seems wrong," I said, "but I am sure."

"What about Sirius? I assume he gets along with her?"

"Peas in a pod," I said.

"That makes me feel better."

"My judgment is iffy, but Sirius's is spot-on?"

"Something like that."

"I'll see you tomorrow," I said. "Give my best to Deborah."

"And you give my best to Emily."

She heard my kiss and I heard hers, good sounds to end our conversation. Then I returned to the desk area. Emily seemed to know that something special was in the works. She was looking at the happy humans and reading their vibrations.

Heather handed me a packet. "Here's a list of the medications that Emily is currently taking, and a schedule for when they should be given to her. Dr. Misko just signed off on the adoption, but she wanted to warn you that Emily still has a low-grade infection, and she wants to make sure that gets favorably resolved. You're also supposed to keep her cast dry, and the cone needs to stay on for at least one more week."

"Okay," I said, trying to get everything clear in my head.

Heather must have known I was on sensory overload, because she said, "All that information was put in your packet."

"Great," I said.

"What would probably be best for Emily is if you transported her by pet carrier," Heather said. "You can borrow one from us."

I have never had the fortune of bringing a newborn home, but have known many parents who have. First-time parents always look shocked at the huge responsibility that suddenly enters their lives. Babies don't come with manuals, and I've heard many parents confess that they felt woefully unprepared to take on the responsibility of looking after another life.

Bringing home a dog isn't the same thing as bringing home a newborn, but it's still a big-gulp moment. Sirius and I had been a team for years, and when Lisbet came into our lives we became a family. Now we were bringing a stranger home. What would Emily's demands be, and could I meet them? Would she fit in the existing routine, or would we have to create a new formula? Was Emily housetrained? Had she ever been part of a family before? There were all sorts of questions. The only sure answer was that life wouldn't be the same.

We put Emily and her carrier inside my car. Sirius sat next to her, and I think his steadying influence helped keep Emily calm.

"I always said that if I ever had a daughter I would play Stevie Wonder's "Isn't She Lovely" on the ride home," I said. "I guess you're going to be the closest thing to that, Emily."

I made my hands-free song request, and Stevie started singing. Once upon a time I had thought Jennifer and I would be going home with our own bundle of joy and I'd be playing this song, but that's not what life had in store for me. During my marriage there had been times when I had imagined myself looking into the rearview mirror and seeing my wife and baby.

Now, years later, I looked through that rearview mirror. Almost, I could see them now, but then they disappeared into the ether.

"Bye-bye, love," I said, but I didn't call out to Bluetooth for the Everly Brothers song of the same name. There had been a time when that was my song, and my lament, but I had held on long enough for there to be a second act. Thankfully, Fitzgerald had been wrong when he said there were no second acts in American lives.

In my rearview mirror I took stock of Sirius and Emily. They might not have been the vision I once expected, but it was good to see them there.

I pushed a button and said, "Call Shaman at home."

"Calling Shaman at home" was my electronic genie's response. Her pronunciation made it sound like "Hey man."

Seth picked up on the third ring. "I'm about to stop at El Pollo Loco," I said. "Are you in the mood for some chicken and fixings?"

"As a matter of fact I am," said Seth.

"I'm about twenty-five minutes out," I said. "How about we dine at my place?"

"I'll put some beers on ice," he promised.

"Great minds think alike," I said, and ended our conversation.

I turned my head for just a second and waved at Emily. "That's your uncle Seth," I told her. "You're going to love him."

Five minutes later I pulled up to the order window of the drive-through line, and Sirius joined me in putting in our order. "Let's go with a grande meal," I said into the intercom, "with sides of pinto beans, black beans, and Mexican rice."

Sirius gave my ear a lick. "And a three-piece leg-and-thigh combo," I said.

I cradled his head in my left arm and said, "I know, that order wasn't really for you. It was what Emily told you that she wanted."

At the pick-up window I was handed two bags, and I immediately became the most interesting person on the planet. Sirius and Emily did their sniffing in stereo. My partner went so far as to stick his nose over the seat so that he could inhale the bag.

"*Pfui*," I told him, the German word for *shame*. "You're supposed to set a good example."

He withdrew his nose but didn't appear shamed at all.

When we pulled into the driveway, Seth's front door opened and he walked over to the car. Sirius was making his happy sounds as Seth opened the door. Normally Sirius jumps out of the car, but tonight he stayed put for a few moments, licking Seth's hand and then turning to Emily's cage and licking her through its openings. It was almost as if he was telling her, "This is a good friend of mine. I am sure you will like him as well."

"You're an uncle for the second time," I informed Seth.

"So I see."

"I'll need some help carrying Emily's carrier into the house."

"I'm attached to my fingers, you know," said Seth, mindful of putting them in harm's way.

"They'll only be in danger of being licked," I promised.

I raised my right arm out to the side, and then gestured inward to my chest, and Sirius followed my hand signal by coming to my side.

"The carrier is bulky but not that heavy," I told Seth. "I'll pull it out so that we can both get a good grip on it."

Before doing that, I leaned in toward Emily so that the two of us could have a little conversation. "How did you like your ride, cutie-pie?"

Inside the cage, her docked tail thumped. I pulled the carrier out far enough for Seth to get a grip, and then the two of us walked it into the house.

"Let's put her out back in case she has to go," I said.

"Lead the way," said Seth.

We carried the carrier to the back yard, and then I opened its door. Sirius was there to greet Emily as she came outside, and he decided to play tour guide. He went over to the Valencia orange tree and lifted a leg. And then he did an encore on the Meyer lemon tree.

"Why don't you watch the two of them while I retrieve our dinner?" I said.

Seth waved his approval. A minute later I returned with the bags and Seth said, "Emily decided to join Sirius in his watering. And now he's leading her on a tour of the house."

"While he's doing that," I said, "I'll make their dinners."

"And I'll get the beers," Seth said.

I went into the kitchen and was halfway through deboning the leg-and-thigh combo when I was joined by company. The dogs watched carefully as I mixed the chicken into two bowls of kibble. The senior dog had priority, so I called Sirius over to a corner and put down his bowl. I was glad that Emily didn't try to horn in.

"Emily, come," I said.

I'm not sure if she followed the command or the bowl of chicken and kibble. Either way, she moved toward the opposite side of the kitchen from where Sirius was eating. I removed her cone so that she could more easily eat.

"Good girl," I told her, and Emily began eating. It was a positive sign that she didn't appear possessive of the food, nor did she exhibit any food anxiety.

Seth reappeared with the beer. After he flipped two caps, we took seats on bar stools at the kitchen counter and lightly clinked the tops of our bottles.

"To your new girl," said Seth. "I'll have to get you a pink collar."

"I'm not sure if pink is her color," I said. "Right now she seems to be more into the Goth look."

"Is Emily a permanent addition to the roost?" he asked.

"That's the plan," I said. "But you know what they say about plans."

"Man plans and God laughs," said Seth.

I nodded.

Both dogs finished eating. Emily began touring the kitchen, sniffing at the cupboards. Her broken leg didn't seem to be inhibiting her tour. Since she wasn't trying to lick her wounds at the moment, I decided to hold off putting on her lampshade.

"Hard to imagine she was on death's door not very long ago," I said.

"Dogs are amazingly resilient," said Seth.

"When Sirius and I took down Ellis Haines," I said, "Sirius's wounds were much more serious than mine, yet he recovered in about a third the time that I did."

"And with a lot less whining," said Seth.

"Isn't that the truth," I admitted.

Hearing his name, Sirius came over to where we were sitting and decided to grace us with his company. He plopped down on the floor, and a short time later Emily joined him.

"You never mentioned that you were contemplating having a second dog," said Seth.

"That's because it wasn't on my radar."

"What changed your mind?"

"Emily did," I said. "I've been trying to turn up the heat on the asshole that left her for dead. Whenever I talk to him he's all smiles, and without admitting his involvement, makes a case for animal fighting, saying that it's normal, even instinctual. He also likes to make a case that those who are opposed to such activities are hypocrites."

"The human animal is wonderful at justifying its behavior," said Seth.

"I'm no exception," I admitted. "Anyway, late this afternoon it suddenly struck me that just nailing this guy won't even the scales. Sure, it will get him off the streets, and it might put a dent in Southern California dogfighting, but it won't atone for what he's done. That's when I decided the best way for me to work on the karmic scale of atonement was to love Emily and give her a good life. Besides, that's the best *eff you* I could think of to give the bastard that tried to kill her."

"When did this wisdom suddenly manifest itself in you?" he asked.

"Don't expect it to linger," I said.

"You told Lisbet about Emily?" he asked.

I nodded. "She has her reservations, which is to be expected. But what I neglected to tell her was that I didn't feel I had a choice in the matter."

"What do you mean?" asked Seth.

"A funny thing happened on my drive home. My subconscious mind directed me on an alternate route that just happened to take me to Angie's Rescues. That's why I decided to stop in. At first I just assumed I had been preoccupied with work, but now I'm thinking it was more than that. I know it doesn't make any sense, but it felt like I was being directed to adopt Emily without any delay."

"You decided, to hell with logic?"

"Pretty much," I said.

"There's hope for you."

"That's high praise, indeed," I said. Then I asked, "How about dinner?"

"You really are getting intuitive," said Seth.

I carefully got down from my bar stool, and managed to navigate through the obstacle course of dogs on my way to the kitchen. After making and delivering two plates of food, I asked Seth, "Another beer?"

"Please," he said.

I took two beers off ice, flipped their caps, and slid Seth's along the counter to his waiting hand. Acting like a bartender in an Old West saloon was a totally unnecessary move, but it was something I always enjoyed doing.

The tough part was making it back to my seat. Sometimes, letting sleeping dogs lie is perilous to your health.

"I hope you're not waiting for me to start eating," I said as I finally sat down. "As the Italians like to say, *Mangia*."

"*Buona salute*," said Seth, and translated the words for my sake: "Good health."

We both ate for a few minutes without talking, but I suppose eating chicken made me think of El Gallo Negro.

"My dogfight suspect started with cockfights," I said. "In fact, his nickname is the Black Rooster. He's a successful businessman who runs a junkyard. And what's a junkyard without junkyard dogs? His training ground is right out in the open."

"That must feel like a taunt to you."

I nodded. "He even has a second guise; he supplies guard dogs around LA. Our rooster likes to hide in plain sight. Of course, I'm working on flushing him out."

When I told Seth about the imminent Crime Stoppers commercial, he more than approved. "I like the irony of him being caged," he said.

"That's two of us."

"What about that other case of yours with the missing fiancé?" he asked.

"It's taken some unusual turns," I said, and told him about my two visits to Woodland Hills.

"I think I'm just beginning to understand Mateo Ramos," I said. "It surprised me that he posed nude on at least two occasions, but he was willing to do anything for Luciana. I'm wondering if that somehow contributed to his death."

"Any suspects?" asked Seth.

"I wouldn't go so far as that," I said, "but I have three persons of interest I'll be questioning: Alfred Hitchcock, Martin Scorsese, and Quentin Tarantino."

"Explain," Seth insisted.

Over a third beer, I did. When I finished, Seth said, "You have been a busy boy."

"I haven't even told you about the serial murderer," I said, "or the case I'm trying to build against Ellis Haines."

Normally, I like it when Seth does most of the talking. He knows so much about so many things that he's didactic without even trying. Tonight, though, I was the one exercising my mouth.

"Have you ever found yourself being the odd man out in a conversation because the other two people were speaking a language you didn't know? That's how I feel with Haines and the serial murderer who seems to be paying a strange homage to him. The two of them are communicating through crime scene pictures, and through languages I don't speak."

"It's easy to be paranoid in a situation like that," said Seth.

I nodded. "You'd think they'd no longer have tête-à-têtes with the FBI's involvement, but I get this feeling that the two of them will still be able to pass along things to one another without the Feds having a full interpretation of what's being said. Right now, though, that's only a strong hunch on my part. That's why I need to try and decipher their language, so that I can do my own interpretations and not be reliant on either Ellis Haines or the FBI. I'll have to go over the crime scene photos, as well as learn poker lingo. Do you know anything about Texas Hold 'Em poker?"

"Very little, I'm afraid," Seth said.

"I've been studying all the nicknames for cards and suits," I said, "and how they fit into the game. It's like trying to understand the nuances of a foreign language."

"It would probably be easier for you to learn those nuances by playing the game, rather than by reading about playing the game. Maybe you should spend some time in a card room."

"You know how to make a small fortune playing cards?" I asked.

He knew the punch line and said, "You start with a large fortune."

"WC Fields once said, 'I spent half my money on gambling, alcohol, and wild women. The other half I wasted.'"

"I imagine that line was a thousand years old," said Seth, "before WC Fields appropriated it."

"Probably," I agreed.

"Black aces and black eights," Seth suddenly said.

"What about them?"

"I just remembered those four cards are called 'the dead man's hand.'"

"Why?"

"Legend has it that those were the cards in Wild Bill Hickok's last poker hand. He was shot and killed in Deadwood while playing poker, and never got to collect on that last big pot."

"What was his hole card?"

"I don't know if he was even dealt a hole card."

"So Hickok might have died waiting for a full house."

"Maybe so."

I reached down and took turns scratching Sirius and Emily. My dogs were happy to be included in the conversation. *My dogs*, I thought. Emily was already part of the family, part of the household, part of our full house.

"They call a king-nine 'the dog hand,'" I said. "Or at least that's one of the names for it."

"Your lucky cards," said Seth.

Or were they? I thought. In the back of my mind, there was some image that wanted to come to the fore but eluded me.

"Not against pocket aces," I said.

CHAPTER NINETEEN

BEWARE ENTERPRISES THAT REQUIRE NEW CLOTHES

I suspected I might have a fire dream, as the onset of my PTSD seems to occur when I'm unsettled. Because of that, I dreaded the prospect of sleep, but on this night I had only the dreams of the innocent.

As usual, Sirius slept on the floor next to the bed. Emily decided her place was at the foot of the bed. Her pain meds must have offered her relief, because, like me, she slept through the night.

In the morning I gave each of my charges a piece of chicken jerky, and then stuffed a few more pieces in my pockets to use as rewards while doing obedience training. Because of Emily's injuries, I limited her activities, focusing her workout in a very limited area. I didn't stint on praise, though, and tried to make her abbreviated training fun. As her wounds healed, I would continue to challenge her more and more.

The stitches on her skin, and all the scabs from the healing gashes, were playing havoc on her coat. I rubbed some Vitamin E oil on the rough, scaly areas, and Emily tried to reward me with mostly unsuccessful licks because of the barrier of her e-collar.

I was thinking of having a second cup of coffee, when my cell phone rang. The display told me Heather Moreland was calling.

"Your girl has been doing great," I said, jumping right into what I thought was the expected conversation.

It took Heather a second to respond. "That's so good to hear," she said.

Checking on the welfare of Emily, I realized, was clearly not the primary reason for her morning call.

"I don't mean to bother you, Detective," Heather said, "but I guess I'm calling to ask you what we should do."

"What happened?"

"Every night, the shelter closes at six o'clock, and then reopens again at eight in the morning. We have volunteers who are on property after the shelter closes, as well as before it opens. Those same volunteers take home animals that need watching at night. Most of our animals, though, don't leave the shelter. Because of that, we have a security service that periodically patrols our property. In addition to that, we have CCTV cameras. We don't have signage yet advertising those cameras; that's on my to-do list. And because the cameras aren't spotlighted in any way, they're easy to overlook. That's what I think happened last night. Our visitor didn't know he was being recorded."

"When did your trespasser show up?"

"Just after ten. I'm hoping you can come in and look at the footage. You'll see that it shows an individual with a dark hoodie closed tightly around his face. I say 'his' because the intruder appears to be a man, even though I suppose it could be a woman."

"Did he steal or vandalize anything?"

"Not that the footage shows. And that's not what was upset-
ting. I called you because he was armed with a gun. In fact,
you'll see the way he moves around makes it look like he's a hit
man. There's even one of those silencers on the end of his gun."

"You're sure about that?"

"I am. I've looked at the footage several times."

"I'll be there within the hour," I said.

I debated bringing the dogs with me, but decided to leave them
on their own for the morning. Thus far Emily hadn't exhibited
any desire to chew on anything other than some of Sirius's toys.
The two dogs were also getting along better than I could have
hoped. Sirius now had a little sister and a playmate.

The traffic was heavy, and I almost didn't make it to the
shelter in the promised hour. During my drive, I thought about
the shelter's late-night visitor. I wasn't surprised that someone
might have been casing the shelter and looking for an easy score,
but the intruder's walking around with an exposed gun, especially one with a suppressor, made no sense to me. Being caught in
possession of a suppressor brings a felony charge in the state of
California. And why would you have a suppressor on your gun at
an animal shelter? Had the intruder expected to use his gun? And
if so, who or what had he planned to shoot?

Heather was waiting for me in her office. Angie was with
her, and the two were staying close to one another. Each was being protective. I imagined seeing a man with a gun had brought
back bad memories for Heather. She had survived a prolonged
encounter with a monster.

She smiled at my appearance and pretended not to have been shaken by the invasion of her workplace, but her unsteadiness could be seen in her right foot's unconscious tap dance.

"I'm having to rethink the idea of any of our volunteers being here by themselves," she told me.

And Heather's being here by herself, I thought.

"After we talked," I said, "the first thing that struck me was that your intruder might have been looking for veterinary drugs, like ketamine or morphine or diazepam. Even animal steroids are targeted by thieves."

"Kate doesn't leave any prescription drugs here," said Heather.

"You might want to post signs saying there are no drugs on the property," I said.

"You think that's what our trespasser was looking for?" she asked, sounding hopeful.

"I think that's more likely than someone coming here after hours to get a puppy. But I'd like to see the tape before jumping to conclusions."

Heather had me sit at her desk while she downloaded footage from the night before. Angie came over and joined me. First she took a few good sniffs of me, determined exactly what I'd been doing all morning, and then she stuck her big, drooling mug on my slacks. Well, Thoreau did say we should beware of all enterprises that require new clothes. Having a bloodhound essentially eliminates ever attempting such enterprises.

The laptop finally lit up, and I found myself following the movements of the trespasser. As Heather had told me, the prowler was wearing a hoodie that completely shrouded his features. There was something masculine, though, about his movements, and I agreed with Heather's assumption that he was male. He looked to be of medium height and build. As he approached the dog compound, he reached into the folds of his hoodie and pulled out his gun. By its shape, the gun appeared to be a semiautomatic nine-millimeter; what was unmistakable was the sound suppressor attached to it.

Different cameras showed his walk through the dog compound. He stopped and looked at every cage and enclosure, studying the dogs within.

He moved, I thought, like the angel of death.

Instead of raising the roof at the intruder's movements, most of the dogs remained silent in his presence. Maybe they sensed that death was walking among them. In a few frames it appeared that the dogs slunk back into the recesses of their cages; only a few lunged and barked, choosing to fight in the absence of a chance for flight.

On two occasions the prowler brought out a penlight and shined it into the interior of a cage.

"What the hell is he looking for?" I said aloud.

"That's what I kept asking myself," said Heather.

"Do you know which animals occupied the cages that he was illuminating?"

"The first cage was Tony's," said Heather. "We call him Tony the Tiger because of his dark striping."

"What kind of dog is he?"

"Judging from his looks, he's mostly boxer."

"And the second cage?"

"Lotta is in there. We like to say she's a whole lotta dog."

"What breed?"

"We think she's Rhodesian ridgeback and pit bull."

I continued watching the intruder. It almost looked as if he was making rounds. When he finished walking through the dog compound, he made his way over to the quarantine area, checking on the dogs there.

He didn't try and open storage closets, nor did he make an attempt to break into the vet's office. His sole interest seemed to be in the dogs. When he finished his walkthrough, the man hid his handgun inside his hoodie, and then made his way out of the shelter.

"Do you have cameras out in your parking lot?" I asked.

"We have one camera," Heather said. "He didn't park on our grounds."

"So either he lives in the neighborhood or he knew enough to park away from the place he was casing."

"That's what I was thinking," she said. "My hope is that he doesn't live nearby."

"Not the kind of neighbor you'd want," I agreed.

"Do you still think he might have been after drugs?" she asked.

I shook my head. "If this had been a burglary, he would have taken anything of value he could find."

"So what was his purpose here?"

"I have no idea."

"I'm sort of at a loss as to what I should do," she said.

Angie must have heard her uncertainty; she left my side to join her mistress.

"I'd start by putting up more lighting," I said. "That's a great initial deterrent. And I'd increase your signage. Advertise that you have surveillance cameras and that there are armed security patrols. Tell would-be thieves you don't have anything they'd want. Post that there are no veterinary drugs on the property, as well as no money on the premises."

Heather took notes. The prospect of taking action seemed to put her more at ease.

"Can you send this footage as a file to my computer?" I asked. "And if so, can I forward that file?"

"Neither of those things should be a problem," she said. "What are you going to do?"

"I want to study the footage some more," I said. "And I want to get the file to our techs. They'll be able to make a positive identification on what kind of handgun our intruder was carrying, as well as the sound suppressor. It's also possible that they'll be able to break down the frames and get us a face shot of the prowler. Or maybe they'll pick up on a scar or tattoo we couldn't see."

"I'll send it to your LAPD email," she said.

"Good," I said.

Heather kept running her hand through Angie's coat. I didn't want to give her false reassurance, but I did want to comfort her. You can't come out on the other side of what she went through without feeling the world is a less secure place than you once imagined.

"Whatever the gunman was looking for," I said, "he didn't find it. Since that's the case, I doubt he'll bother to come back."

"You think so?" she asked.

"I do," I said.

But I still wondered what had brought him to the shelter in the first place.

CHAPTER TWENTY

DON'T CALL US, WE'LL CALL YOU

Before leaving Angie's Rescues, I made a call to Vincente Calderon, a tech I know who works in the Firearm Analysis Unit of LAPD's Forensic Science Division.

"*Qué pasó*, Vincente?" I said. "This is Michael Gideon."

"Neither wheedling, nor sweet-talking, nor cajoling will move you up in line, Gideon," he said. "If it's not time sensitive—and those parameters are defined very narrowly—we'll get to whatever you want us to look at based on the date of your request."

"'Cajoling'?" I said. "'Wheedling'? I think you must have me mistaken for someone else."

"Uh-huh," he said. "What's the purpose of your call?"

"I wanted to give you a heads-up about a file I'm sending your way. It's CCTV video of a man walking around an animal shelter brandishing a gun with a sound suppressor. I'm hoping you can use your magic to determine the make and model of the gun, as well as the suppressor. From what I could see, there wasn't any good face shot available, but maybe you can slow it down and find something. Short of that, I'm curious if you can give us your best guess as to the height and weight of the intruder, and whether you can determine if there is anything else that might help us identify the suspect."

"Identifying the gun and suppressor shouldn't be hard," he said. "However, if you want face shots or anything of that nature, we'll have to pass on the file to Photography."

"What's most important to me is getting the make and model of the gun. Any advice on expediting that process?"

"Yeah," he said. "Fill out the paperwork correctly."

"Don't call us, we'll call you?"

"I couldn't have said it better myself."

"That's because I'm just quoting you from the last time we talked."

"And who says you don't listen?"

"What's the expected wait these days?"

"Three, four weeks if you're lucky."

"What if you unofficially look at the tape for two minutes, and then send me the Vincente best guess on the gun?"

"Remember when you were a kid waiting in line and someone else tried to cut in? That's when you and everyone else would start yelling, 'No cutsies.'"

"I'm not cutting in line. It's more like I'm asking for clarification on something you might be able to tell me at a glance."

"You should have been a lawyer, Gideon."

"Now, that's a low blow. But I'll forgive you if you look at the tape."

"I can live without your forgiveness."

"Thank you for your consideration."

Calderon hung up on me, which wasn't totally surprising.

In the subject line of the email containing the file footage, I wrote, *Pretty please with a cherry on top*. And in the body of the email, I added, *Forget two minutes. I'd even be happy with a one-minute thumbnail sketch.*

Confessions of a squeaky wheel, I thought. I wasn't sure if Calderon would budge in his timeframe; time would tell.

My next call was to a fish restaurant in Calabasas that Chase Durand—one of the three wannabe directors of *Macho Libre*, who referred to himself as Marty—had conveniently provided as his workplace on social media. The hostess confirmed that Chase was working that day. After learning they were a dog-friendly restaurant, I made a reservation and requested that Chase be my server.

There was time enough for me to do some shopping, so on the way home I stopped at a pet-supply store. I had in mind a specific animal carrier, and though they had various crates, cages, and kennels, there was nothing like what I wanted. The year before, I'd use my garden cart to help transport a wounded Angie, and I decided to employ it once more. It had been big enough for Angie, so it would easily accommodate Emily.

After I got home, I made a bed inside the cart, and then lifted Emily inside. She made no move to try and get out, and seemed pleased with me doing the pulling of her rickshaw. Sirius jogged at her side as we wheeled it out to the car. Then Emily was lifted onto a seat in the car, and her transportation was stowed in the back.

Our destination was the Commons at Calabasas, one of those outdoor malls with a little bit of everything. We arrived before noon and got a parking space near the restaurant where I'd made the reservation. I pulled my makeshift buggy. Passersby probably expected to see a baby inside; instead, they got a scarred pit bull.

Despite the good weather, no one had yet opted for outdoor dining at the restaurant. I lifted Emily from the cart, and she and Sirius did their sniffing of the patio. Finally, they settled on a table. I tied Emily's leash to one of the table legs, and with a voice command told Sirius to lie down and await my return.

After cutting through the patio, I walked up to the hostess stand, where a young, petite blond woman greeted me. "My name is Gideon," I said. "I had a reservation for the patio and requested Chase as my server. My entire party is here."

The hostess's brows furrowed. "Aren't you a single?" she asked.

"Yes and no," I said. "I was told I could dine on the patio with my two dogs."

"Oh, that's great!" she said. "I'll make sure the busser brings out two water bowls."

"Much appreciated," I said.

"No worries," she said. "Chase should be out to see you very shortly."

I retraced my steps to the patio and received a standing ovation and tail wagging commensurate with my time away. Since Emily was already up, I removed her e-collar.

There were saltines and oyster crackers on the table. I opened the oyster crackers, popped a few in my mouth, and then threw one Sirius's way. He nonchalantly snagged it out of the air. Then I threw one to Emily. It was apparent no one had ever tossed a treat to her, as she had not yet developed any mouth-eye coordination and it bounced off her head.

"It's a bad habit anyway," I said, and took one of the crackers and carefully offered it up to her. Some dogs aren't very mindful of fingers when being given snacks; Emily comported herself like a well-trained lady, carefully taking the oyster cracker out of my hand.

"Your full name must be Emily Post," I said, and turned to Sirius. "Perhaps she'll teach you manners."

He was watching me carefully, ready to be tossed another cracker. I obliged him.

Our waters were served by a cheerful Mexican busser who looked to be about the age of Mateo Ramos. In a thick accent he said, "Good morning."

"Morning," I said.

He paused in his reply to think. "I guess it is afternoon," he said.

I looked at the time, saw it was just past noon, and nodded. "*Buenas tardes*," I said.

"*Buenas tardes*," he agreed.

Chase Durand appeared right after the busser left us. He had long hair, styled and parted down the middle, brown with blond highlights. Unlike the busser, he didn't seem at all pleased to see me, or the dogs. His pout grew even more pronounced when I put my wallet badge down on the table. I didn't read him his rights, but I wanted to make sure he knew who I was. Apparently, that wasn't necessary.

"I've been told I shouldn't be talking to you," he said.

"Who told you that?"

He didn't directly answer, but instead said, "I should have a lawyer present when you ask me questions."

"Fine by me," I said. "Is your lawyer available now?"

"I'm working," Chase said.

"We're both working. That means I don't have time to play social secretary with you, me, and your lawyer. If you want, I can assign a time for the three of us to talk tomorrow."

In a surly voice he said, "What do you want to know?"

"You can start with today's specials," I said.

That threw him off for a second, but then he transitioned from suspect to server. "We have grilled salmon with a beet-top salsa verde and a lemon-ginger yogurt. And we also have a grilled Mediterranean-style swordfish with artichokes, kalamata olives, capers, roasted red peppers, and grape tomatoes, served on a bed of rice."

Neither special made me salivate. My two friends were salivating, but I suspected that was because of the oyster crackers in my hand.

"I'll have the fish and chips," I said. "And they'll have the fish and chips."

"Two separate orders?"

I nodded.

"Anything to drink?" he asked.

"The water is good."

"Anything else? An appetizer, soup, or salad?"

"Caesar salad," I said. "No anchovies."

"Very good," he said, resorting to server speak. "Will that be everything?"

"As tempting as it might be," I said, "I'd ask you to not spit in my food. That's a felony. Last year a server learned that lesson the hard way when a DNA analysis was done on some food that a table asked to be boxed up. The diners grew suspicious that their food might have been adulterated after opening one of the take-out containers and seeing what looked like expectorant. That's a roundabout way of me warning you that cops frequently work with DNA, and we're naturally suspicious."

"That warning wasn't necessary," said Chase, assuming a posture of rectitude.

"I'm sure it wasn't," I said.

And it probably wasn't, but at least I'd have some peace of mind when the food arrived. Servers have a tough job, and I know it's not wise to get on their bad side. Still, like it or not, I had a reason for being there, and I didn't want Chase to retaliate against me with anything other than cold food and bad service. I could live with those.

There are some jobs I know I'm woefully ill-equipped to handle. Being a waiter is one of them. Servers need to have the patience of Job. That's not me. I would be a Sweeney Todd kind of server and spend much of each shift fantasizing about how to go about killing my patrons and recycling them.

As the minutes passed, the patio area began to fill up with other diners, but none of them had dogs. Chase brought out my Caesar salad. "Pepper?" he asked.

"Please," I said.

He did some grinding, and I said, "Thank you."

Instead of taking his leave, Chase nervously shifted his pepper grinder from hand to hand. In a low voice meant just for me, he said, "I was just helping with Jason's film. I wasn't even paid."

"So it was charity work on your part?"

"Not exactly," he said. "There was an informal agreement that if the film or films were released, I'd get twenty-five percent of the profits."

"I thought Hollywood accounting made sure there were never such things as profits."

"That's true in theatrical movies," Chase said, "but not necessarily in shorts or direct to DVD."

"So *Macho Libre* was going to be a short?"

Chase opened his mouth, and then closed it. "That's something you'll need to ask Jason. I think he was envisioning a series of shorts. He talked about putting teasers on YouTube, and then streaming the film for money, or making it available through DVD."

"You didn't pay for anything?"

He shook his head. "It was financed by Jason and . . . "

Chase reconsidered saying the second name. I wasn't as reticent. "Brad Steinberg?" I asked. "Aka Hitch? And Jason was Quentin and you're Marty?"

His face reddened. "Those names were just in fun," he said, trying to explain.

"So Brad and Jason financed the film?"

"Brad paid for most of it. It must be nice being a trust fund baby."

"I wouldn't know."

"I wouldn't either. You think I'd be working this job if I was?"

"Brad has a trust fund?"

"His family has money. Right now, he's going to USC film school and getting his MFA. That will cost a boatload of money."

"Did you go to film school?"

He nodded. "That's where I met Jason. The two of us graduated last May."

"Where did you go?"

"We were undergrads at Cal State Northridge, majoring in film production. Neither of us could afford USC, so we went to what's called 'the people's film school.'"

I didn't bother to tell him I'd also gone to CSUN, where I'd been an undeclared major for most of my too many years there.

"Did you get your degree?"

Chase nodded and said, "For all the good that's done me. That's why I've been trying to do some shorts on a shoestring. If I don't get an entry-level job in the industry, the shorts might help me get into graduate school."

"But not USC?"

"The University of Spoiled Children?" he asked. "Don't get me wrong, it's a good school, but I could never go there without a scholarship."

Then he took his leave of the table by saying, "Duty calls."

I chewed on my salad and on our conversation. Chase hadn't clung very long to his threat to lawyer up. Of course the cynic in me guessed that he had decided to act out the role of the sincere-but-poor film student, all the while minimizing his involvement with *Macho Libre*. But why was he reluctant to talk about someone else's failed movie that had been shut down, purportedly for lack of funds? Why was it a sensitive subject for all those involved? Jason Cunningham had clearly called Chase and Brad, warning them about talking with me.

The busser came around with a water pitcher. He refilled my glass, and then poured water in the two water bowls.

"Ah, poor doggie," he said to Emily. "You hurt?"

Emily waved her nubbin, glad for his attention. He offered his hand and she licked it. Then he ran his hand along her neck.

"Her leg was broken," I explained, "but it seems to be healing well."

He gestured to all the stitching and scabs. "What happen?"

My Spanish wasn't good enough to explain adequately. My English was probably not good enough either. Evil is not easily expounded upon. It's an ugliness like a bad cancer, and too often, like cancer, it's hidden from view.

"Bad people," I said. "They caused her to be hurt."

"That is a shame," he said.

The way he said the word *shame*—casting it in evil and sorrow—was just right.

"Yes," I said, "a shame."

Chase appeared right after the busser left. He carried out a tray with my orders of fish and chips. The entrees came with coleslaw, malt vinegar, several lemon slices, and tartar sauce.

"I brought two plastic plates for the dogs," he said. "Do you want me to serve them?"

"Thanks," I said, "but I can take care of that."

"Can I get you anything else?" he asked.

"I'm good," I said. "Although I am curious as to what *WW* is."

"WW?" he asked.

"On social media you referred to the movie that you and your friends were doing as *WW*. I've been wondering what that stood for."

"I—I can't recall," Chase said, and then hurried off.

He couldn't pull off the scene. It was probably a good thing that he wanted to be a director instead of an actor.

At the appearance of the fish and chips, my dogs roused themselves from their sleepy stupor and were suddenly alert. I cut up the fish my friends were having, making sure there were no bones. I also scraped away the breading so they were getting mostly fish. It was a case of do as I say, not as I do, as I ate my fish with all the batter intact. Fish and chips are comfort food; all of us were comforted.

With full stomachs, we enjoyed the warmth of the sun. Eventually, Chase reappeared and asked, "Can I interest you in dessert?"

"No, thanks," I said. "Just the check."

He returned with it a few minutes later. Instead of giving him a credit card, I offered him my business card.

"I don't know what happened during the shoot," I said, "but I do know that whoever talks first always gets the best deal. Call me."

He didn't say anything, but he did take my card. I ended up paying in cash and gave him a twenty-five percent tip for presumably not spitting in my food.

CHAPTER TWENTY-ONE

ONCE UPON AN OCTOPUS

I opened the car windows, fired up my laptop, and wrote a report of my lunch meeting. Whenever possible, I always try and get everything down while it's still fresh in my mind. The reports aren't only for my own record keeping. If a case goes to court, defense lawyers always request copies of any reports. That's reason enough to try and get everything right. The prospect of having defense lawyers hold your feet to the fire is always great motivation.

Now that I'd talked to both Jason Cunningham and Chase Durand, there was only one member of the "tres amigos" wannabe directors' club left to contact. I called the number I had for Brad Steinberg but got a recording. It was possible he was in class, or he might have been ducking my calls. Either way, I was confident I could track him down in the next day or two. I had his home address, a good idea of his school schedule, and I knew his favorite haunts based on his social media postings. In fact, he made a habit of posting from one particular Starbucks on Ventura

Boulevard in Tarzana most mornings at 8:30 and most afternoons at around 4:30. He must have liked both the coffee and the complimentary Wi-Fi; from what I could determine, it was his home away from home.

My cell phone rang, and on the display I could see Bud Bennet was calling. "Budweiser," I said.

"Wiser, no," he said, "but we might have gotten lucky."

"I'm listening."

"Yesterday you asked me to expand my search and see if in nearby counties there were reports of any dead dogs suspected to have been involved in dogfighting. Lo and behold, I hit pay dirt in San Bernardino County. Two years ago, half a dozen dogs were left in a remote desert location about thirty miles from the Nevada border. As it so happens, three of those dogs had bullet wounds."

"What did ballistics say?"

"Ballistics said nothing," said Bud. "The bullets were dug out of the dogs, but because there was no gun at the crime scene, they never went to San Bernardino's Firearms and Toolmark Identification Unit. Instead, those bullets have been in storage in the Property Division Unit."

"Whisper sweet nothings in my ear and tell me tests are now being run."

"How about I forgo the sweet nothings and just tell you the bullets have been moved out of Property and are now in the possession of Firearms and Toolmark ID. I was promised that they'll soon be conducting the tests."

"What's 'soon'?"

"Three or four weeks."

"I think all evidence techs get trained to say that their work will take three or four weeks."

"You sound like a suspicious cop."

"You can only be told 'the check is in the mail' so many times before getting a mite suspicious."

"When I used to work traffic," he said, "We had this sign posted in our locker room that said, *Drinking? Why, no, Officer.*"

"You hear about the traffic court judge who summed up his career by saying that in most instances he had to make his rulings between two parties, each of whom swore they were driving the speed limit and on their side of the road when the accident occurred?"

"It's hard to tell if people know they're lying," said Bud, "or if they've successfully lied to themselves. When my first two wives served me with divorce papers, both of them said the same thing: 'We can still be friends.'"

"'I stopped looking for a Dream Girl, I just wanted one that wasn't a nightmare.'"

"I like that."

"Credit Charles Bukowski," I said, "LA's unofficial poet laureate."

"Never heard of him."

"He was a character. Mickey Rourke played him in the movie *Barfly.*"

"Never heard of it."

I probably wouldn't have heard of him, I thought, if not for my playing with fire. While I was recovering from my burns, a cop friend gave me a volume of poetry by Bukowski titled *What Matters Most Is How Well You Walk Through the Fire.* I'm pretty sure the cop only gave me the book because of its title. There is no profession that appreciates gallows humor more than law enforcement officers.

"Someone once asked Bukowski if he hated people, and he said, 'I don't hate them . . . I just feel better when they're not around.'"

That got a little laugh out of Bud. "There's a reason we wanted to work with dogs, Gideon," he said. "There's a reason."

I remained in the parking lot. There was information to process, and Bukowski to think about. He'd once offered up words that I imagined were his own litmus test, saying, "If you're losing your soul and you know it, then you've still got a soul to lose." I believed, and hoped, some of my soul was still intact. It was something I was trying to cling to.

The *Peter Gunn* theme started playing on my phone. In an old-school moment, I'd returned to that ringtone. The display told me Vincente Calderon was calling. I knew not to hope that he'd be getting back to me with information so quickly.

But if he is, God, I thought, I am going to take this as a sign I should no longer be as cynical about my fellow man.

"If you're getting back to me on the gun video this quickly," I said, "I just made a promise to God that I'd be a better person."

"I should probably hang up right now, then," said Vincente, "so that you don't break your promise to God."

"You'll invoke divine retribution if you do. What do you have?"

"Unofficially," Vincente said, "and given the disclaimer that my analysis lasted less than a minute, per your begging email, I'm pretty sure the weapon is a Heckler and Koch USP Tactical forty-five caliber. The sound suppressor attached to it is definitely a Brugger and Thomet Impuls-IIA."

"Was the gun modified for the silencer?"

"Hardly," said Vincente. "The barrel is designed for the suppressor to thread right into it."

"That kind of barrel is illegal, right?"

"Yes and no," he said. "In California you can have a threaded pistol barrel, but it can't have a normal magazine release, because then it would be considered an automatic weapon. If you have a fixed-magazine gun of ten rounds or fewer, it can have a threaded barrel. However, it's easy to switch out an unthreaded barrel with one that's threaded. And you don't have to drive far to get either a threaded barrel or a suppressor. They're sold in Nevada and Arizona."

His words made me feel that I was missing some obvious connections, and that only increased my frustration that I couldn't get those thoughts to surface into my conscious mind. Still, there was something there, even if I couldn't put my finger on it. For now, I would have to take comfort in that.

"I owe you big time, Vincente," I said.

"Don't expect to hear from me officially for another five weeks," he said.

"Five weeks? I thought you said three or four."

"That was before this call to you. I can't have you thinking you can get what you want, when you want it. The extra week is your penalty."

It was more than fair, so I didn't complain. Instead, I asked, "You didn't happen to isolate a frame with the suspect's picture, did you?"

For the second time that day, Vincente hung up on me.

The feeling of having this logjam in my head continued to plague me. I had the sensation of all these thoughts wanting to come out, but being obstructed in such a way that nothing was passing through.

My mind kept replaying my interactions at Best Scrap. For some reason, though, this time I wasn't thinking about Tito but

Fausto. Maybe it was his eye patch that caused me to fixate on him. In our culture, the eye patch was once thought to have sinister connotations. What's a pirate without an eye patch? But popular culture has somehow made the eye patch heroic, as seen in such movie characters as Nick Fury, Rooster Cogburn, and Mad-Eye Moody.

Fausto and I had said very little to one another. Now that I thought about that, I realized that Tito had intervened, explaining that Fausto spoke little English. Because of that, I had curtailed the questions I might have asked. In fact, Tito had cut me off just as I was about to ask Fausto something. But what had it been? I thought back to our conversation. We had been talking about guns. I had never gotten around to asking Fausto if he owned a licensed firearm. That would have been my next logical question, and Tito had to have known that. I wondered if there was any reason for his hijacking the conversation. After all, those with green cards could legally buy a gun in California.

I pulled up my notes from my visits to Best Scrap and looked at what I had entered on Fausto Alvarez. It was a long shot, but I decided to do a firearms inquiry through the National Crime Information Center. I entered Fausto's name and ran a search on any firearms registered to him. Moments later I got a bingo. Six years before, Fausto had purchased a Heckler & Koch USP Tactical .45.

The same kind of gun had been waved around by an intruder at Angie's Rescues. Although it's a commonly sold gun, I didn't think it was a coincidence that Fausto Alvarez owned an HK Tactical. Still, I didn't think it was Fausto on the tape I'd seen. The hoodie had prevented facial identification, but based on his stature it seemed unlikely he'd been the intruder. Fausto couldn't be any taller than five foot four. On the CCTV footage the trespasser looked taller and thinner than Fausto. There was also the matter of Fausto's eye patch. Even the hoodie wouldn't have been able to hide that.

The obvious suspect was Humberto "Tito" Rivera. Based on his height and weight, he could easily be the shrouded figure in the video. But why would he break into Angie's Rescues with a silenced gun?

There didn't seem to be a logical answer. I thought about the two cages where the intruder had stopped to shine his light. Neither Heather nor I could figure out what had interested him, but now I thought I knew. One dog had been a big boxer, and the other had been part pit bull. That suggested the intruder had been looking for a pit bull.

Had he been targeting Emily? And if so, why?

"That doesn't make sense," I said.

Emily raised her head, thinking I was talking to her. I reached out a reassuring hand and started scratching under her cone.

"Why would Tito be looking for you?" I asked. My tone was friendly and high pitched.

"It's not as if you could testify against him," I said, continuing to work my fingers under the lampshade she was wearing. Emily responded almost joyously, making sure I kept scratching under the cone.

"I can't imagine your survival would matter to him one way or another. You escaped death. Is it a matter of some sick pride that he'd want to kill you for having done that? He's definitely twisted, but there's no profit in trying to kill you a second time, and that's what he's all about."

Emily was a sympathetic listener. I could speculate on grisly matters for hours at a time and she would happily commiserate as long I scratched away.

"I'm tempted to pay another call to Best Scrap," I said, "but the potential risk might not be worth the reward. Right now Tito doesn't know about the videotape, or that I'm aware Fausto owns an HK Tactical. He also doesn't know about the remains of the three dogs shot near the Nevada border. It's possible we'll get lucky with those ballistics. Maybe they'll match up with Fausto's gun. If that happens, then I'll regret spooking Tito. What I don't want is for that gun to suddenly go missing."

I wondered if Emily would still be alive if I hadn't listened to my gut and adopted her.

"I want you to be a happily-ever-after story," I told her. "You have the makings of a classic fairy tale. The good girl prevails over the villain. Is that too much to ask?"

Emily didn't think so, but Sirius decided he should be consulted. He intercepted my hand with his muzzle, making sure he got his fair share of affection while we deliberated.

"Did I neglect to mention the hero of this story?" I asked. "Mea culpa, mea culpa. It's time to talk about Sirius the Noble. You see, a wise queen named him after a star, and not just any star, but the brightest star in the sky. And when she bestowed that name, a little bit of that stardust entered his being and made him special. It is Sirius who has to guide his plodding and pedestrian partner. In fact, Sirius telepathically communicated what needed to be done to the rather slow detective, and because of that, Emily was adopted."

It was a plot twist that Sirius approved of, especially as it came with scratching. Emily also became enamored with the story when a second hand was brought into play and took to scratching her as well.

"And it really was happily ever after for Sirius and Emily," I said, "especially after their servant Gideon was recast in his bodily form so that he had six arms like an octopus, which was all the better with which to scratch them."

The dogs thought it was a great story.

CHAPTER TWENTY-TWO

NEVER BEEN TO SPAIN

I left another message with Brad Steinberg, although I wasn't expecting a call back. He hadn't responded to my previous messages, making me believe that he was now officially ducking me. That meant I was now officially getting annoyed. If you want to get on a cop's bad side, attempt a disappearing act.

My next call was to another fledgling director, Jason Cunningham. I didn't want Jason to think I'd forgotten him. I wasn't surprised when my call went directly to his voice mail. My message was simple: I provided my name and my telephone number and said, "Call me."

Since no one was willing to talk to me, I decided to call Lisbet. At least she took my call. "I'm glad you're not avoiding me," I said.

"That happen often?"

"Occupational hazard," I said.

"In that case," she said, "to what do I owe the *pleasure* of this call?"

I appreciated her emphasis and decided to offer tit for tat. "I'm just confirming the *pleasure* of your company tonight, and wondering when I might expect you."

"I still have a lot of work to do," she said. "Is seven too late?"

"That's perfect," I said.

"Do you need me to bring anything?"

"Just you," I said.

"Is that all?"

"That's more than I ever could have hoped for."

As much as recent events had made me glad at the timing of Emily's adoption, I still felt bad that Lisbet hadn't been more involved in the decision. The two of us spend most nights together. Common sense, not to mention courtesy, suggested that I should have consulted with her before bringing another dog into our lives.

Even though she hadn't voiced any explicit disapproval, I wanted Lisbet to know I didn't take her for granted. To try and show that, I decided to serve her favorite meal in the world. Although I'm a pretty fair cook, I know better than to try and make certain meals on my own, especially when such an endeavor would require utensils, ingredients, and expertise I don't have.

In the words of Dirty Harry, "A man's got to know his limitations." Mine are many and sundry.

A man's also got to be able to gauge LA traffic. That's what prompted my decision to drive to Lisbet's and my favorite Spanish restaurant in West Hollywood before doing anything else.

When I called in my to-go order for paella marinara, I was warned by the order taker that the food wouldn't be ready for forty minutes.

"Perfect," I said, knowing it would take me about that long to drive to the restaurant.

"Sir?" she said, surprised by how amenable I was to the wait.

"Forty minutes is fine," I said. "I'll see you then."

Some of Lisbet's favorite dishes, I think, have to do with her unrequited wanderlust. In lieu of traveling, she loves to watch travel shows, especially those that highlight a country's cuisine. Neither one of us has traveled outside North America, so when we dine on certain dishes we let ourselves be magically transported to that country. For Lisbet, paella is Spain, as are sangria, vibrant colors, landmark basilicas, Salvador Dali, flamenco, and Antoni Gaudí.

"Never been to Spain," I mused to the dogs, and without thinking about it, started humming the Three Dog Night song of the same name.

"I just figured out our playlist for our drive," I told them.

We started with "Never Been to Spain," went to "Easy to Be Hard," segued to the loneliness of "One," picked up the pace with "Eli's Coming" and "Mama Told Me (Not to Come)," and ended up in the mythical kingdom of "Shambala."

I saved one particular song for the homestretch to the restaurant: "This one is for Lisbet," I said, and called out for "An Old Fashioned Love Song."

"Dogs," I said, getting used to saying the plural, "this should be your favorite musical group. The band was named for how to deal with the cold. On a cold night you need one dog to snuggle up with and stay warm; on a really cold night you need two dogs. And when it's a freezing night, you need three dogs. Since we live in Southern California, and since it rarely freezes here, our household need only consist of two dogs. Do I hear a second on that motion?"

I looked in the rearview mirror and saw Sirius raise an ear.

"The motion has been seconded," I said, "and passed with unanimous consent."

I found a parking space closer to the restaurant than I dared hope. Even though it was a temperate day and I didn't expect to be gone for long, I knew just cracking open the windows wasn't enough. My latest gadget is a portable, battery-operated air conditioner, and before leaving the car I turned it on.

My order was all ready for me, and as it was being rung up, I took a deep breath and tried to inhale all the packaged offerings. I could smell the toasted rice and how it was just on the verge of being burned, as it should be, seasoned by the saffron and paprika. Notes from the sea combined with tomatoes, artichokes, and fava beans.

"Good?" asked the dark-haired woman taking care of my order.

"*Muy bien*," I said.

As good as the Spain of my imagination.

I thought about ending my workday early. Brad Steinberg hadn't returned my call, and I wasn't hopeful that I'd find him sitting at his favorite Starbucks at 4:30. However, my stubbornness won out over the certainty of bad return traffic. The only good thing I could envision in regards to my homeward commute was that Lisbet wasn't going to be over until seven, which would give me plenty of time to get ready for her.

I thought about playing some more Three Dog Night, but decided I'd had enough of a good thing. Still, their instrumental song "Fire Eater" made me think about a recent conversation I'd had with Seth. We'd been discussing how my life seemed to be divided into before the fire and after the fire. For short, Seth suggested we refer to it as BF or AF. Or, as he added, "From the time you became a fire-eater."

"'Fire-eater'?" I'd asked.

"I don't mean fire-eater like a street performer," he'd said, "but more as the opposite. Like the archangel of your name, you went up against the dragon and you vanquished it. You took on the fire and absorbed it; that makes you a fire-eater. In some ways, it's like being a sin-eater."

I had never heard of a sin-eater either. Seth told me about the tradition of the sin-eater eating food and supposedly absorbing the sins of those recently deceased. There were traditions very similar to this, he told me, in some of the South American tribes he had worked with.

"Not that we need to go very far afield to see it in our own culture," Seth had said. "Think about Jesus. Is he not purported to be the ultimate sin-eater?"

My shaman friend does not think like most people, and I'm very grateful for that. Still, I am not at all convinced he's right about me being a fire-eater. What I am is a fire survivor. And I'm glad I'm *not* a sin-eater; I can barely digest my own.

I resisted the temptation to call out for the song "Fire Eater," and the three of us rode in silence.

As it turned out, going to Tarzana was a wild-goose chase. Brad Steinberg never stopped at his favorite Starbucks to get his late-afternoon caffeine, and neither did he broadcast his whereabouts on social media. I suspected Chase had probably contacted his friends, telling them I'd been questioning him at lunch. The time wasn't totally wasted, though. When it appeared Steinberg would be a no-show, I took the dogs to a nearby park and we had a work-and-play session. Emily was happy when I removed her cone, and even with the cast on her leg she was able to amble around. She already had mastered "sit," "come," and "down." "Stay" was a work in progress, so I had Sirius show her how it was done. I had him sit and stay, and emphasized the command while throwing a ball. He watched the bouncing ball, and then waited, and waited, until I finally said, "Go ahead."

We drove from the park back to Starbucks and I made sure Brad hadn't snuck in during our absence. After that, we began our drive home. The stop-and-go was to be expected, but it was a little more go than stop, and we puttered along the freeway at between fifteen and twenty miles an hour.

We made only one detour, my favorite wine shop in Sherman Oaks. I left with a Cava, a Spanish sparkling wine, and some Tempranillo that the clerk assured me would make a great sangria.

Usually Lisbet has to endure "Gideon time," a condition where I'm perpetually running about thirty minutes late for whenever we agreed to meet. For once, I arrived home with almost half an hour to spare. That gave me time to warm the paella, chill the Cava, and make the sangria. Then I jumped in and out of the shower, and even did some tidying up before the ever-punctual Lisbet arrived at seven.

Sirius alerted me to her arrival, making his happy sounds. Behind him was Emily. She didn't bark, but watched the way Sirius greeted Lisbet. Then it was her turn. She was sniffing Lisbet's leg, or doing the best she could with her cone, and wagging her nubbin. Lisbet got down on one leg and extended her hand so that the e-collar didn't interfere with the necessary sniffing. Emily looked delighted to meet the mystery woman whose scent was everywhere in the house.

"Hello, Emily," said Lisbet. "Welcome to the household. I'm glad I'm no longer the lone female here."

Maybe on some level Emily understood she was now family; maybe it was Lisbet's tone; maybe it was Emily's desperate need to be loved; maybe Lisbet was even better in person than she was in her scents; maybe it was all the above. The scarred-up pit bull melted in Lisbet's arms, leaning her weight against her body. Lisbet laughed, Sirius barked, and Emily melted a little more.

"Home sweet home," I said, and bent down and gave Lisbet a kiss.

Lisbet was in no rush to be disentangled, so I went out to the kitchen and returned with a flute of the Cava. We clinked glasses and said, "Cheers."

"Am I sniffing what I think I am?" she asked.

"Yep," I said. "Mung beans, tripe, and haggis."

"My favorites," she said.

"There is also humble pie as an accompaniment to the meal," I said.

"Is that so?"

I nodded. "I apologize for not consulting with you when it came to adopting Emily."

It was a good time to beg forgiveness; Emily had managed to work most of her body onto Lisbet's lap.

"She seems to be as sweet as you said she is," said Lisbet. "But . . . "

The sound of Lisbet's having reservations concerned me. "But what?"

"But I'm in danger of dropping my glass and being smothered. Help!"

Lisbet's arm was pinned to her side by Emily's weight, and she was barely able to hold her half-filled glass aloft. I took it from her and helped her up.

Before putting the paella in the oven, I had sprinkled a little chicken broth atop it, hoping that the seafood and rice wouldn't dry out during reheating. Whether my trick worked or the dish was so good it defied my attempts to ruin it, the paella was wonderful.

There were just a few grains of rice left now, morsels we unashamedly vied for. Lisbet feigned poking me with her fork, and then swooped in with her fingers, getting all the remaining rice.

"Foul," I said. "No fingers allowed."

She smacked her lips, swallowed, and said, "You no longer have any evidence with which to convict me."

"The proof is in the pudding. Or to be specific, it's in the crema catalana, which you won't get unless you confess your crimes."

"I'll confess to Lincoln's assassination," Lisbet said, "for crema catalana."

While I went to retrieve dessert, Lisbet put down her fork and stroked Emily's head. For both her sake and the dog's, she had removed Emily's cumbersome lampshade halfway through dinner. Now Emily was able to more easily rest her head in Lisbet's lap.

"How's your new BFF?" I asked.

"Great," she said, running a hand along Emily's head, but then suddenly pulling it back and examining what was there. "Gross."

"What?"

"I'm afraid Emily is still oozing from some of her wounds. In fact, there's puss coming out of one of her head wounds."

I nodded and said, "I've got lotions and potions and pills for that."

"And I've got soap and water for my hands," Lisbet said, rising to go and wash.

I put our desserts down on the counter while the two of us washed our hands. "I know it probably would have made sense to leave Emily at the shelter while she healed," I said, "but if I had done that, I'm pretty sure she would now be dead."

Lisbet finished with her washing and turned off the water. "Did you just say she would be dead?"

"I did."

"From what cause?"

I told her about the videotape of the man with a gun, a suspect I was all but certain was Humberto "Tito" Rivera.

Lisbet considered what I'd told her and tried to make sense of it. "So you think the man who left Emily for dead," she said, "then sought her out at the shelter to kill her?"

"I can't think of any other reason why he'd be there with a gun. At the same time, I haven't yet been able to figure out what would compel him to try and kill her for a second time."

"What's the best reason you can come up with?"

"There's probably not a better way for him to tell me to eff off. And maybe by killing Emily, he thought that would scare me."

Lisbet half nodded but clearly wasn't sold. Unfortunately, neither was I.

CHAPTER TWENTY-THREE

VERDADES (TRUTHS)

Over cups of espresso, Lisbet and I discussed the disappearance of Mateo Ramos.

"The three directors are trying to close ranks," I said, "so now I'll need to convince once of them that it's time to play 'let's make a deal.' I know one of them has a conscience. Someone filled Mateo's wallet with twenty-five hundred dollars and sent it to Luciana Castillo. Since money is tight for Jason Cunningham and Chase Durand—aka Quentin and Marty—that leaves Brad Steinberg—aka Hitch—as Luciana Castillo's anonymous donor.

"What I think played on Brad's conscience was seeing Luciana's pictures in Mateo's wallet and reading his love poetry. Without knowing much about him, I'm guessing Brad is a romantic. I can use that as his Achilles' heel."

"It seems wrong to target the one person who did the right thing," she said.

"You're probably right," I said, "but my concern is what happened to Mateo Ramos. Even an accidental death has consequences."

"I suppose so," said Lisbet. "It just seems sad."

"It is that. This will probably be one of those cases that has no good outcome."

"What's your plan for exploiting that Achilles' heel?" she asked.

"Love poetry," I said.

"That's your secret weapon?"

"It is when I'm using words from the grave," I said. "Tonight I thought I'd translate the three poems that were in Mateo's wallet."

"I'd better help you," said Lisbet.

"My Spanish isn't good?"

"There's that," she said.

"And what else?"

"You've heard of being a hopeless romantic?" said Lisbet.

I nodded.

"You're more of a clueless romantic," she said.

Luciana had allowed me to make copies of everything in Mateo's wallet. Two of the poems meant for Luciana looked like works in progress. There were scratch marks on the papers and crossed-out words. The third poem was typed out and much longer than the others. It was unclear if Mateo had written that poem or if it had been authored by someone else. Because it was typed, or copied from some book, I suspected it wasn't original to Mateo.

Lisbet began working on one of the shorter poems, transcribing its words into the laptop in their original Spanish.

Luciana, Mi Amor

Mi sueño es simple,
Quisiera estar contigo,
Mi sueño es mi mundo,
Quisiera estar contigo.

Te he dado mi corazón,
Lo es tuyo siempre,
Ha dejado mi ser,
Y ahora palpita contigo.

Tus ojos son mi universo,
En los cual logro verlo todo,
Déjame perderme en ellos,
Y vivir en tu eternidad.

I was lucky Lisbet was helping me with the translations, as she seemed to have an intuitive sense for interpreting what Mateo had wanted to say in his poem. For her it wasn't only taking a word from Spanish and finding the English equivalent; she made it more personal, as if trying to draw the words from Mateo's heart.

"I think that's about as good as I can do," she said.

I thanked her, and then picked up her translation and read.

Luciana, My Love

My dream is simple,
I want to be with you,
My dream is the world,
I want to be with you.

I gave you my heart,
It is yours forever,
It left my chest,
And now beats in yours.

Your eyes are my universe,
I look into them and see everything,
Let me fall into them,
And be lost in you for eternity.

"You did a great job," I said.

"How do you know?"

"It feels right," I said. "And I met Luciana. What Mateo wrote about her eyes, and what you translated, describes them. They're the first thing you notice about her. She's a tiny woman, probably under five feet. It would be easy to mistake her for a girl but for her eyes. They're large, and they are filled with sorrow. The first time I looked at them, I thought of one of those Margaret Keane paintings."

"Eyes easy to fall into," Lisbet said.

"They were eyes I didn't want to further disappoint," I said.

Lisbet nodded, and I nodded. Then she said, "I'm ready to tackle the next poem."

"You sure?"

"I wouldn't want to disappoint Luciana," she said.

As before, Lisbet typed the poem in its original Spanish. Although she was using a computer program that translated the words into English, she continued working on the poem and formulating her own translation. Finally, she was done.

"It's titled," she said, "'On the Day We Wed.'"

She wiped a tear from her eye. Strangely enough, there was something in my eye as well. This time she read the poem aloud in Spanish:

En el Día de Nuestra Union

He contado los momentos,
Demasiados sin duda,
Pero sé que serás mía,
Por siempre solo mía, Amén.

She continued reading the stanzas, and though I didn't know many of the words, the love came through. Lisbet read with emotion, and when she finished had to blink away the tears. Several seconds of silence followed her reading. Then she said, "And now what feels like the inadequate English translation for 'On the Day We Wed.'"

I hadn't realized that translating Mateo's poetry would be such a personal endeavor, and I wondered if I should have involved Lisbet.

She started reading, and I listened carefully:

I count the moments,
They seem far too many,
But soon you will be mine,
Forever and ever, amen.

Lisbet read about how Mateo had loved Luciana from the first moment they met and was made forever a hostage to her heart. The love-struck suitor said that he settled for having Luciana in his dreams for now, but he longed for the reality of waking with his bride at his side.

After what I felt was an appropriate silence, I said, "Thanks so much for your translations."

"Thank you," she said, "and thank Mateo for his poems." Then she asked, "Didn't you say there was a third poem?"

"There is," I said, "but I'm pretty sure Mateo didn't write it."

"Why is that?"

"The first two poems were simple and earnest and handwritten. The third poem is a copy of some sort. It's also longer and more complicated than the first two poems. I suspect it was someone else's love poem."

"Let me see it," said Lisbet.

I handed her the copy of "Verdades." As soon as she saw the poem, Lisbet nodded and said, "You're right. Mateo didn't write this poem."

"How are you so sure?"

"'Verdades' is a classic Spanish love poem. The title means *truths.*"

"You're familiar with it?"

She nodded.

I had this sense that there was more to her story. I also had this sense that I wasn't sure I wanted to hear more. But then again, the poem was supposed to be about truths.

"A man once gave me a copy of the same poem," she said. Her smile was small, and maybe a little sad.

"He was in love with you?"

"He was," she said. "But I also think he wanted to comment on the way I sneezed."

"Your sneeze?"

"Didn't you once refer to my sneeze as 'a kazoo meets a hissing cat'?"

"I might have said something like that."

"David was also amused by the sound of my sneeze."

She said the name the way Hispanics do, making the I in his name a hard E, so the second syllable rhymed with the word *need.*

"You see this line here?" she said, pointing.

I read the words: "*Me gusta verte estornudar.*"

Lisbet nodded. "It says, 'I even like the way you sneeze.' I always found that funny, especially after the poet extolled so many other things about this woman."

"Did David write you love poetry?" It was a question I was afraid of asking.

"Yes, he did."

"*Verdades*," I said, thinking about truths. "Even though I don't write poetry, you're still my muse. For me, poetry is like a foreign language, with all the words untranslatable."

"I know that."

"Whatever happened to you and David?"

"I broke up with him."

"Why?"

"He wasn't you."

"If you were trying to make me feel better, you just did."

"I'm glad."

"When were the two of you together?"

"More than a dozen years ago."

"For the record," I said, "I, too, am a huge fan of your sneezes."

"Really?"

"You doubt me?"

"Whenever I sneeze, you always laugh."

"I will not deny it's a funny sound. In fact, I always thought it was a shame that Dr. Seuss never heard it, because I'm sure he would have immortalized it in one of his books."

"What would the title have been?"

"*Goodnight Gesundheit?*" I said.

"Not bad," she said.

"*A Snozzle of Snorkeling Sneezes?*"

"You're not a poet," she said, "and you're not a romantic, but you do have your moments."

CHAPTER TWENTY-FOUR

LOOKING FOR TARZAN

Even though it's only about a ten-mile drive from my home in Sherman Oaks to Brad Steinberg's preferred Starbucks in Tarzana, I allotted an hour for the commute. In the event Steinberg wasn't there, I also brought the dogs along; at a minimum we'd get another workout in his absence. And since it was likely to be a bumper-to-bumper drive, I'd at least have the dogs to complain to.

I lowered all the windows an inch or two, so as to allow the dogs to sniff the news of the day. It wasn't easy for Emily with her lampshade, but I didn't want her to ride without it. For the most part her wounds were healing, but given the opportunity, she liked to dig at some of her injuries and chew on her cast. That morning I'd spent ten minutes rubbing her with one of the lotions Dr. Misko had prescribed. It had helped most of her scaling skin, but there were a few wounds I was worried about and wanted a vet to look at. There was still discharge coming from Emily's head wound where it looked like she had an abscess.

Maybe it was time to schedule Emily to see Sirius's vet, Dr. Wolf-Fox. The hyphenated last name had come about because of her recent marriage. The last time Sirius and I had been in to see her, I had encouraged Dr. W-F (as I was now calling her) to start a family, and suggested if they had a boy, he should be Jack Russell Wolf-Fox, and if they had a girl, to name her Kerry Blue Wolf-Fox. Dr. W-F seemed to find my suggestions equal parts funny and intriguing.

The traffic seemed a little more merciful than usual, and we arrived in Tarzana earlier than I had expected. Visitors to the area are always curious about the city's name. Yes, Jane, there really is a Tarzana, and the city really was named after Tarzan. In 1919, Edgar Rice Burroughs, author of the Tarzan books, bought a 550-acre ranch in the San Fernando Valley and renamed the spread Tarzana Ranch. In 1950, Burroughs's ashes were buried under a walnut tree located in front of his office on Ventura Boulevard. I heard the location was now private property, and I wondered if there was currently any memorial to Burroughs.

"If I don't connect with my suspect today," I said, "what do you say we go pay homage to Burroughs?"

The tone of my voice must have sounded like there was a potential outing in the offing, which got some tail wagging.

As a kid, Tarzan had been a big deal to me and my friends. It's a wonder none of us were killed trying to duplicate his swinging through the jungle. Whenever we'd go swinging on a rope, usually with the object of landing in a body of water, we'd shout out bawdry Tarzan rhymes. Even Ronald Reagan had recognized the comedic value of Tarzan. "A hippie," he said, "walks like Jane, looks like Tarzan, and smells like Cheetah."

I parked, made sure the dogs were comfortable, and went to get a cup of coffee. Just in case Steinberg was there, I had some paperwork I wanted to share with him, including Mateo's poems.

It wasn't until I joined the line of the caffeine deprived that I casually looked around the place. Brad Steinberg was sitting at a table by himself. Whatever he was looking at on his tablet had him immersed, and he took no notice of my presence. I wanted to make sure that didn't change, so I turned my back to him and pretended to study all the coffee and tea offerings as if they were of great interest to me.

Of course, I ordered a plain old coffee.

While I waited for it, I found a vantage point from which I could see Steinberg's reflection in the window. He was still busily typing into his tablet.

My coffee was ready at the same time the table next to Steinberg opened up. I grabbed my cup and went to claim the table. When I sat down, Steinberg looked up at me, and then returned his gaze to the tablet. After a moment or two, he must have made the connection as to who I was, because he suddenly turned my way.

"Morning," I said.

His hands appeared to be frozen just above his tablet, while his eyes remained locked on me. It was a classic fright-or-flight pose.

I extended my hand and said, "Michael Gideon."

Habit drew his hand toward mine, and we shook.

"I left you a few messages," I said. "I'm glad I caught up with you this morning. We need to talk."

He ran a hand through his thick, dark curls and sighed. His brown eyes went basset hound on me and were suddenly full of worry.

"I can't talk," he said, and then looked away.

"Why is that?"

"My lawyer has advised me to say nothing. Would you like his name and number?"

"Not particularly," I said, taking a sip of my coffee.

He maintained a rigid posture, unsure what he should do.

"So, do you like to be called Brad, or Mr. Steinberg, or do you prefer Hitch?"

"Brad," he said. "The Hitch thing was sort of a joke."

I nodded. "Chase said the same thing. But I got to admit I liked your choice of directors. Hitchcock was something, wasn't he? I'll bet you I've seen *Rear Window* half a dozen times. That's my personal favorite, but I also love *The Birds* and *North by Northwest* and *Vertigo*. And let's not forget *Strangers on a Train*. That's right up there as well. Do you have a favorite?"

I wasn't sure whether he was going to answer or not, but after a few seconds he said, "*Psycho*."

"I can understand that," I said. "In fact, most people would probably answer that. But for me, the shock value grew old after the first viewing. With a lot of his other films, it seems like there's more nuance, and you see new things every time you view them."

Steinberg didn't answer, just continued to stare straight ahead.

"I guess the movies I like best, I need to engage with the characters," I said. "That's why I go back to *Rear Window* as my favorite. How can you not want Jimmy Stewart and Grace Kelly to make it as a couple? There's also the mystery that draws you in. What happened to Raymond Burr's wife? And you get this great cast of characters that live in the apartment complex.

"*Vertigo* was almost as good. Maybe I like that one because I'm a cop. You know how Jimmy Stewart got obsessed with the Kim Novak character? I can understand that kind of obsession. A good cop feels this need to get answers. It's almost like a hunger. Do you understand what I'm saying?"

The stiffness hadn't left Steinberg's posture. "This is police harassment," he said.

"How is it harassment?"

"I told you I didn't want to answer your questions without my lawyer present."

"That's why I haven't been asking you questions. I've just been offering up a few Hitchcock observations."

"As I told you," he said, "if you want to talk, I want my lawyer to be present. If you'll excuse me, right now I need to get to class."

I shook my head. "I don't think that's in the cards."

He turned to me and asked, "What do you mean?"

"You've been avoiding me," I said. "If you'd called me back, I would have been amenable about scheduling a time and place to talk with you, and your lawyer. That time has passed."

"Are you arresting me?"

"If I have to, I will. To make it easy on you and your lawyer, we can arrange for your booking to occur at the West Valley station on Vanowen Street in Reseda."

"Jeez," he said. "Can we slow down a little?"

"We can slow down a lot. If you want to sit here and talk to me, I'm good with that as well. But that has to be your decision. And I need you to go on the record that you're good about not having a lawyer present."

He thought about that and finally said, "Okay."

"Just to show you that I'm not coercing you against your wishes," I said, "I'd like you to sign this paper, which stipulates that."

He read the paragraph I'd prepared the night before. I had anticipated that initially he would ask for counsel to be present.

"I'll sign," he said, "but I really do have schoolwork I need to get to."

"I'll try and make it short."

"You know," he said, "I'm not the one you should be talking to. This was Jason's film. He and Chase were much more involved than I was."

222

"I understand you bankrolled the film."

"That way overstates it. In fact, the money I put in the film was essentially a loan to Jason."

"How big a loan?"

"I covered the expenses for the props and the set. Jason said he could do it for under ten thousand. I gave him that seed money."

"Were the day laborers paid with your money?"

"I don't know," he said. "To tell you the truth, I felt sorry for Jason and Chase. Both of them graduated last May, and neither could find work in the film industry. I was accepted into graduate school. That's been my emphasis. I know they resent me for pursuing the same dream we all have. That's why they wanted to work on their short. They had this idea they could do most of the shooting in a week, and scheduled it for when I had spring break."

"What was the original name of the script?" I asked.

"Ask Chase and Jason," he said. "They wrote it."

"*WW*," I said.

He rubbed his chin and then said, "As a joke, they originally referred to the project as *Wetback Wars*."

There had been a time when undocumented aliens were referred to as *wetbacks*. It was a seldom-used term now, and for many good reasons.

"From the time they first conceptualized the idea," Steinberg said, "things changed. Chase wanted to have crazy boxing matches going on in *lucha libre* outfits. It was supposed to be a *Fight Club* kind of comedy, with lots of south-of-the-border stereotypes."

Steinberg must have read the distaste in my eyes. "I know it sounds stupid," he said, "and offensive."

"What audience could possibly want to watch that?" I asked.

"Jason was planning to market it to lowlifes," he said. "There's always been an underbelly, people who buy DVDs of bums fighting or spring-break girls flashing for the cameras."

"Sex and violence sells," I said. "And for good measure, let's add in a little racist comedy."

"Don't you think I know how stupid it all sounds?" he said. "But I was busy in graduate school, and this is all my friends had. Jason also had this idea that they could do certain outtakes for YouTube and rack up enough viewers to get advertising money. But do you know how I looked at the money I put up? I thought of it more as a contribution than an investment. To tell the truth, I never expected to get paid back. I felt guilty that I was continuing on with my career, all while my friends were feeling like they'd spent the last four years with nothing to show for it."

"Guilt money," I said.

"I suppose."

"Is guilt the reason why you put twenty-five hundred dollars into a wallet and sent that money to a woman you'd never met? Or should we be calling it blood money for the death of Mateo Ramos?"

The "aha" moment didn't fly. Steinberg turned away from me and withdrew into himself, going very still. "I don't know what you're talking about," he said.

I decided to back off, at least for the moment. "Before you leave today," I said, "I would like you to have these."

He didn't reach for the papers, so I placed them in front of him.

"Those are copies of Mateo Ramos's poetry," I said, "and their translations. Do you speak Spanish?"

"*Un poco*," he said.

"Same with me," I said. "My girlfriend helped me translate these. It gave me a better sense for Mateo. He was a young man deeply in love. And his fiancée loved him just as much. Have you ever been in love?"

Steinberg didn't answer.

"I'm not sure if you have or not," I said, "but I believe you are a romantic. And I also believe you tried to do what was right."

I let those words register with him.

"This was a tragic love story," I said. "As a student of film, I would think you could appreciate that. An undocumented worker comes to America with the sole goal of making money and sending that money back to his family. But things change while he's here. The worker falls in love with a woman who just so happens to have been born less than a hundred miles from where he was born. And in this supposed land of opportunity, in the place where the two of them meet, they set a goal for themselves. They want to save ten thousand dollars. Their plan is to go back to their birthplace and get married in the heart of Mexico. They're getting closer and closer to that goal, but then something terrible happens. And now the woman won't be going home for a wedding; she'll be going home for a funeral. But one thing prevents that: she needs the body of her fiancé to take back with her.

"You might ask why that is. What difference does it make where someone is buried? I know I don't have any great plans for my own remains, but different people and different cultures view death very differently.

"A few years ago I struck up a friendship of sorts with a Palestinian deli owner named Adnan. And one day I went into his deli right after there had been this horrific traffic accident on the street outside. And he told me, 'That is why I drive so carefully in America.' And I said, 'What do you mean?' And that's when Adnan explained to me that he was afraid of dying in America. He said funerals here were sterile and artificial and devoid of emotion. Adnan said that was very different than funerals back home, where there was loud mourning and crying and displays of bereavement.

"I suspect when Mateo returns to his village, he will be remembered in the way that Adnan prefers. But first I have to locate his body.

"*Verdades*," I said. "It means *truths*. It's also the title of one of the three poems found in Mateo's wallet. He didn't write that poem. The author is anonymous, but I suspect whoever wrote it was a young man in love. I think my favorite line is when the poet says, *Sometimes it scares me to think where I'll put so much love, when it doesn't fit in my chest*. I think that was Mateo's love. It was overflowing. I'd like you to read that poem, and the two poems that Mateo did write.

"Read them, and I'm pretty sure you'll do the right thing."

Brad Steinberg did his best to keep a neutral expression. He didn't look at me or the poetry, but stared straight ahead.

"I am going to close this case, Brad. What I would suggest is that you come clean with your lawyer. He'll know how the system works. Inevitably, the first person who talks gets the best deal."

I placed my business card atop Mateo's poetry. "My cell number is written on that card," I said. "Call me anytime, but I strongly advise you to call me soon."

I picked up my coffee cup and exited the Starbucks.

CHAPTER TWENTY-FIVE

A SHALLOW GRAVE

I second-guessed myself on the ride back, thinking about what I could have done better during my talk with Steinberg. There are a lot of moving pieces to consider when you're trying to make a suspect confess. I had bet on Brad Steinberg's better nature. He had demonstrated that he wanted to do the right thing; he had passed on Mateo's wallet to Luciana, and had added money of his own. Still, as much as Steinberg likely wanted to confess, he was restrained from doing so because it would impact his friends.

There was also Steinberg's own future. At a minimum, it was likely he'd be charged with involuntary manslaughter. It was possible the three young men could get probation, but it was also possible they could get jail time. Confessing might also result in his getting bounced from graduate school and having to give up on his dream of working in Hollywood.

Maybe I should have used more stick than carrot, I thought. Maybe I should have waved the possibility of a get-out-of-jail card. I wouldn't have explicitly promised anything, but I could have said that the deal I was offering came with a limited-time offer. Often, it's only a ticking deadline that gets lawyers to respond.

When I joined the ranks of law enforcement, I had no idea that sales was part of the job. Many experienced cops, many of the best cops, are salesmen in blue. They know that you have to close the deal to close the case. Some of those closers are great at reading body language. Others are expert at the fine art of manipulation.

To try and close Brad Steinberg, I'd used the love card. I wondered if that would prove enough.

It was my hope that Steinberg was reading Mateo's poetry at that very moment. He knew that happily ever after was no longer possible for the couple, but he could still do something for them. He could bestow peace in the form of a body. The story I'd told about Adnan being afraid of dying in America wasn't made up. Many cultures focus their memorial services around a body. I was hoping I had sold Steinberg on the idea of making amends by giving up the location where Mateo was buried.

As more time passed, though, I was sure I hadn't succeeded, and critiqued myself much as an actor would. How had I delivered my lines? Was what I had said believable? How convincing were my words? How effective was my entrance, and my exit?

By the time mid-afternoon came around, I had decided that I wasn't much of a salesman or an actor. That didn't mean I couldn't be a good old-fashioned cop, though. I didn't need a confession in order to make a case. There was plenty of evidence for me to rework, and I still hadn't even had a face-to-face with Jason Cunningham, or his mother. It was just a matter of time before I found something I had overlooked.

"Back to the old drawing board," I said.

For most of the afternoon, I reviewed case notes. I was figuring out my moves for the next day, when my cell phone rang.

The display said Alex Eisen was calling, a name unfamiliar to me.

"Detective Gideon?" he said. "This is Alex Eisen. I'm a lawyer representing Brad Steinberg."

Before cutting a deal, I insisted Brad Steinberg provide a formal written statement describing the circumstances that resulted in Mateo Ramos's death. I read his account several times. I wish I could say there was some purpose for Mateo's death, but there wasn't. Mateo didn't die in the middle of some epic bout. Javier Moreno and some of the other fighters had to be induced to go into the ring through a combination of money and drugs, but not Mateo. Boxing was just another job, another means to his end. That wasn't what killed him. He'd died from something that shouldn't have killed him. His death was a fluke, a one-in-a-million tragic occurrence.

According to Steinberg's statement, Mateo was a proud man. When asked, he refused to kiss the pig or pretend she was his love. He wore a costume, a rooster mask with a pronounced cockscomb, but did so reluctantly. As an actor, he was wooden, unenthusiastically delivering the lines he was prompted to say. He was a man with a purpose. Mateo had agreed to fight for money, and to that end he lived up to his bargain.

To the best of Brad's recollection, Mateo's bout was with a man named Juan Carlos. Both men were of similar height, age, and weight, but the fight was dominated by Mateo. There was plenty of blood, but all of it belonged to Juan Carlos. The three directors did what they could to prolong the fight; still, the beat-down of Juan Carlos was just what they wanted to get on film.

Mateo didn't strut around after his victory, as did most of the winners. He was interested in getting paid and returning to

Home Depot. Mateo's eyes were on the prize, and that was Luciana. The money he'd earned fighting would get them that much closer to their wedding.

After the fight, the directors told Mateo not to change into his work clothes, because they would need to shoot more footage of him both inside and outside the ring. For the time being, though, they told him he could take a break.

No one was looking at Mateo, let alone filming him, as he made his way out of the boxing ring. The boxing shoes he was wearing were large on him, so he might have slipped; maybe his mask made it difficult for him to see. Experienced boxers have miscalculated entering and exiting through the ropes in the ring. Mateo was not experienced. He might have tried to vault the ropes and gotten his feet tangled up. Maybe he decided to climb the ropes and push off from the corner post, only to have one of his feet catch. It's possible he got tripped up on the ropes and stumbled downward.

What was known was that the boxing ring was on an elevated platform, and when Mateo tried to exit from the ring, he fell. And while no one saw this fall, everyone heard his head hit the boulder that was right next to where they'd put up the ring. The thud was sickeningly loud.

No one knew what to do. None of the three wannabe directors had ever taken a first aid class. They huddled around Mateo's still body, hoping someone would take charge. Their first instinct was to call 911, but all of their cell phones had been stowed away and turned off so as to not interfere with the filming.

It was this, Steinberg wrote, that stopped them from immediately calling for help.

Durand checked for a pulse and didn't find one. With his hand shaking, Cunningham placed a quarter under Mateo's nose.

There was no condensation; he wasn't breathing through his nose, nor did it appear his chest was rising and falling.

"He's dead," Jason whispered.

That wasn't part of their script.

No one could believe how quickly everything happened. One moment a man was winning a boxing match, and the next moment he was dead. And that was where their dilemma began, and the first of many bad decisions.

Luciana wanted to be there for Mateo's disinterment. I had tried to talk her out of it, but she was insistent.

We stood and waited about twenty feet from where the others were working. There had been no need to bring in a cadaver dog or any machinery. This was spadework.

All three of the young filmmakers were now fully cooperating. As a group, they had volunteered to take us to where Mateo was buried. After pointing out the spot where he'd been placed in the ground, all three of them had retreated back to the police cars. That's where they were doing their watching from. I think they were glad of the insulation the vehicles provided. Luciana's grief was raw, and it made them fearful to be close to it.

The grave was shallow, only about three feet deep. Woodland Hills still has a few woodlands, and they'd found one that suited their purposes. Mateo had been buried in the midst of scrub oak and manzanita and laurel sumac.

LAPD would process the body and get it to the coroner's office. Even though none of the wannabe directors believed Mateo had been hurt during the fight, the coroner would be making his own determination. Only after that would I assist with the body's being shipped down to Mexico.

Luciana sobbed as Mateo's body was lifted from his make-shift grave. I thought of his love poem to Luciana, and how he had written, *your eyes are my universe.*

His universe wept and wept.

CHAPTER TWENTY-SIX

SOMEDAY MY PRINCE WILL COME

Santa Fe, New Mexico
848 miles from Los Angeles
April 10

When Diana Robinson began dating Stephen Prince, her friends teased her that she was "dating royalty." As the couple became more serious and marriage was discussed, Diana discovered another name-game wrinkle.

Diana Prince was the alter ego of Wonder Woman. Luckily for Diana, few people seemed to know that. All that changed, of course, when the very successful Wonder Woman franchise of films reintroduced a new generation of filmgoers to the Amazonian's history, and name.

By that time, though, Diana was long settled into her name. She and Stephen had brought five Princes into the world. Her children were grown now—the youngest was twenty-three—and so far, Diana was the grandmother of three. She and Stephen had retired to Santa Fe, New Mexico, before they were sixty. They had bought Diana's dream home, a 4000-square-foot pueblo-style house made of adobe, located in the historic district of town.

Diana liked to say she was busier in retirement than she had been when she was a working mother. In a town known for its art, Diana worked as a docent in the Georgia O'Keeffe Museum. Stephen, meanwhile, golfed three days a week and played with a doubles tennis group. Today was one of his golf days. Usually, he also stopped for a drink at the nineteenth hole.

That meant he probably wouldn't be home for at least two more hours. It was too pretty a day to do housework, Diana thought, but she could at least vacuum. The blue skies of Santa Fe never got old. They were high up at more than seven thousand feet in elevation, giving a special luster to the sky. The climate of Santa Fe was considered high desert. It was cold in the winter—brisk, Diana liked to call it—but rarely below freezing. The city's altitude kept it from ever getting too hot. It was a locale that Goldilocks would have approved of.

Diana began her vacuuming. Now that they no longer had a dog, it was considerably easier to vacuum the house, especially with its tile floors. Diana finished with the master bedroom and started in on Stephen's "retreat," where he liked to watch sports. That's when she first heard the music.

The tune sounded familiar, but Diana couldn't quite place it. She wondered where the music was coming from. They had neighbors on both sides, but both were generally quiet, and the houses were spaced well apart. It was unusual to hear noise.

The music, Diana decided, sounded as if it was coming from their guesthouse. That was strange because, at the moment, it had no guests. For much of the year it was occupied. The casita, as they called it, had proved popular with children, friends, and relatives. Everyone always commented on how cozy it was, with its kiva fireplace and enclosed patio. No one ever seemed to stay without threatening to move in.

Maybe a television was playing, or the radio. Of course that still didn't explain how one of those devices might have gotten turned on. Electronic gremlins weren't unheard of, though. Her computer always seemed to be doing strange things. Maybe some rogue electronic signal had kicked on the TV.

Diana opened the front door of their house. There was no question but that the music was coming from the casita. And now she recognized the tune: "Someday My Prince Will Come." It was the Barbra Streisand version, not the version sung by Disney's Snow White. Streisand's version had been popular while Diana was dating Stephen. Her friends used to hum it around her as a joke. Everyone always remembered the first line—*someday my prince will come*—but it was rare anyone remembered beyond that.

Then it struck Diana that Stephen's golf game must have fallen through, and that he was announcing he was home with "his" song.

Her Prince had come home.

Diana went and opened the patio door to the casita. Its front door was ajar, and the music coming from inside was overloud.

"Stephen?" she called.

Diana made her way through the patio into the casita. Barbara sang, "'Somewhere waiting for me, there is someone I'm longing to see.'"

A shadow emerged from behind the curtains. It was not someone she was longing to see. The short sledgehammer the figure held came up off the ground, rising like a cobra.

Her caller was sure as hell not her prince.

CHAPTER TWENTY-SEVEN

CIRCLING AROUND THE RABBIT HOLE

"We're pretty sure we've got another one," said Special Agent Ben Corning.

"I assume you're talking about the Stormy Weather Killer. Or did the card-sharp contingent win and is the murderer now known as the All-In Killer?"

"The winning hand went to the card sharps. Our serial murderer is now referred to as the All-In Killer."

"Tell me about the latest one."

"We're preparing a case packet for you with pictures and details," he said.

The other shoe dropped an insinuating moment later: "Any way you can hand-deliver a packet to him?"

I didn't want to tell Corning about how Detective Charles and I were trying to tie Ellis Haines to one or more Las Vegas homicides. Seeing Haines wasn't anything I enjoyed doing, but I was especially wary about seeing him now. Haines picks up on things in an almost preternatural way. On the face of it, he seems to be incredibly intuitive. That might just be the result of an overactive mind. Like the poker player he is, Haines is always thinking of odds and angles. He is part prescient, part suspicious animal, using his senses to monitor everything around him. Because of his paranoia, he is always alert to the wrong body language or the misspoken word.

"I am going to have to decline your invitation," I said.

"What can we do to change your mind?" asked Corning.

"I'm trying to put the finishing touches on one case," I said, "while at the same time being in the middle of two other cases."

"We wouldn't ask if this wasn't important. Haines seems to have honed in on the killer's wavelength. If he can give us a few things, it's possible he could be a lifesaver. Playing catch-up isn't a good position for us to be in. Playing catch-up means we're looking at another body. We need to try and get ahead of the killer."

"I understand that, and I sympathize, but I'm still going to have to say no."

"I warned the assistant director that you might not cooperate," Corning said. "The AD told me if that occurred, he'd be calling your Chief Ehrlich."

I'm okay with prodding but don't react well to outright bullying. "Tell your AD that if he doesn't have Ehrlich's direct number, he can call me and I'll give it to him."

"I value not having my head chewed off, Gideon. How about throwing me a bone? Can't you give some positive spin for the AD?"

I didn't envy Corning's position. At the same time, I wanted to be further along in the Las Vegas investigation before seeing Haines again.

"I know you think it's important that Haines gets the pictures and report on this latest case," I said. "I'd like to go on the record, though, and say that I suspect Haines is using you for his own purposes, even if I don't know what those are. Still, if you go ahead and give Haines this latest material, I will communicate with him by phone later this week."

"That is great," said Corning, not even trying to hide the relief in his voice. "When can we arrange the call? Are you good for the day after tomorrow?"

I sighed. "Give me at least three days," I said. "And I'll expect those case notes today."

"Roger that," said Corning.

I wondered if all Feds enjoyed talking like pilots. "I'll take a short synopsis in the meantime," I said.

"Female victim," said Corning, "aged sixty-two. She was bludgeoned to death."

"Where did this happen?"

"Santa Fe, New Mexico," he said. "It appears the woman was ambushed inside the guesthouse of her luxury home."

"What links her with your All-In Killer?"

"The killer didn't bother with any meteorological symbols this time. The woman was found with four black croquet mallets in her hands. Red lipstick was used to draw a heart around her lips. And there was a flamingo brooch pinned to her blouse that her husband never remembers seeing before. We believe those clues translate to the queen of hearts and the four of clubs."

"A queen-four hand," I said.

"There are poker players that call that hand 'the prince maker.'"

"Why is that?"

"What's a queen for?" he said.

"Ruling," I said, "knighting people, being a figurehead—"

Corning interrupted me. "To make princes," he said, and then quickly added, "That's not the FBI's interpretation. We know it's sexist. That's what poker players call it."

"That seems like a bit of a stretch."

"It might be until you learn the victim's name: Diana Prince. She was a mother of five."

"Shit," I said.

"There's more," he said. "In the book *Alice in Wonderland*, there's a character named the Queen of Hearts. Supposedly, she has two passions: she likes to order beheadings and she enjoys playing croquet with a flamingo mallet, like the bird. That explains the flamingo brooch, which further identifies Diana Prince as the queen of hearts."

This was the kind of measured madness, I thought, that Ellis Haines would love.

"Add to that the four black clubs left behind."

"I get the picture," I said.

What I didn't say was that I wished I hadn't.

"I'll get you those case notes," he said. "How about we talk tomorrow and firm up details for your call?"

I was already regretting having agreed to that. "I suppose," I said.

Corning clicked off.

Alice in freaking Wonderland, I thought. It was a rabbit hole I would have preferred not going down.

CHAPTER TWENTY-EIGHT

CELEBRITY ENDORSEMENTS

Even though from my end the Mateo Ramos case was officially closed, that didn't mean I was done with it. It wasn't enough to have confessions, statements, and even a body. The DA's office had my number on speed dial, and ADAs kept calling me with questions. A few times I referred the callers to my report. There are some lawyers who seem to think reading about the case is optional.

Reporters wanted to interview me, especially as all I had offered them was a brief written statement. They kept calling LAPD media relations, as well as the chief of police's office, hoping to flush me out into saying more.

To my thinking, it was better that media relations do the talking than me. The brass was also of the opinion that when it came to me making statements in public, less was more.

The word from the DA's office was that it looked like they were going to reach a plea deal with Marty, Quentin, and Hitch, but not until the coroner weighed in that Mateo had died hours before he was buried. I hoped for their sakes that Mateo had been as dead as they said he was. No one wanted an Edgar Allan Poe story of burying Fortunato while he was still alive. That kind of miscalculation could be the difference between probation and life in prison.

Thinking about the coroner's office reminded me that they were also on my callback list.

Most of my incoming calls I was letting go directly to voice mail, but when the display showed Bud Bennet was calling, I picked up.

"I need you to block off next Wednesday or Thursday. It looks like we'll be shooting one of the commercials that day. Maybe you can take Sirius to the doggie beauty parlor on Tuesday. And shine his medal, would you?"

"That's wardrobe's job," I said. "And speaking of wardrobe, tell them that Sirius will need a forty-long jacket, and his pants waist size is thirty-six, with a thirty-four inseam."

"I suppose you want me to ask, 'Left or right?'"

"I'll ask him and get back to you. Are you planning on using the pit bull for the shoot?"

"No final decision has been made. I heard someone in production was worried that the dog might be vicious."

"The dog is sweet," I said. "After all she's been through, she still thinks humans are the good guys. Full disclosure: I adopted her."

"People are going to start thinking you're soft-hearted, Gideon."

"Those who know me know better than that."

"If you want, I'll vouch that you're an SOB."

"I knew I could count on you."

"In all seriousness, you did a good thing."

"Emily deserved another chance. Hell, she deserves a first chance. You should see her just being part of everyday stuff; she seems so grateful."

"Emily got her forever home."

"I prefer to say she found her pack."

"Motley as it is," he said.

"Or mutt-ley."

Bennet groaned. "I should hang up," he said, "but there's one other thing I called about. The reward flyers are in. They look great."

With the promise of a Crime Stoppers commercial, not to mention the public service announcements on dog abuse and dogfighting, I had forgotten about the flyers.

"How many do you have?" I asked.

"I think we ordered a hundred."

"Do you have extras?"

"How many do you need?"

"A dozen would be good."

"That shouldn't be a problem."

"I'll stop by your office later this morning and pick them up."

As it turned out, Bennet left me more than the flyers. There was also a bumper sticker in my packet that read, *My Rescue Dog Rescued Me.*

With Sirius and Emily riding with me, we took a drive to Boyle Heights and made several stops. I put the dogs on leashes and visited several businesses, talking to employees and owners. Everywhere we went, I asked to hang a flyer. Without exception, every business agreed.

During the visits, I made a special point of introducing Emily, telling them she had been one of the dogs who were dumped. As far as I could tell, everyone was sympathetic to her plight. I pointed out the reward that was being offered and gave out my business card with my cell phone number.

My last stop was Best Scrap. As I pulled into their lot, I saw Tito leaving the trailer office carrying a box. I parked in the customer lot, angling the car so as to watch where Rivera was going. There was a Ford F-350 hitched to a fifth wheel. Rivera opened the trailer's door and placed the box inside. From what I could see, the trailer looked packed up and ready to go. Farther into the lot, I could see a second truck and trailer that appeared to be full of cargo. A tarp was draped over the bed of the second truck, but it didn't completely cover the space, and I could see some of what was there. There were benches, what looked to be a generator, and dog crates.

Both dogs had been asleep in the back seat when I parked but were now beginning to stir. It was almost like Emily had awakened from a bad dream to a worse reality. She started whining, and I reached back to reassure her. Sirius joined me in the comforting, but our joint efforts didn't soothe her. I wondered if she had spent time on this property, or if she had caught the scent of the man who'd tried to kill her.

With Sirius acting like a protective big brother toward her, I went back to my observing. The last time I'd been at the business, I had seen at least half a dozen dogs in various spots around the property. A few of the dogs had been on long chains; others had been housed in the kennels. Today there were fewer dogs on display.

Emily whined, and then whined again. "It's okay," I told her, "it's okay, girl." But it wasn't. I hadn't thought of how she might react to this place. I probably should have driven away and parked elsewhere, but I wanted to finish up my business.

With a flyer in hand, I got out of my car and walked toward the office. An unsmiling Fausto looked up when I entered the trailer. As far as I could tell, Fausto wasn't carrying a gun.

"Good morning," I said.

Fausto nodded. His one visible eye stared me up and down, looking hard and suspicious. By comparison, his eye patch side looked almost charitable.

"I brought this flyer," I said, showing it to him. "I'm wondering if I can hang it here."

I stopped talking at the sound of something banging against glass outside, and throaty growling and barking. Having worked with dogs most of my adult life, those are sounds that immediately get my attention. This wasn't casual barking. These were calls with an urgency to them, and a voicing of threat. The barking was rapid and low; the sounds, I realized, were being caused by the impact of a dog collar against glass. Emily was responding to the threat she perceived.

The office door flew open. Tito closed the door behind him, making sure it was secure. In the distance, Emily continued to throw herself against the car window.

"I've never seen my dog act like that," I said. "It's almost like she's telling me something, wouldn't you say?"

Tito didn't bother putting on his carefree islander act, and shucked his Caribbean accent. "What do you want?"

I was glad to hear Emily's fierce response subsiding. She was no longer throwing herself against the window. Her warning barks were still sounding, but now that Tito was out of sight, they weren't as frantic.

"Like I was telling Fausto here," I said, "I was hoping you'd let me post my flyer in one of your windows."

I held one of the flyers up for Tito to see. What caught the eye more than anything else was the green-hued promise of a $5000 reward.

Tito glanced at the flyer. What he saw made him frown even more. When his body shifted, I was fairly certain that under his windbreaker was the outline of a holstered gun. But was it the right gun? There were no ballistics in yet on the dogs dumped near Nevada, and I wanted those reports before I popped him on possession of a firearm, even if it was officially Fausto's.

"I spent the last two hours talking to business owners around here," I said. "They were all cooperative about letting me put up a flyer.

"Most of them hadn't heard about the dogs that were dumped. As you might imagine, they were horrified. They told me they'd be glad to help in whatever way they could. In fact, everyone around here has been cooperative. I talked to people at the Laundromat and the bus stop. And I posted the flyer at that bulletin board area a few blocks over. Frankly, I wondered if people would even care. Or if the only thing that motivated them was the promise of a reward. That didn't prove to be the case, though. I found that very heartening."

"Take your flyer and shove it," Tito said. "And get the hell out of here."

"No need to get hot," I said. "I just wanted to give someone in this neighborhood a chance to cash in first. The phone lines will probably get crazy once the Crime Stoppers ad starts running, especially as it will air throughout Los Angeles County and beyond. You never know who might have seen something or heard something.

"And the exciting news I just heard today is that Selena Gomez is going to lend her voice to our efforts. Can you imagine that? I can't really say I'm a fan of her music—I mean, I liked her vocals in "Good for You," but let's face it, her demographic is pretty far removed from me. Still, I think it's great she's on board. Usually, I'm not big on celebrity endorsements, but her involvement will definitely focus more eyes on what occurred. And I understand she'll do at least one spot in Spanish."

The door to the office opened. A man in work clothes stepped inside. It looked like he'd come from demolition work. He had on heavy-duty boots and worn jeans. His long-sleeve cotton shirt was stained and dusty. In his hands were construction gloves. He looked around, expecting a greeting he didn't receive.

"I got a truck full of scrap," he said.

"Fausto will help you," said Tito.

As the two men made their way out of the office, I said to Tito, "It looks like you're busy today. Are you doing some kind of move?"

"If you don't leave the property right now," he said, "I will call the chief of police's office and register a formal complaint that you're trespassing."

"If you want me out of here," I said, holding my hands up as if protesting my innocence, "then I'm out of here. And don't worry, I'll take my dogs with me. But for your own sake, I'd stay in this office until we're gone. For some reason my pit bull really doesn't like you. It's like she hates you. Strange, isn't it?"

CHAPTER TWENTY-NINE

THE CHESHIRE CAT

When I got in the car, I could see Emily was still unsettled. Her slobber was all over one window, and the glass was scratched where her nails had clawed. It was my fault, of course. I shouldn't have put Emily in the position that I had. I was lucky she hadn't broken through the window, or that Sirius hadn't decided to open the door for her. If that had happened, it was likely either Emily or Tito would have ended up dead.

"I'm sorry, Emily," I said, reaching to comfort her.

As I touched her, she began to tremble. It was PTSD, I was sure. The two of us apparently had that in common, and I felt bad that I had helped bring hers on.

"Let's get out of here," I said.

I knew the faster and farther we got away from Tito Rivera and Best Scrap, the better Emily would feel. We made our escape from the lot, and during the drive I continued talking to her, hoping the sound of my voice would make her feel better.

"We'll stop at a park," I promised. "And I'll spring you from your e-collar, and then I'll give you a rubdown. And you can roll in the grass, and Sirius can roll in the grass, and I'll roll in the grass. And that's how we'll wash that bad place, and bad man, out of our minds.

"We'll even make it a little picnic. The three of us can all get turkey subs. How does that sound?"

There was no question but that it sounded good to Sirius. And it looked as if Emily was coming around as well. Her trembling was diminishing, and she appeared less traumatized.

"You showed him, Emily. When the bad man ran into the office, he couldn't hide his fear. That's why he was so angry. Sick men like him have sick definitions, and one of them is that a dog is only considered game if it will fight on command, fight all the way to death if necessary. But most dogs aren't any different in that way from humans. Who wants to fight without good reason? But there's no shortage of game in you."

I know it wasn't the words but the tone of my voice. I know Emily didn't understand a thing I was saying, except the most important thing: she was loved.

And love is worth fighting for.

One of my favorite delis in the Sherman Oaks area features what is called a Thanksgiving Sub. The sandwich consists of mashed sweet potato with turkey on a hoagie roll. The cranberry sauce is optional, and I don't get it if I'm sharing with a four-legged sort. It's a great dog dinner if you're on the run. Add some spinach, and it's a pretty balanced meal for both humans and dogs.

I called ahead and arranged for our subs to go. After getting them, our next stop was the Van Nuys–Sherman Oaks park. All the picnic tables were vacant, so I let the dogs sniff out their favorite one. Two of the sandwiches had been cut into quarters. My idea was to dole out the subs to the dogs; their idea was to bolt whatever I gave them. We compromised, which allowed me the chance to eat some of my own sub. Afterward, with full bellies, we stretched out in the afternoon sun. As promised, I took off Emily's e-collar and gave her a rubdown. With the passage of time she was beginning to look less and less like a Frankenstein dog. As I applied lotion to her, I checked her wounds to make sure she was properly healing. Everything was looking good on her save for the abscess near the top of her head; that wound hadn't fully closed, and there was still some discharge coming from it. I was sure that battering her head against the window while trying to get at Rivera hadn't helped the wound any, but I suspected the underlying problem was a lingering infection.

The day before, I remembered, I had come to the same conclusion. My other conclusion had been that Emily needed to see my vet. It was past time to act. I pulled up Dr. Wolf-Fox's contact information, and then called her office. After four rings, the receptionist answered and said, "Please hold."

If I'd known the hold music was going to be "Let It Go" from the animated movie *Frozen*, I probably would have hung up then and there. What ended up being even worse was that my time in purgatory wasn't rewarded; when a human came back on the line, she told me that unless my animal's condition constituted an emergency, all the afternoon appointments were taken. We agreed on an eight-thirty appointment the next morning.

"'Let it go, let it go,'" I said to the dogs.

It was the brainwashing from the hold music talking, but they seemed fine with the sentiment.

. . . .

On the drive home, I heard the sound of ringing. The display told me Ben Corning was calling. Knowing the reason he wanted to reach me was to arrange a time for my talk with Ellis Haines, I decided to let his call go straight to voice mail. Psychologically, I wasn't yet ready to commit to a time. Before I did that, I wanted to look at the crime scene photos the FBI had sent over the day before. And like anyone trying to put off the unpleasant, I wanted to procrastinate as long as possible.

Once home, I filled up the water bowls, then made myself an iced tea. My preferred reading spot is an easy chair in the family room, and I set myself up there. I took a deep breath, leaned back in the chair, and opened the folder. From experience, I knew it was necessary, if not easy, to be a dispassionate viewer. This was the third time I was venturing into the polluted waters of the All-In Killer. The killing spree had been announced with a variety of playing card and poker terminology. Because aces are called bullets and twos are called ducks, the ace-two hand is known by poker players as hunting season. Jim Grinnell had died so that the killer could announce the game was at hand. That murder had been followed up by an association with the king-three, a hand known as King Crab. The latest was the queen-four, or a prince maker.

I looked at the first picture of the latest victim: Diana Prince. Just like the previous victim, she had been killed because her last name fit the pattern of Texas Hold 'Em slang. She was believed to be the first female victim of the All-In Killer.

The Feds provided an extensive write-up, along with dozens of pictures from the crime scene. The bulk of the report dealt with the latest kill, although the previous two murders were also referenced. The All-In Killer seemed to change his methodology with each kill. The first victim had been shot (according to the figures provided, almost half of all serial murderer victims died that way); the second victim had been axed (which, according to the FBI, only occurred in 1.46% of serial murders); and the third victim had been bludgeoned (the methodology used in 9.2% of serial murders). So far, two of the victims had been male and one female. Statistics kept over the last century noted that 51.5% of serial murderer victims were female, and the majority of those were Caucasians. Thus far, all three victims had been white.

One seeming anomaly among the All-In Killer's victims revolved around the ages of the victims, compared to the national average of other serial murderer victims. The youngest of the victims was fifty-eight and the oldest eighty-four. Diana Prince was sixty-two. The median age of those killed nationally was substantially younger, hovering around thirty-three years of age.

Almost a third of all serial murderers said the primary reason they killed was "enjoyment." The FBI believed the All-In Killer's murders fit that category, even though the deaths were also clearly a way to communicate with Ellis Haines.

Sick games, I decided, must qualify as enjoyment. The All-In Killer's primary motivation appeared to be communicating with Haines.

I studied the next picture of Diana Prince. The murder weapon was believed to be something heavier than the croquet mallets; tests were now being conducted to see if an engineer's hammer had been used, at least for the initial blow. I flipped to the next photo. Ben Corning had said lipstick was used to paint a red heart on her face. What he hadn't mentioned was how pervasively her lips had also been painted. So much ruby-red lipstick had been applied, I thought of Heath Ledger's face when he'd played the Joker in the movie *The Dark Knight*.

Maybe that wasn't happenstance, I thought. It was possible the killer was offering up multiple meanings. The queen of hearts wasn't a concept confined only to cards or to the landscape of Wonderland. Over the years, a number of singers had covered the song "Queen of Hearts."

What Corning hadn't mentioned to me was that the red lipstick had been used for something else. Pictures had been taken where the lipstick had been applied to the white drywall. The photos showed two upturned lines that extended about six inches in length, parallel to one another. The FBI had several guesses as to the purpose of the lines; it was also thought they'd been drawn to make it easier to apply the lipstick on the cadaver, much in the manner that someone might scratch a pen on paper to make ink flow.

I had another theory. The killer was bragging. He was also winking at Ellis Haines.

To my thinking, the two lines formed a grinning mouth. In the world of Wonderland, that conjured an image of the enigmatic Cheshire Cat. And when the Cheshire Cat disappeared, the last trace of him that could be seen was his smile.

It was the Cheshire Cat who had said to Alice, "I'm not crazy. My reality is just different than yours."

The All-In Killer, I suspected, was saying the same thing. There was a lot more subtext in his crime scenes, I was beginning to believe, than I had imagined. I would need to study the first two crime scenes much more carefully.

I wondered what else the killer had been communicating. And I wondered what else Ellis Haines had been withholding.

CHAPTER THIRTY

POSITIVELY CREEPY

I let Special Agent Corning leave two more messages before I called him back. By then he was getting close to frantic. He had already talked to San Quentin prison officials and arranged an eleven o'clock call for the next morning but was waiting for me to confirm. I told Corning the time worked for me but that I would need something in return. He actually sounded relived when I told him that what I wanted were the up-to-date case files for the three homicides attributed to the All-In Killer.

"The fastest way I can get them to you," said Corning, "is by sending electronic files for all three. The only caveat is that unless you have a special printer, the clarity of the photos won't be nearly as crisp."

"Blurry works even better for me," I told him.

Corning seemed to find that funny and promised to send the files within an hour.

My next call was to Detective Andrea Charles of the Las Vegas Police Department. "This is getting sort of creepy," she said. "Just like the last time we talked, I was reaching for my phone to call you, only to have you call me."

"Last time, did I say, 'Great minds think alike'?"

"It was either that or something equally nonsensical."

"It's good to hear I'm consistent at least. Since I've been sitting here venting about Ellis Haines, I decided misery needed some company."

"What's Haines done now?"

"I told you how he and that scumbag killer had forged a relationship. Now I'm beginning to think it goes a lot deeper than that. They have a dialogue going via the bodies, and I don't think it's one-way. I am pretty sure that even from behind bars, Haines is managing to get word to this All-In Killer."

"How do you know that?"

"I'm just beginning to realize the extent of the subtext in the crime scenes. This might sound paranoid, but I think I'm part of their discussion."

"Are you sure?"

"My gut is. But you're the first to hear my speculations."

"You almost sound betrayed," she said.

"Haines and I have a complicated history," I said. "He's even intervened on my behalf. Of course, I've always suspected he acted in his own self-interest, because he didn't want anyone else to have the pleasure of killing me."

"Isn't that a good thing?"

"It is," I said, "but it comes with survivor's guilt. As long as Ellis Haines is alive, I'm going to feel responsible for any and all evil he commits, even if it's secondhand. I could have, and should have, put a bullet in him years ago."

"You missed your opportunity once," she said, "so let's not miss a second time."

"You got something?"

"I'm not ready to celebrate," she said, "but I did find a potential witness who links Haines with one of our victims."

I could hardly hear my own voice over my suddenly pounding heart. "How credible is the witness?"

"When I went into Dino's Lounge, two different employees said I needed to talk to Darlene DeVito, or Dee Dee as everyone seems to know her. As they told me, her memory is legendary."

"Dino's," I said. The lounge had been one of the "old" Las Vegas haunts recommended to me by Ellis Haines.

"It's sort of a dive," said Andrea. "In fact, its motto is 'Getting Vegas drunk since nineteen sixty-two.'"

"Catchy," I said.

"Anyway, today I caught up with Dee Dee. She's been a cocktail waitress at Dino's for the last thirty years. Dee Dee was acquainted with Carol Shipley, one of the victims we identified as fitting our criteria. She said Carol was a karaoke regular and would come in about once a week. In fact, when Dee Dee heard about Carol's homicide, she claims the first thing that came to her mind was Carol's Creep. She wondered if he might have been involved in her murder."

"And you think Carol's Creep is Haines?"

"Dee Dee picked him out of a six-pack," Andrea said. "And she referred me to some old karaoke regulars who she's sure will be able to do the same."

"Did she remember his name, or the name he went by?"

"No," Andrea said, "all she could remember was her own nickname for him: Carol's Creep. After Carol's homicide, Dee Dee said she never saw him in the lounge again."

"Why did Dee Dee think this guy was a creep?"

"'Insincere' and 'oily' is how she described him, but her nickname for him came from his song selection. Every time he came in, the song 'Creep' was part of his karaoke repertoire."

"The song by Radiohead," I said.

"You got it. Dee Dee said he always nailed the song in a perfectly eerie way. She said the lyrics sounded all too natural coming out of his mouth."

I am a creep, I thought, *I'm a weirdo*.

"Dee Dee said there's a falsetto part to the song, and the way he'd sing those notes would send shivers down her back. To her, it sounded like he was voicing equal parts menace and desperation. She was convinced that there was something dangerous about him."

"But she never made the association between Carol's Creep and Ellis Haines?"

"She did not and has not. And I made sure Haines's name never came up in our conversation."

"What else did she have to say about Carol's Creep?"

"Dee Dee said she often associates karaoke customers with their favorite songs. Haines also regularly sang 'Space Oddity' by David Bowie and 'Africa' by Toto."

I considered my visits with Haines and tried to recollect if I'd ever heard him singing either of those songs.

"'Ground Control to Major Tom,'" I said.

"He is a spaceman of sorts," she said.

"No argument here. I imagine a lot of Bowie songs are in his wheelhouse. The man does love to sing. It sort of surprises me to think he'd be singing something from Toto, though. They're too easy-listening for him."

"I just listened to the song 'Africa,'" she said. "It's possible he sang it for the one line."

"Which is?"

"I won't sing it, to spare your eardrums, but it's something to the effect of how the singer's seeking a cure because he's frightened of this thing he's become."

I remembered the line. It was a note of darkness, and maybe desperation, amidst a song of remembering and longing.

"What's your next step?" I asked.

"I'll be making rounds of places that Haines mentioned to you, like Hugo's Cellar, Bootlegger Bistro, Batista's Hole in the Wall, and Bob Taylor's Ranch House. I'll also circle back to Dino's and see if some of the old regulars can identify Haines as Carol's Creep through a six-pack."

"I wonder if Carol introduced him to others as Ellis. Or maybe he never offered up his real name to her."

"As I mentioned," she said, "I've kept Ellis Haines's name out of any questioning. But two people who looked at the six-pack commented that Haines's face appeared familiar to them. And a third individual asked if the man in the picture wasn't the Weatherman."

"I guess there's no avoiding that," I said, "but do your best to keep the genie in the bottle as long as possible."

CHAPTER THIRTY-ONE

A LATE-NIGHT PICNIC

I spent the evening going through the All-In Killer files and making notes. What I found didn't make me feel any better, but it was still progress of sorts.

At a little before eight, my cell phone started ringing. The display said, *Private Name, Private Number*, but I answered anyway.

"Gideon," I said.

"Yeah," said a male voice. "You the cop?"

"Who's calling?" I asked.

The caller had a thick Mexican accent. "I call about the money."

At the bottom of all the posters I'd dropped off at businesses in Boyle Heights was the number for Crime Stoppers. I had also decided to write my cell phone number with a Sharpie in case someone wanted to talk to me. This was my first bite.

"The reward?" I said.

"Yeah. You pay cash?"

"I'm sure that can be arranged. Do you know something about those dogs dumped in Boyle Heights?"

"Yeah. El Gallo Negro no like losers."

"Are you saying Humberto Rivera killed those dogs?"

The line was silent for a few seconds. "Hello?" I said.

"I'm not saying nothing," the man said. "You talk, you die."

"Then why are you calling?"

"The poster ask for information about dogfights. If I tell you when next dogfight is, I get the money?"

"If you provide the location of when and where the fight is taking place, and we make arrests resulting from your information, you would be entitled to the reward, yes."

"And you no tell El Gallo who tell you?"

"That's right. Your anonymity is assured."

"You arrest all the peoples at dogfight?"

"Yes," I said. "It's illegal to even watch."

"So you arrest me, and El Gallo sees, and he never know I not arrested for real?"

"I can arrange that," I said. "I will make sure all the charges against you get dropped."

"Okay," he said.

"Okay?" I asked.

"I think about it."

I spoke quickly, afraid he was about to hang up. "If you want the money, you'll need to act before anyone else does."

He didn't respond, so I pushed a little harder. "You don't want someone else to get that reward money, do you? If you hesitate, that might very well happen."

"I no know," he said.

"What are you unsure about? Five thousand bucks is a lot of money."

"Ay yi yi," he said under his breath. Then he apparently came to his decision. "Next time."

"What do you mean next time?"

"I call before next fight."

Next fight, I thought. Now his questions and worries made sense.

"A dogfight is taking place tonight, isn't it?" I said.

"Yes."

"Then talk to me now," I said. "If you wait until next time, someone else might get the money. We still have time to make arrangements. What time does the fight start?"

"We no know yet."

"What do you mean you don't know?"

"We wait to hear from El Gallo. He not send out last text."

"So he already texted everyone to say there would be a fight tonight, but you don't know when and where it's taking place?"

"It be somewhere near Sunland-Tujunga," he said.

I thought about what the man was saying. Tito's caution made perfect sense. He had provided enough information for those involved in his dogfighting ring to begin driving toward Sunland-Tujunga. Before too long, they'd be texted with the final details. The information was being parceled out on a timely need-to-know basis. By operating in secrecy and limiting the timeframe, Rivera was minimizing his risk.

I began to put everything in context. Earlier in the day I had seen the loaded trucks in the recycling yard and noticed the absence of dogs. Pop-up restaurants are popular in LA. Having a pop-up dogfighting ring allowed Rivera a mobility that would make it extremely difficult to ever nail him.

"Let's meet up somewhere in Sunland-Tujunga in forty-five minutes," I said. "You can pick the spot to make sure no one sees us. By that time I'm sure El Gallo will have sent out the text saying where and when the dogfight will be taking place."

"You give me my money tonight?"

"I can give you a hundred dollars tonight. You'll get the rest of the five thousand after we make the bust. Okay?"

I listened as he took a deep, uncertain breath and considered my proposal. I didn't like the sound of his wavering.

"Listen," I said, "we need to meet face-to-face anyway. That way I can get your name and information so that the arrest charges get thrown out. Do you understand what I'm saying? Tonight everyone will see you being arrested along with them, but I'll make sure you get released later, with all of those charges dropped."

He let out some air, and once more he said, "Ay yi yi."

I joined him in taking a lungful of air. Not breathing, I waited on his decision. Finally, he said, "Okay." Then he told me where to go for our meet-up.

My mind was racing as I dressed. I chose dark clothing and work boots. As a precaution, I put on a Kevlar vest and wore a shoulder holster with my Glock. Going into this alone was stupid, I knew, but my informant was already skittish enough. As it was, I couldn't be sure he'd show up. And if I came with backup, he might very well be scared off. Not that I planned to be solo any longer than necessary. If the info was good, I'd call in LAPD's Foothill division to assist me.

My informant had told me we'd be meeting up in Sunland-Tujunga, an area about twenty-five miles north of where I lived. I'd been told to park at a pullout along Big Tujunga Canyon Road, and then proceed on foot to the exit for the Wildwood Picnic Site in the Angeles National Forest. Although the area was closed to cars, my informant said I would be able to walk down the road, although he didn't recall its name. Before leaving, I took a hurried two minutes to study the area on Google Street

View. I followed Big Tujunga Canyon Road, found the pullout where he wanted me to park, and using the street view, I continued up the road a few hundred feet, finding the sign for the Wildwood Picnic site. The name of the road my caller couldn't remember was Doske. On my computer screen, I followed Doske Road down to the picnic area. That's where my informant said he'd be waiting.

Both Sirius and Emily were watching all my movements with interest. I think they were hoping for a walk, but instead I asked them, "Do you want to go for a drive?" Judging by their enthusiastic response, they very much did.

"Let's go," I said.

The merged towns of Sunland and Tujunga have a mixed reputation. Although the town is only half a dozen miles north of downtown Glendale, in many ways it's another world. The area is up in the hills, with its northern border the San Gabriel Mountains. For a time, Sunland-Tujunga was the hub for biker gangs in LA County. Perhaps hand in hand with that, it also had the dubious distinction of being LA's meth capital. Proponents of Sunland-Tujunga like to tout the area's open space, rural atmosphere, ranches, and horse country. Its detractors claim it has a disproportionate amount of crime-related activities.

From Sherman Oaks, you ascend into the hills. Twenty years ago, when LA's air pollution was at its worst, some residents relocated to Sunland-Tujunga as a respite from the bad air. Located in the foothills of the San Gabriel Mountains, its area includes Mount Lukens, which tops out at more than 5000 feet in elevation—the highest point in Los Angeles.

I had only been to Sunland-Tujunga a few times. From memory, I knew Foothill Boulevard was the only major road in the city. The route ran east to west, but depending on where the dogfight was to take place, Sunland-Tujunga could also be reached using Interstate 210.

During the drive, I began to choreograph in my mind the best way to go about meeting with my informant. The street view that I'd studied electronically had allowed me some limited insights into the lay of the land, but I wished I had a better idea of what I was walking into. I had been so intent on making sure my informant wouldn't back out that I'd neglected to ask basic questions. I'd agreed to meet at a spot of his choosing, allowing him to dictate terms.

My qualms grew as I closed in on the town. I could turn around, I told myself. No one would be the wiser if I backed out. But just because I hadn't dictated the conditions of this meet-up didn't mean it wouldn't ultimately be worth it. If all went right, I could shut down a dogfighting ring and arrest Tito.

On my steering wheel I punched a button. One day, I'm sure, some car company will adapt Barbara Eden's voice from *I Dream of Jeannie* into its audio system. I responded to the prompt of a mechanical voice and said, "Call Shaman."

When he answered, Seth anticipated that I was calling about having a drink. "I'm afraid I have company tonight, Michael," he said. "How about tomorrow evening?"

"Tomorrow evening sounds good," I said, "but I'm actually calling about something else."

"Everything okay?" Seth asked.

My friend already sounded alarmed. I tried to strike a calm, nothing-is-out-of-the-ordinary tone. "I'm going to be meeting with an informant in a few minutes," I said, "and since the spot is a little bit off the beaten path, I thought it only made sense to give you the address."

Cary Grant probably could have made what I said sound like something reasonable. Judging by Seth's response, I was no Cary Grant.

"Why are you meeting an informant in a remote spot without backup?" he said.

"A short time ago I got a call saying that a dogfight is taking place tonight. I'm meeting with the informant to give him a down payment on the reward and get its location."

"You're taking an unnecessary risk."

"Today I saw two large trucks at Best Scrap that were filled to the gills. And even though those trucks were covered with tarps, I could see what looked to be a generator, as well as tables and chairs and benches. At the time I didn't put two and two together. Now it makes sense. This is my chance to nail a mobile dogfighting ring."

"What's the name of this informant?"

"He didn't give it to me. He spoke in broken English with a Latino accent."

"Where are you meeting this guy?"

"In Sunland-Tujunga," I said. "There's a spot off Big Tujunga Canyon Road called the Wildwood Picnic Site. It's part of the Angeles National Forest."

"And the purpose of your call was to tell me that?"

"It only makes sense to have someone know my whereabouts."

"It only makes sense to not go through with this meeting. I think that's the real reason why you're calling me. You wanted me to point out the obvious."

"Thanks for your concern, Seth."

"I can leave now and join you in about half an hour."

"I appreciate your offer, but if you'd heard how shaky my caller was, you'd know I have to do this alone. He'll no-show if he spots anyone else."

"If I were trying to set you up," said Seth, "I'd probably think up something just like this."

"I'm armed," I said, "and I'm also wearing a Kevlar vest that must weigh about ten pounds and provides no ventilation. And as soon as I learn the whereabouts of tonight's dogfight, I'll be calling for backup."

"At least you haven't taken complete leave of your senses."

"Thanks much."

"Call me after your meeting so I know you're all right," he said.

It was dark, the kind of dark someone who lives in a city doesn't experience. I was less than twenty-five miles from downtown Los Angeles, but it felt as if I had landed in a foreign country. There were few cars traveling along the two lanes of Big Tujunga Canyon Road. It was a winding road that discouraged speed. Looming over me, and accentuating the darkness, was the inhospitable stone that lined much of the roadway.

On this section of Big Tujunga, which was mostly uninhabited canyon country, there were no lights from houses or businesses. If I were to continue on the road, it would end up running into the Angeles Forest Highway. I wasn't traveling that far, though. If the GPS was right, I'd be pulling over in about a mile.

There was little in the way of signage. Here and there were warnings about curving roads, with speed limits not to exceed thirty MPH. Most road signs usually overstate the danger of what's ahead; these seemed to understate the hazard potential, especially at night.

My nervousness didn't go unnoticed by the dogs. Sirius made a sound that I call his questioning whine. He wanted to be reassured.

"It's all right," I said, trying to fool my partner.

The truth is I was having second thoughts about the arrangements that I'd agreed to. But it would all be worth it, I told myself, after I got the information that would take down Tito.

The pullout suddenly appeared, and I pulled over and turned off my lights. It had been more than five minutes since I'd seen another car. There was no second car in the pullout, and I wondered if my informant had decided not to show up. I took a deep breath, not sure what I thought about that. My heart was already pounding, and I was still in the car.

Both Sirius and Emily were standing up and looking at me expectantly. I considered taking Sirius with me, but then decided against it. It would be better to leave him with Emily. Besides, if the terrain allowed for it, I wanted to avoid the direct approach of walking down Doske Road. If an ambush had been planned, I didn't want to walk into it. Sirius knew the command for silence—usually he made no sounds after I called out "*ruhig*"—but a dog's natural inclination is to bark at the unknown, or any potential threat. My best chance for silence was to go in solo.

"You both need to stay here," I said.

Sirius gave a sharp, high-pitched single bark. That was his *come on, you've got to be kidding* bark.

"I'll be back soon," I said.

My partner tried his bark on me once more. Emily decided to back him up.

"Hush," I told them.

So much for a silent approach.

The night was on the cool side. I opened all four windows almost a third of the way down so that there would be plenty of ventilation. Then I took Emily's lampshade off so that she would be more comfortable.

"You two be good," I whispered.

In my right hand I held the heavy Maglite, but I didn't turn it on. The night was cloudy and there was little in the way of moonlight, but I hoped it would provide enough light for me to make my way to the picnic site.

I walked forward along Big Tujunga Canyon Road, glad I'd electronically visited the area, especially with the darkness. The drop-off was too steep, and there was too much brush, for me to consider bushwhacking over to Doske Road. Keeping hunched down, I approached the closed gate across the road that led down to the picnic area. I could see that, past the barrier, Doske Road was paved but in a state of disrepair. There were potholes and loose asphalt and plenty of potential stumbling blocks. I tried to be a silent shadow, moving off the asphalt and following a rain-carved gully downwards. My boots crunched in the loose grit, sand, and hard dirt.

In the distance I could see the outline of a large pine tree. It was breezy, and the wind was stirring up the needles of the tree so it sounded as if it were whispering. The temperature was on the cool side, but I was producing a puddle of sweat. Part of that was the Kevlar vest; the bigger part was my uncertainty.

I moved slowly, letting my eyes adjust to the darkness. Every few steps I found myself holding my breath and listening. There was nothing to be heard except for the occasional clicking of pine needles. Those sounds didn't explain the hairs on my arms rising up or the prickle I felt along my spine. My veneer of civilization had been quick to fall away, and my primordial instincts were screaming caution.

In the distance I saw a flashlight go on, then off, then on again. Instead of signaling back, I hunched down low, trying to disappear from view. Using the brush as a barrier, I moved farther away from the road and hoped the foliage and the darkness were now shielding my movements.

The light flashed again. Maybe because of my new angle, I saw something that I hadn't seen before: next to where the light was being shined, two pairs of eyes glowed green in the dark.

These were nonhuman eyes. These were eyes that were tracking me with senses of hearing and smell and night vision far better than mine. These were eyes that came with huge, cutting teeth.

I wanted to tell myself that the ghoulish-looking eyes, and all that I imagined accompanied them, were but a momentary illusion. Still, the realist in me knew the purpose of the light was to draw me in toward those waiting eyes.

The gun I'd brought was meant for a human opponent or opponents. I'm an adequate marksman, but hitting two moving targets in the darkness would take more than luck; it would take a miracle. That wasn't something I was ready to count upon.

I considered flight or fight, and which was the better option. The car was too far away. I probably wouldn't even get to the top of the road before being run down by the dogs. *Fight* didn't seem much more feasible. I would need some kind of barrier or fort, something I could hide behind and shoot from, but nothing showed itself as a possibility.

The breeze kicked up and the pine needles started their whispering again. This time I listened to what they were saying. If I could get to the pine tree before the dogs ran me down, I might find both safety and high ground.

I was running through the chaparral even before I was aware I'd made my decision. The ground was uneven, prime territory for twisting an ankle, but I couldn't slow down. My legs pushed through brush and high grass. I kept my eyes on the prize. Though I tried to keep the sound of my breathing in check, I was soon gasping for air. The Kevlar vest cut into my side like a lead corset. Still, the pine tree was getting closer. Maybe the element of surprise had worked; maybe my race to safety had gone unnoticed. There was no barking, but then I heard something off to my side—the crackling sound of brush separating. *It's the wind*, I prayed, but a quick turn of my head realized my fears. A streaking dark shadow was on an intercept course to take me down.

One dog, I could fight, but I didn't like my odds going up against two. I was now committed to the tree.

A dozen steps separated me from it, then nine, then seven. Now I was close enough to see that there were no low-hanging branches. I would need to throw myself at the tree's thick trunk, and then start shimmying upwards. From four feet away I took off, leaping toward the tree, my arms outstretched. The first impact I felt was the tree. The trunk was thicker than my extended arms, but I managed to get a good grip. Without an instant's hesitation, I dug my boots into the bark and pushed upwards. That's when the second impact hit.

I screamed, a cry of both pain and fright. One of the dogs had his teeth deep into my calf.

That's when the second dog leapt at me. The force walloped my torso and head against the tree, and I screamed again. The second dog's target had been my back, but the Kevlar vest saved me from being ripped open. For an instant, I almost lost my grip on the tree, but then I tightened my bear hug.

The second dog fell to the ground. I knew he'd be up and at me again; my only hope was to try and get out of his reach. Gritting my jaw, fighting off the pain, I used two arms and one leg to hoist myself up another foot. Covering that distance was made all the harder by the anchor I was dragging. The first dog hadn't loosened his grip on my leg. His teeth were deep in my sinews and flesh, and he was not about to be shaken off. The dog's additional weight put a toll on my waning strength. In fact, just holding on was tough enough; trying to climb higher up the tree was quickly taxing all my reserves.

The second dog came at me again. He must have used the first dog as a ladder of sorts, climbing up its back and using its body as a springboard. I screamed again as the dog's teeth opened up my lower back, but again my vest mostly rebuffed the attack, causing the dog to fall.

Even though my arms were beginning to twitch, I managed to hoist myself up another foot. I hoped I was out of range of the second dog, but even if I was, all I had managed was to buy myself some time. The dog that had the bite on me didn't even appear to be winded. He was just waiting for his prey to fall.

I tried not to be terrified, and to keep a clear head. If I could get at my gun, I might have a chance. But time was running out. In another minute or two, it was likely the dogs would have human company joining them to take down their quarry. Could I cling to the tree with just one arm for long enough to get my gun? I shifted, trying to find a position that would allow me to loosen my hold, but then found myself slipping. Panicked, I reestablished my hold. For how long could I hang on, though? It was like riding the back of a tiger and not being able to get off.

I thought about the best way to drop to the ground, and what I would need to do to survive. If I was able to land on my feet, there might be time to draw my gun before the two dogs were on me. I'd likely have only an instant's reprieve.

But if the fall from the tree resulted in me losing my balance, then I'd have to roll and try to come up with my gun. From there I'd need to fight to my feet. Even if I couldn't get my gun free, during my time at Metropolitan K-9 I had been trained in how to best defend myself from a dog attack. None of the instructors had ever thrown a second dog into the equation, though. Going up against two dogs that had been trained to kill changed everything.

That's when I heard something. At first I doubted my ears, thinking it was wishful hearing, but then there was no mistaking the sweet, sweet sound of sirens. There was no guarantee those sirens were coming for me, but I wanted to believe they were. Still, I quickly learned my mental celebration was premature.

The second dog came at me again. Vaulting off the first dog, he pushed off high enough to bite my upper thigh. It was all I could do to scream and cling to the tree. My pants ripped, and once more the dog fell to the earth, taking some of my flesh with him.

I didn't have the strength to climb higher, and the sirens were still too far away. That was when I heard the roar of an engine. What sounded like a motorcycle was making its escape up Doske Road. The hellhounds were too intent on finishing me off to even notice their ringleader's exit.

As desperate as my grip was, I could still feel myself slipping. The next hit, I was sure, would bring me down, but I tried to prepare myself anyway. *Protect the throat*, I thought.

Survive.

Up until that moment, the battle had been fought mostly in silence, punctuated only by my screams. That suddenly changed. There was a roar, followed by cries of throaty rage. A life-and-death battle of vicious intensity broke out below me.

Somehow, my shepherd had arrived.

The dogs were rolling, biting, lunging, growling, and screaming. It was the meeting of Sturm *und* Drang, the frenzy of kill or be killed.

But as brave and determined and fierce as my partner was, his opponent was a trained killer, and I feared Sirius would not survive this fight.

I readied to drop. I would take on my attacker, and then try to help my partner. But suddenly I saw another shadow enter the fight, and the sounds of war redoubled. Emily had joined Sirius, and the two of them acted in tandem. They attacked as a team, each of them coming at the second dog, lunging with a ferocity that was driving the hairy assassin back.

My grip was about to give, so I decided to act before my strength gave out. I pushed off from the tree, dropping down about six feet. Even with the first dog's weight pulling at me, I managed to keep to my feet. It took me only a moment to pull free my Glock with my right hand; my left hand grabbed the Maglite from my belt. And then the dog was up, jumping at my throat.

I clubbed him first with the Maglite, and then my gun, and before he could jump at me again, I jumped at him and kicked with all my strength. A sound came out of my throat that I had never voiced before, something feral and savage and wild. And then I was the aggressor, coming at the dog and screaming my rage. I took the battle to him, swinging at his forelegs, slashing at his eyes. I was ready to use my fingers and nails and teeth. Civilization's veneer was gone.

The first dog bared his teeth and backed up, but I didn't pause, and was able to club his nose with my heavy flashlight.

Dogs are good at suppressing and hiding their pain. It's how they evolved. Despite that, there's no better way to get their attention than to strike them on their nose. That is a sensitive spot for them, and a most painful place to be struck. And I wasn't done. I followed up with another limping, but aggressive, step forward. I was attacking. As loud as the dog's growls were, mine were louder.

And that's when he turned tail and ran.

A part of my mind recognized that there were flashing lights coming from Big Tujunga Canyon Road, as well as shouting voices. But at the moment, I was a berserker. Had I not been seeing red, I probably would have thought to shoot my gun into the air. That might have scared off the remaining dog. I was in attack mode, though, and ready to join in with my pack.

You never get into the middle of a dogfight. You will only get bit if you do. Those words had been indoctrinated into me. So, naturally, I stepped into the middle of a dogfight. Sirius and Emily had done well against this fighting machine, but both were bloody. Two against one had allowed them to survive. But now it was three.

I didn't fight by the Marquess of Queensberry Rules. I blindsided the dog, aiming a kick at his balls. What works on human males also works on male dogs. I ignored the pain in my savaged calf for long enough to step into the kick and punt with everything I had. That actually lifted the dog into the air. He didn't land on his feet but fell to his side. As the rest of my pack attacked, he got to his feet and, for a moment, faced off against the three of us.

As our united front came at him, the last assassin fled into the night.

CHAPTER THIRTY-TWO

TO COME TO A HEAD

When an LAPD officer made his cautious approach to the three of us, we were in the middle of a group hug and I was telling the dogs how brave they were, and how no one could hope to have better friends, and how they were the best dogs in the world, and how they had saved my life.

I heard no arguments from them, and they seemed to take joy from all my praise. It was a paltry enough offering for their loyalty and the wounds they'd suffered.

All of us were the worse for wear. As scarred as Emily had been, she now had new wounds. Sirius was carved up as well. It had been a hell of a fight, but we'd survived.

I was holding up my wallet badge for the cop to see, even as I was hugging the dogs and doing a post-battle inspection of their wounds. I wanted to make sure LAPD knew we were the good guys.

The cop called, "Detective Gideon?"

"That's right," I said.

I gave Sirius and Emily a last hug, extricated myself from our group huddle, and rose from my knees. Now that the fight was over, I was finding any movement hurt like hell.

A light shined on me. "Are you all right?" the cop asked.

"Bloodied but unbowed," I said. "My two dogs are the same."

"An ambulance is on the way," the cop said.

"Cancel it," I said. "Our next stop is an animal hospital. In the meantime, you need to put out an alert about two vicious pit bulls that are loose in this area. Maybe you can roust someone from animal control to come out at this time of night."

"What happened here?" asked the cop.

"I was stupid enough to be ambushed," I said, "and almost paid the price. Your sirens and my dogs saved my life. Let me guess: an individual named Seth Mann contacted you."

"That's correct," said the cop. "Dr. Mann told us that immediately after you supplied him with your location, your phone conversation was suspiciously terminated. According to Dr. Mann, he suspected it was a situation of an officer down."

Dr. Mann, I thought, had invoked words that guaranteed a police response like nothing else. The next time we were together I would ask him to never ever do that kind of manipulating in the future. Of course, I would make that request right after thanking him for saving my life.

"I'll call Dr. Mann and tell him I'm all right," I said.

"You said you were ambushed," said the cop. "Do you know who did this to you?"

"I know who arranged it," I said. "And I hope to soon be arresting him."

The officer opened his mouth, but I spoke before he could ask his question. "Right now I am going to drive the dogs for medical treatment, and then I will also be making a trip to the ER to get my own wounds treated. Your questions will have to wait until tomorrow."

"Fine," the cop said.

He asked to look at my ID, and took down the best numbers on which to reach me. By that time, a second cop had joined us.

"I'm going to need a favor, guys," I said. "I don't think I can get up that hill by myself. But if I can use both of you to brace me, I think I can swing and hop my way to my car."

It took almost fifteen minutes of stopping and starting to get to my car. The adrenaline was long gone, and I was cold and hurting and weak. I was also as stubborn as ever and refused the ambulance that was waiting for me at the top of the hill.

Once the dogs and I were inside the car, I did a quick study of the interior door handles. The handle nearest to where Sirius always sits showed scratches and what I was sure were bite marks. Houdini's talents weren't only limited to doors and windows at my house. Sirius had figured out the car handle all on his own. I was glad I hadn't locked the doors, and had left all the windows at least six inches open. My partner would have heard me being attacked. Hell, the way I had screamed, he would have heard me from a mile away.

I touched the scratched-up door handle. Despite the videos I'd seen of dogs opening car doors, Sirius's springing himself from the confines of the car still seemed like a miracle. And damned if I didn't get all teary-eyed and insist upon another group hug.

Before calling *Dr. Mann*, I wiped those tears away. Then I told my friend that we were all alive, but that drinks were definitely in order for tomorrow night.

My next call was to Dr. Wolf-Fox's answering service. I explained the emergency and said I knew it was long after office hours, but that I was sure Sirius would prefer seeing his own vet. If Dr. W-F could accommodate him, I said, she should call me on my cell.

Two minutes later, Dr. Wolf-Fox called. She has a soft spot in her heart for Sirius. Everyone loves a dog in uniform. Dr. W-F was given an abbreviated story of what had happened and the wounds involved on both dogs, and then told me she'd be ready to see us at the clinic in half an hour.

"What a brave, sweet boy you are," Dr. Wolf-Fox said to Sirius.

"And you," she said to Emily, "couldn't be any sweeter than you are."

Both dogs were showing off for Dr. Wolf-Fox, doing all they could, and more, to be everything she said they were.

"What about me?" I asked.

"You should have known better," she said, "than to put these two in danger."

"I didn't put them in danger," I said. "It was Sirius who opened the car door with the handle, and Emily who chose to follow him."

"Incredible," she said.

"What?"

"Your whole story. First, that Sirius opened the door to get out of your car. And then your rescue dog, with a broken leg and still-healing wounds, follows him into battle and comes to your rescue."

"The bastards that hurt her," I said, "that left her for dead, said there was no fight in her. You should have seen her tonight when she was saving my ass."

My voice caught, and I turned away from Dr. Wolf-Fox. She pretended not to hear, or see, my tears splattering on the floor.

She gave shots, stitched up wounds, whispered sweet nothings, and checked the two heroes from head to toe. I watched her eyebrows wrinkle as she examined the abscess on Emily's head.

"That's why we were supposed to see you first thing tomorrow morning," I said. "We had an eight-thirty appointment. I guess we can cancel . . . "

I stopped talking. And then the piece of the puzzle that I had always known was there suddenly revealed itself. It had been there in front of me all along, but I hadn't seen it. Dr. Misko had overlooked it as well, because Emily's head wound had presented as a dog bite.

"We need to take an X-ray of that head wound," I said. "I think you're going to be surprised at what we see."

The other three dogs dumped at Boyle Heights had been shot. Everyone had assumed Emily must have appeared dead already, with no reason to shoot her. But Emily *had* been shot in the head. At the time of her shooting, the bullet must have knocked her senseless.

Thank God she has a hard head.

Removing the bullet proved surprisingly easy. Dr. Wolf-Fox said it was almost as if the bullet wanted to come out. Using specialized forceps, she took it out while I documented her handiwork with pictures.

When she finished, Dr. Wolf-Fox held the bullet up for me to better see it.

"You sure you want to throw in your lot with me?" I asked Emily. "You've had a hole in your head with a bullet in it, and I was too stupid to figure it out."

"As much as Emily probably appreciates the sound of your mea culpa," said Dr. Wolf-Fox, "the bullet's entry wound actually presented as an abscess. I wouldn't beat yourself up over it."

With her forceps, she dropped the bullet into a small jar, and then covered it with a lid.

I reached for the jar and held it up to the light.

"You're right," I said. "It's time to beat up someone else over this."

It was almost one a.m. when I awakened Lisbet. "I'm okay," I told her, "but I'm going to need some medical treatment tonight."

She was instantly awake. "What happened?"

"Long story short," I said, "I was bitten by a dog in several spots, but primarily on my calf."

"It wasn't Emily, was it?"

"Quite the opposite," I said. "In fact, Sirius and Emily saved me from getting bitten up much worse than I did. Both of them were just treated for their wounds. Now it's my turn. I'm on my way to the Sherman Oaks Hospital. Since I doubt they allow dogs in the ER, and since after they shoot me up with pain meds they're going to insist I have a driver, I'm wondering if I can impose on you."

"Impose? I would have been furious if you hadn't called me, Michael."

"Just hearing your voice makes me feel better."

"Are you sure they haven't shot you up with those pain meds already?"

"Not yet," I said, "but soon, I hope. My leg has stiffened up to the point where I think you'll have to wheel me in."

"You're making me worried."

"Don't be. Believe me when I say it was worth it."

"I believe you. And it shouldn't take me more than twenty minutes to get to the hospital at this time of night."

"Drive carefully," I said.

CHAPTER THIRTY-THREE

A SERVING OF SOUP

It took me several days to get everything buttoned up before returning to Best Scrap. Not only did it take me time to get my ducks in a row, it also took me that long to be ambulatory. A pit bull had put a serious bite on me. Now it was my turn to bite back even harder.

As I limped up to the Best Scrap trailer, Humberto Rivera didn't hide his amusement. Fausto was also in the office. Judging by their expressions, neither man was surprised to see me. In fact, they had probably been expecting me for days.

In order to open the trailer's door, I put the bowl in one hand and did my pulling with the other. I entered the trailer and limped over to Tito's desk.

"For you," I said, putting the steaming bowl down in front of him.

"What is it?" he asked, looking confused.

"'It is not always the bull who loses,' I said, quoting his punch line back to him. "Of course, this soup"—I pointed to the bowl—"isn't quite complete yet. All it lacks is your huevos. And you're about to serve those up to me."

Tito wasn't smiling now. I was. And that was before the two squad cars came charging into the recycling center's lot with their lights flashing.

"Humberto 'Tito' Rivera," I said, "and Fausto Alvarez, you are both under arrest."

I read them their Miranda rights, and then to be sure they understood what I had just said, I handed them cards containing the Spanish translation.

"I advise you to carefully look over what's written on those cards you're now holding," I said. "I want to make sure you understand your rights."

"This is a joke," said Tito. "My lawyer will have me out in less than an hour."

I shook my head and said, "I don't think so."

By that time the two uniforms had entered the trailer, and the confined space seemed that much smaller.

"Do you understand your rights?" I asked them.

The two men made eye contact, and then both nodded.

"I don't want either one of you to move," I said. "So, are you holding the gun? Or where is it?"

I saw Fausto's eyes look to a spot behind the counter. That was enough for me to limp forward and retrieve the hidden gun.

"That's Fausto's gun," said Tito. "Don't try and say it's mine."

I dropped the firearm into a plastic bag. "An HK forty-five," I said. Then I asked Tito, "Where's the suppressor?"

"What are you talking about?"

"We have videotape footage of you walking around Angie's Rescues waving this gun. At the time, though, the gun had a sound suppressor attached to it."

"You got me mistaken for someone else."

I shook my head. "No, Tito, it's definitely you, and it's definitely this gun. We have footage and pictures that just this week identified you and this gun."

"Like I said, that's Fausto's gun."

I turned to Fausto. "Is that so?"

"Don't say a word," said Tito. "Let the lawyers do all the talking for you."

"I think that's good advice, Fausto," I said, "at least for Tito here. You see, we've been able to determine that this gun has been used in the commission of multiple crimes. And that's going to mean serious jail time for the shooter."

"That's bullshit," said Tito.

"When I saw the videotape of you walking around Angie's Rescues," I said, "I couldn't understand what you were doing there. What was motivating you to trespass on private property while carrying a firearm? At the time, I didn't realize that the reason you were there was to destroy evidence. You knew there was one thing left to connect you with the murder of those dumped dogs: the bullet in Emily's head.

"We have that bullet now and were able to conduct ballistics tests. After we do tests on this gun, I'm confident it will show that this is the weapon that fired the bullet retrieved from Emily's head."

"That still doesn't give you the shooter," said Tito.

"You hear that, Fausto?" I said, turning to the man with the eye patch. "I think we just heard the legal defense that your boss's attorney plans to put forward. And I suspect you'll be the one who's hung out to dry.

"What your boss doesn't know, though, is that we're also going to link this gun to a crime scene not far from the Nevada border. That's where several other dogs were shot with an HK forty-five. I am quite sure tests will show this is the gun that fired those bullets."

"He's lying," said Tito.

I shook my head. "No, I'm not. And both of you know I'm not. You're just hoping Fausto here doesn't give you up. Yes, he's the registered owner of this gun, but you're the one who's been using it. Of course, that's not the only lethal weapon at your disposal. There are the two pit bulls you sicced on me. Did you know both those dogs have been captured?"

"I don't know what you're talking about."

"I got to hand it to you, Tito. You played me perfectly. The last time I visited here, you set things up so that it looked like your mobile dogfighting ring was ready to roll. You played me hook, line, and sinker when you called me up asking about the reward, and all the while you spoke in pretend pidgin English. It was perfect, the way you acted, making it seem like you were so afraid of being found out. The more reluctant you played it, the harder I worked to land you. You suckered me, and then you tried to kill me."

"I don't know what you're talking about. Are you saying someone tried to kill you? When was this?"

"You missed your calling as an actor," I said.

Then I told Tito that the attack on me had taken place four nights ago, at which point he vehemently proclaimed his innocence.

"I was at a party that night," he said. "I can get you a dozen witnesses to that fact. And if that's not good enough for you, I can produce video and pictures showing me there."

"What a surprise," I said, my words more for Fausto than they were for Tito. "It's almost like you prepared the perfect alibi for yourself. What about you, Fausto? Do you have a perfect alibi as well, or were you set up as the fall guy just in case something went wrong?"

Tito was staring at Fausto. He was holding his index finger up to his lips, discouraging the man with the eye patch from saying anything.

"Even if you both contest the charges," I said, "we already have more than enough evidence to convict the two of you, and we're in the process of adding even more."

I placed some paperwork on Tito's desk, careful to keep the pages away from his bowl of broth.

"That's a search warrant," I said. "It allows us free run of your property. I'm wondering what's going to turn up on all those video cameras you have. Do you think there will be footage of those two dogs that attacked me? And let's not forget the DNA and blood evidence we'll be collecting. It's amazing how a few follicles here, and a bit of splatter there, tell stories that are most convincing. If you used this site to dispose of dog remains, there will be plenty of evidence to show that."

I turned to the officers and nodded. "Please handcuff your prisoners and take them to be booked."

"I want to make a call," said Tito.

"You'll get that opportunity," I said.

I took out my business card, circled my phone number, and handed the card to Fausto.

"You can make a call, too. My advice to you is to dial this number. By now, I imagine you realize that you're supposed to be Tito's sacrificial lamb. If you don't want to spend the next ten years in jail, though, you had better tell me what you know. And I wouldn't hesitate if I were you. As soon as people hear about the arrest of El Gallo Negro, and that he's safely behind bars where he can't hurt them, they'll be calling for the reward. You'll want to act before then, while you still have some bartering power."

The suspects were handcuffed. As they were being led out, I called to Tito: "You sure you don't want your soup?"

CHAPTER THIRTY-FOUR

SOMETHING WICKED THIS WAY COMES

The only good thing that came out of being chewed up by a pit bull was that it allowed me to back out of my scheduled call with Ellis Haines. My convalescence provided even more excuses to put off that call, as did the demands that came with trying to close two cases.

And, of course, there was the third case I'd been working, that of Haines potentially committing a murder or two while spending time in Las Vegas. Detective Charles and I were now calling our investigation the Karaoke Creep case. She had found two more witnesses who remembered a man who looked like Haines being friends with Carol Shipley, the woman we suspected Haines of murdering.

Even though I had avoided talking with Haines, I had kept current with the goings-on of the All-In Killer case. The FBI now had me in the loop on all their reports and crime scene investigations. It was their belief that Diana Prince—the queen-four killing—had been the most recent victim. Of course, the more I studied the cases, the more I became convinced the FBI had missed some significant clues.

That was why I agreed to return to San Quentin to meet with Ellis Haines.

I waited for him in the lawyers' room. For whatever reason, it took the correctional officers longer than usual to bring Haines to me. Once more, I wished I wasn't there. Prisons bring out the claustrophobic in me. I found myself breathing through my mouth, not wanting to inhale the pervasive odor of desperation. To me, it's worse than cigarette smoke and even more toxic.

Finally, I heard the sound of approaching chains. For whatever reason, Haines had chosen not to sing today. I thought of the lyrics to "Creep" and imagined Haines singing it. By then, Haines had murdered a number of women and knew exactly what he was. His singing was a way for him to confess to the world, all the while riotously laughing inside. I wondered if he had sung the song expressly for Carol Shipley, knowing he would one day murder her.

As Haines drew closer, I tried to think about something else. I was probably being irrational, but I was afraid of his psychic bloodhound abilities. I didn't want him to sniff out my thoughts.

When he came into view, I put on my best poker face but immediately wondered if I was offering up a tell. Whatever Haines saw made him smile.

"Detective Gideon," said Haines, "I'm so sorry to keep you waiting, but you know how the help is around here. It took forever for the staff to muster up a contingent to walk me over here. I volunteered to walk myself over, but they declined my offer."

Haines kept up his chatter as the cell was unlocked and his bracelets were removed. As he was seated, I declined the offer from the correctional officer to have Haines shackled to the table.

After the officer vacated the cell, Haines and I sat looking at one another over the table. He was still smiling.

"No pictures for me today?" he asked.

"The FBI gave me this month off from courier duty," I said. "They tell me you were given pictures of the queen-four killing, as well as from some other homicides."

"So many murders," he said, "and so little time."

"I read your write-up on the Diana Prince killing."

"A write-up," he said, "that was made necessary when you didn't call me for our scheduled meeting of minds."

"You mean you didn't get my flowers and note of apology?"

"I understand you were wounded in the line of duty. And if the story was relayed to me correctly, we now have something else in common: each of us carries the scars of dog bites on our bodies."

He stared me down, his smile long gone. "I'll show you mine," he said, "if you'll show me yours."

"I get the feeling you're not talking about scars," I said.

"How perceptive of you."

"Is that anger I detect?"

"I would categorize it more as disappointment."

"Funny," I said. "When I talked to Special Agent Corning, I used that same word to describe what I thought of your analyses of the All-In Killer homicides. I told him that today I'd be asking you why you've been less than forthcoming with the FBI in your write-ups."

"Forthcoming," he said, almost like he was chewing on the word. "You are questioning my being forthcoming? Isn't that like the pot calling the kettle black?"

"A club flush is called 'puppy feet' because the clubs supposedly look like the paw prints of dogs. The croquet mallets left at the queen-four crime scene constituted puppy feet. You never commented on that. You never brought up the subtext in the All-In Killer's crime scene. And that wasn't the first time."

"Do tell," said Haines.

"The All-in Killer likes to offer layers of riddles. That's why you've been asking for such detailed crime scene reports. You want to know what was in the room where the victim was found, including titles of books, or songs being listened to, or brochures left on a table. You were curious about brand names and the names of plants. No detail was too small, including the perfume or aftershave worn, fruit or food left out, and what was on display.

"The obvious clues were easy to pick out; the well-known poker hands and meteorological symbols. And clearly you were the intended target for those messages; the killer was speaking in tongues you were familiar with. But his messages continued beyond the surface clues.

"For example, I never realized that I was a point of discussion from the first murder. When hunting season was announced in the ace-two staging, you pointed out the umbrella, but not the MP3 player also lying nearby. Like you, I've also been asking questions about the crime scene. What I recently discovered was that the song the victim was supposedly listening to was Elvis Costello's 'Watching the Detectives.' I think there was a double meaning in that. Card players, as you pointed out, refer to a king as Elvis. And I'm pretty sure I was the detective in question."

Haines lightly clapped his hands. "Excellent, Detective. And now the two of us can definitively say that Elvis has not left the house."

"How do you think the FBI is going to respond to your having purposely withheld information?"

"I expect they'll forgive and forget, especially when I intimate that their killer has struck again since Mrs. Prince. They were expecting an obvious play on the jack-five with the next homicide. They were thinking the killer was going to murder someone with the surname of Jackson. They should have remembered that the first victim wasn't murdered because of his last name; his death was simply a statement. Besides, did they think they would always have clues so linear, so simple? Why should they expect something as easy as ABC?"

He didn't try and hide his gloating, or his clue.

"The Jackson Five song 'ABC,'" I said.

"Follow the alphabet soup to the killing," he said. "The police didn't even recognize last week's death of that elementary school teacher, directly under the classroom's ABCs, as a homicide."

"Where?" I asked.

"Albuquerque," he said.

"Is there any significance to this trail of murders?"

"Follow the map, Detective. It tells you the killer is progressing along a certain route."

"Am I going to find in this latest homicide that I'm still part of your discussion with the killer?"

"Regrettably, you've given me no choice."

"What do you mean?"

"When our paths first crossed, you were doing your job. I respected that. I respected you. Both of us experienced the baptism of fire. We were marked as brethren. Since then I've done nothing but save you from those who would do you harm. And that is why your betrayal is so terribly unforgivable."

He stared me down with eyes that blazed with hatred and disappointment. I wasn't surprised that he knew about Las Vegas and the investigation, and I wasn't surprised by his ferocity; what surprised me was that I had apparently managed to hurt him so deeply.

"I've always been doing my job," I said. "Then and now."

"We met on the battlefield and you brought in your prisoner. Wasn't that enough?"

"No," I said. "I should have killed you when I had the chance. That would have been justice. Years later I'm still dealing with the families of your victims. I see firsthand the pain you caused, and how it's still so hurtful. To my thinking, justice delayed has been justice denied."

"You've opened Pandora's box, Detective. You've inspired even more evil in the world in the form of this avenging murderer. Did you think I wouldn't find out about your Las Vegas investigation?"

"I assumed you would hear about it sooner or later."

"You think by getting me convicted in Nevada that I'll be moved to Nevada's death row, is that right?"

"That's the hope."

"If you hope to live, then you must cease and desist in your efforts. The pale horse rides the land. It comes at a trot. With each death, it comes closer. The countdown has begun."

"Is that so?"

"Houston, we have a problem," he said.

"Are we done here?" I asked.

"We are," he said.

I called to the waiting correctional officer, and he radioed his team. During the time it took for the officers to gather, Haines and I stared at one another.

After his shackles were reapplied, Haines began shuffling down the hallway. That's when he decided to start talking again.

"Can you feel it, Detective Gideon? It's out there. It's stalking you. And I'm the only one who can commute your death sentence. Yes, you're right, the two of us have found a way to talk. And there's so much to talk about. Know that if you kill me, you kill yourself. Once again, the two of us are walking through the fire and need each other to survive. Will you dream tonight? If so, perhaps you will sense that the killer is drawing nigh. With each murder, he moves closer to you. Something wicked this way comes. And you will only avoid certain death through my salvation."

It seemed to me I listened to the sounds of his chains for a long time before they could be heard no more.

ACKNOWLEDGMENTS

Thanks go to Will Richter for being my Los Angeles tour guide. Whenever I am thinking up a scene, I invariably ask Will, "Where do you think would be a good spot for this to take place?" Will has even been kind enough to go with me to some of these sites. It is a strange life being a mystery writer and considering the right locations for your mayhem.

Once again I must acknowledge our family vet, Dr. Sue Spray. I call upon Sue to vet the vet scenes. It's a good thing I don't have anyone vet my wordplay.

When you write about a cop, it's nice to have the resource of cops. Thank you to longtime sheriff's deputies Dave Putnam and Russell Moore for cheerfully answering my law enforcement questions.

Kudos to Brilliance Audio for their desire to have the Gideon & Sirius novels continue. That meant a lot to this author, and provided incentive to keep going.

Finally, thank you to my loyal readers. It was hearing from you that made all the difference. Because of the many notes you sent asking when the next Gideon & Sirius novel would be coming out, I was determined to keep writing their tales (and tails). Luckily, we found a way to do that. *Gideon's Rescue* is my fifteenth published novel. I am sure this book would not have been written if not for you. Readers who want to reach me can write to alanrussellauthor@gmail.com. Please also visit my website at alanrussell.net, follow me on my author page at Amazon, or like me on Facebook at Alan Russell Mystery Author.

And, yes, there will be at least two more Gideon & Sirius novels. Please look for them in the not-too-distant future!

Alan Russell
July 17, 2018

ABOUT THE AUTHOR

 Critical acclaim has greeted bestselling author Alan Russell's novels from coast to coast. *Publishers Weekly* calls him "one of the best writers in the mystery field today." The *New York Times* says, "He has a gift for dialogue," while the *Los Angeles Times* calls him a "crime fiction rara avis." Russell's novels have ranged from whodunits to comedic capers to suspense, and his works have been nominated for most of the major awards in crime fiction. He has been awarded a Lefty, a Critics' Choice Award, and the Odin Award for Lifetime Achievement from the San Diego Writers and Editors Guild. A California native, Russell is a former collegiate basketball player who nowadays plays under the rim. The proud father of three children, Russell resides with his wife in Southern California.

Author photo credit: Stathis Orphanos

Made in the USA
Columbia, SC
12 February 2019